*To my brother Joseph, this book's instigator,
who has the most wonderful laugh in the whole world.*

Chapter 1

Awareness returned to John with an unexpected sense of calm. Eyes still closed, remembering his previous agony, he touched his throat, testing with his fingertips for a wound. No. No blood. No pain. But he found a scar and traced its subtle ridge...slowly encircling his neck. How could it have healed so quickly? How could it heal at all?

Opening his eyes, John found himself in a limitless space of grayed hush. Others were here. He sensed them nearby. One presence in particular—perfect and all-encompassing—permeated this place, lulling John with a peace surpassing any he had ever known.

You are here, he thought to the Spirit. *And I am not where I was.* Again, he touched his throat, still amazed to find it restored. *I am not what I was....*

Memories of the past intruded now, shaking his tranquility. Fears and inadequacies gnawed hard and he cried to the Spirit in anguish. *I have failed!*

The Spirit answered in calm, wordless clarity. *You did not fail.*

But my work is incomplete.

You will complete your work when His time is completed. Until then, rest.

Obedient to the Holy One, John settled into the hush and awaited his liberation, at rest with the righteous souls brought to this place before him.

And with those yet to appear.

A joyous calm slipped over him as the Spirit promised, *Your Redeemer nears!*

***

Joseph understood what had happened.

He was in a place that wasn't supposed to exist: Sheol.

I'm alive! My soul lives! I'm here.... His elation faded as he remembered his vulnerable young family. How could he protect them from this distant place? From beyond time?

In despair, he appealed to the shaded hues of quiet surrounding him. The Lord's Spirit was near. Joseph felt the blessed presence and pleaded with all his soul's might, *They need me!*

The Spirit answered his soul in reassurance, with a promise. *They are remembered. Rest and wait. He is near.*

***

Restless, the Adversary traced the fringes of the place he could not enter, not permitted because of *It*.

Loathsome Spirit.

And pacing from here to stars in protest would avail nothing. Nor would an audience before the throne of Almighty Him, arguing legalities that should be considered. "The earth is mine—it was given to me. This place is also within my realm."

Yet the Almighty sheltered these souls within this place...these pathetic beings, no less contemptible now that they were freed from their dust-formed flesh. Why did He protect them so avidly—as if they were treasure?

The Adversary continued his zealous watch, peering inside, longing to grasp those protected souls and confront them with all their wrongs, to prove their unworthiness of the Almighty's regard.

But they had somehow escaped him.

He must therefore exploit other options.

Anticipating further maneuvers, he departed, calling his shadow-silent followers to ensnare those yet-walking, still-breathing souls bound by flesh and time.

Chapter 2

Jerusalem's House of the Lord dazzled in the late winter sunlight like a bride in purest white, its pristine marble crowned with gold, its whole presence perfumed with incense that beckoned those who loved her.

Feeling like a bride herself, Elisheba climbed the crowded southern stairs to the Lord's House, varying her pace to match the differing treads of each stone step. How difficult it was to conceal her eagerness when each step took her nearer to her love, her husband, Joseph.

And to You, she told the Lord, sensing His presence, delighting in His Spirit.

A small body collided against Elisheba's legs, catching at her blue tunic and veils, almost making her trip. Her four-year-old, Benjamin, righted himself, staring at the Roman soldiers who lingered near the steps, all conspicuous in crimson cloaks, their helmets, weapons, and shields glinting in the sun.

"Watch where you're going," she scolded softly, taking her son's hand.

"I am." But the little boy continued to stare at the soldiers, his brown eyes wide. Clearly their weapons fascinated him.

"Really!" Elisheba began in pretend complaint. Glancing beyond the edges of her sheer blue veils and head-covering, she stopped suddenly, realizing the soldiers were watching them—watching everyone—hard-eyed, as if prepared to attack anyone who caused a scene.

She tightened her hold on Benjamin's hand. Should she should turn around and take him home? Her servants still waited in the huge public courtyard before the steps, guarding her small blue-curtained litter. They could leave almost immediately.

But what if Joseph was in danger?

Elisheba's stomach clenched at the thought. Trying to reassure herself, she prayed beneath her breath, "Please shield us, Almighty Lord." She urged Benjamin up the myriad steps, moving quietly amid the other visitors and worshipers past the temple's usual Levite guards.

By the time she and Benjamin made their way through the huge, double-arched doorways and tunnel and then entered the vast sunlit stone-paved Court of the Gentiles, Elisheba was sweating despite the cold air. People were gathered here and there throughout the pale marble court: bright-clad Greek-Jews and Persian-Jews, boisterous merchants and herders with their animals, somberly robed Pharisees, and aristocratic Sadducees. Some smiling, many grim, all gossiping as Elisheba walked among them.

Threads of conversation reached her in snatches of Aramaic and Greek.

"They beheaded the Baptist in his cell."

"... the Immerser-Prophet, John, for a dance—a *girl's* dance!"

"He spoke against the Lady Herodias," a dark-clad scribe sniffed, gaining Elisheba's attention with his contempt. "The man was a fool if he thought they would tolerate his outbursts. Prophet, indeed!"

The prophet was dead? Elisheba faltered, her steps slowing with her stumbling thoughts. How could this be true? Only ten months past, she and Joseph had listened to John the Immerser proclaiming the truth of their Almighty Lord with such an unquenchable passion that their lives—their souls—were forever changed. How could he be gone?

Swallowing, she crushed her impulse to cry. What would onlookers think? If Joseph's aristocratic father, Lord Pallu, saw her tears, he'd belittle her. Scorn her as a childish female and send her home.

"There's Abba!" Benjamin announced in Aramaic, tugging against Elisheba's grip.

Elisheba looked beyond the money-lenders' tables and saw her own Joseph, slim and handsomely robed in crimson, his rich dark beard neatly trimmed as many young Sadducees' beards—much shorter than the Pharisees deemed proper for a devout Jew. Yet, despite his worldly appearance, Joseph was truly devout. Even now, he was talking seriously to three of his closest friends, his comrades in prayer, Stephanos and Andronikos—who were also Jewish but Greek-born—and Kore, a young prankster whose family had returned to Jerusalem from exile in Persia only one generation past.

Glimpsing her husband's fading color, Elisheba winced. He'd obviously just heard of the Prophet John's death. And like her, he was fighting his distress. If Lord Pallu noticed and suspected that they had followed the Immerser, the Baptist John, and his Prophet-cousin, Rabbi Yeshua, Lord Pallu would all but disown Joseph.

Controlling herself, Elisheba released her son's hand. "Go to Abba."

Benjamin ran happily, his dark curls shining in the light. Her small sweet messenger, announcing her presence to Joseph. Married or not, Elisheba couldn't speak to her husband in public, particularly not here. The Pharisees would take great offense at even the appearance of impropriety between a man and a woman in the Holy Courts of the Lord. But Benjamin could speak for her. He was also her excuse to draw near.

Joseph and his friends straightened, startled as Benjamin scampered into their midst. Recovering, Joseph caught Benjamin beneath the arms and swooped him up protectively. "You can't stay long," Joseph told Benjamin. He kissed his son then cast a subtle worried glance toward Elisheba.

Slight and scholar-gentle, Stephanos also looked concerned. And Kore, twitching with adolescent tension, seemed ready to bolt from the Gentiles' Court at the slightest excuse. But Andronikos, the tallest, spoke quietly in Greek, his bronzed face cool. "We should delay the Capernaum journey."

"I agree." Joseph shifted Benjamin in his arms, turning him toward Elisheba, almost making her smile in gratitude.

The young men resumed their conversation as if they wanted her to hear what they were saying—and indeed they should. They'd been planning to travel to Capernaum after celebrating Passover to hear the Rabbi Yeshua again—Master Iesous, as Joseph's friends named him in Greek. Elisheba's spirit sank. How long would the journey be delayed? For weeks, she'd anticipated sharing the journey with Joseph and Benjamin as soon as the weather warmed. Indeed, her soul had thrived on the hope, for beyond Lord Pallu's strictures, beyond his mansion in Jerusalem, she was free to enjoy her husband's company.

Kore, turning paler than Joseph, asked, "Should we go into hiding? Is Jerusalem no longer safe?"

Elisheba froze. If Herod the Tetrarch, ruler of this particular fourth of Judea, had turned against the Prophet John, then surely his supporters must hide in fear of losing their lives.

But Andronikos shook his dark head, calming Kore. "No. We're probably in more danger from the Romans crushing riots than we are from Herod."

"I'm sure you're right," Joseph said. "If Herod wanted to imprison the Baptist's followers, then he would have done so before news of his death became known."

"Even so…" Kore's whisper went thin. "…what sort of girl would request a prophet's head?"

"No normal person would," Stephanos muttered, glancing around, clearly afraid they'd be overheard and punished. "Someone coerced the girl."

Herod's non-wife, Elisheba guessed. Herodias, mother of the errant girl, had hated the Prophet John for speaking against her publicly. Even if the prophet had simply announced what everyone thought, what everyone whispered within these sacred courts and beyond these walls.

Giving Benjamin a hug, Joseph set the little boy firmly on the slab paving. "You should go now."

Benjamin looked hurt. But as he opened his mouth to protest, Joseph became unusually stern. "Obey me. And obey your Ama. Go home *now*."

Joseph was right, Elisheba realized. If a rebellion developed as this news spread through the city, then the safest place was in their own household, away from the Roman soldiers. Clasping her unwilling son's hand, she gently addressed Joseph through Benjamin, as any proper wife would do when she wanted to make her thoughts known in public. "Come, my son. I pray your father and his friends return safely to their homes. And soon."

"We should go," Kore urged the others as Elisheba turned away.

She didn't hear Stephanos or Andronikos reply.

It wasn't until Elisheba was outside the courts again, preparing to climb into her blue-curtained litter, that she realized Joseph's three friends had cautiously trailed her and Benjamin outside, all the way down the public steps. Her silent guardians.

As she glimpsed their concern, an unaccustomed tremor passed through Elisheba, of near panic, weighted with dread. Throughout their journey home, she prayed for the three young men and for her husband.

Let Joseph be well. Lord, keep him safe!

***

Joseph looked around the crowded Holy Courts for his father, hoping to persuade him that they should go home. It was best to practice caution, never mind how many men owed his father money and favors.

Or perhaps it was best to practice caution *because* so many owed his father money and favors.

One day he would persuade his father to cease his power-grasping schemes, squandering his money on bribes and shaky loans. Such things were foolishness, tempting disgrace and—

No. Joseph stopped himself. Whatever their differences, he must honor his father.

He saw Pallu then, gray and patrician, standing near the tables rented from the priests, laughing with his friends. All the men were perfectly groomed, well-fed, and wearing gold rings and the best robes and cloaks. And all were in good humor because another troublemaker, John the Immerser, had been struck down.

Joseph willed his thoughts into order. Be calm. Reasoning was better than raging.

His father nodded to him and excused himself from his wealthy cohorts. Sauntering over to Joseph, he sniffed. "I saw you earlier, visiting with your...friends. At least they aren't Pharisees. But you spend too much time with them, Joseph. Who *are* they anyway? Plain merchants' sons. You need to look for better friends than those, I'm telling you."

Joseph tensed. Another thing to disagree with his father over. Well, for the sake of honor before Lord, he would keep his mouth closed. For now.

***

Standing patiently in Elisheba's morning-lit bedchamber, Joseph held still as his oldest and most favored servant, Eran, arranged his cloak's blue folds in perfect order. Seated at her small stonework writing table, Elisheba said, "You look wonderful."

Joseph cast a glance at his wife and paused, mesmerized by the temptation of her dark loosened hair, which framed her exquisite face and the delectable lines of her slender throat. If only he could remain with her this morning instead of attending business. "You're partial, beloved."

"Truth is impartial, my love." She smiled and returned to her task—writing a note to her parents regarding tonight's Passover festivities.

Peace reigned until Benjamin charged into the bedchamber like a small crimson-clad tempest, jostling Eran as he capered between them, and tugged at Joseph's sleeves. "Abba! Can we visit you today?"

Eran—wise man—stepped back, his narrow, gray-bearded face brightening, a smile crinkling the corners of his dark eyes.

Giving up on a perfect appearance in favor of his son, Joseph scooped up Benjamin, growling and shaking him until they both laughed themselves near-breathless. Benjamin flung his arms around Joseph's neck and squeezed hard. "Grrr ... surrender! I am stronger than Samson! I will win!"

"Good!" Joseph swung Benjamin around and then knuckled his hair, delighted by the little boy's laughter. "If you are stronger than Samson, you'll be able to carry your Ama and me when we're old and feeble. And *she* will be the loveliest old woman in all of Jerusalem."

"Now *you* are partial," Elisheba protested, widening her beautiful eyes at Joseph.

Grinning, Joseph set down his son. "*I* am right." Elisheba's bright glance and her sweet spirit would never be old. Truly, he was blessed above all men having her as his wife. Glancing down, he answered Benjamin's first question in Hebrew. "You won't be visiting me today, Binyamin, but we'll wrestle tonight before the feast. Until then, I need you to stay here and protect Ama."

To prevent Benjamin's protest and to attain his own escape without a fuss, Joseph snatched a small polished stone jar of pomade from a nearby table. "Now, my son, you must tend your hair. Remember that despite his failings, Samson always groomed his hair."

To Elisheba and Eran's visible horror—and his secret glee—Joseph glopped some fragrant ointment into Benjamin's hands. "Take plenty and rub it into your hair."

While his son was distracted with hair-grooming, Joseph crossed the chamber and kissed Elisheba, permitting himself to linger for an instant and caress her soft face. "Be safe. Don't go into the streets today. There were protests yesterday over Pilate's proposed use of temple funds for that new aqueduct he's building. If he persists, we can expect rioting and reprisals this morning."

"Then you should stay home," Elisheba protested, gripping his arms.

"I won't be long." Gently, Joseph lifted her hands and kissed her fingers. "I've some contracts to sign and witness, and I cannot allow those men to believe I'm ignoring them. Until I return, please remain here."

"Certainly. May the Lord bring you to me again, safely and soon!"

"He will, bless His holy name." Joseph sped through the chamber again, stopping just long enough to kiss the back of Benjamin's neck, avoiding the smears of hair ointment. "Behave, young Samson!" More mischievously, he pretended to kiss Eran. "Behave, venerable teacher!"

Eran flinched. "Master, when do I not?" But then the elderly servant gasped at Benjamin, who was now frowning at his small pomade-smeared hands. "Young master, hold still! Allow me to wipe your hands. No pomade on the clothes!"

They'd be busy awhile, and Benjamin was too distracted by the gooey pomade to protest his departure. Success! Joseph dashed from the chamber, through the ante-chamber, and out to the courtyard, where the servants waited with the saddled donkeys. His father crossed the courtyard, nodded to him, and muttered, "We'll ride out together, but I've another meeting planned. Go ahead with your dealings. I'll follow later."

Why the secrecy? Why all the recent unexplained meetings and the almost drab clothes? Joseph hid his frustration. Why ask questions that his father would scorn to answer? Indeed, the answers would be unwelcomed if Joseph's suspicions were true. As it was, he must depart. Andronikos, Stephanos, and Kore expected him for prayers in the Holy Courts. Afterward, he'd agreed to meet a beleaguered landowner who'd pleaded with him to seal a loan contract, to be followed by a consultation with an advisor handling rents and investments for Lord Pallu. Certain irregularities had appeared in the accounts, and Joseph was determined to flush out the culprit responsible for the current deficits—for surely a culprit existed.

Pondering business, he rode through Jerusalem's bustling streets, which were thronged with travelers who'd journeyed to Jerusalem to celebrate Passover. More than once he was forced to halt and wait as travelers blocked his path. After the din of the crowded streets and the enormous public square below Jerusalem's Holy House, Joseph welcomed the comparative openness of the vast pale outer court as he emerged from the tunneled steps leading up to the Holy House.

He crossed to the magnificent columns sheltering Solomon's Porch, where his friends waited. Andronikos and Stephanos smiled, but Kore pretended to huff. "You're late! We've finished praying, so have a good day."

Andronikos grinned good-naturedly. "Don't believe him. We weren't—"

Clattering footsteps echoed through the court behind them, and men bellowed hoarsely, "To the sanctuary! Go!"

A band of rustic travelers fled past them, running as if their lives depended upon speed. Red-cloaked Roman soldiers followed the rustics, moving at a swift, relentless cadence, their swords drawn, their expressions pitiless. Joseph gasped, "Mighty Lord, save us!"

If any of those soldiers charged him, he was dead. Already, the first Roman swords lifted. The first screams echoed in the vast, light-filled court.

And the first blood splashed crimson over the pale, sacred stones.

Chapter 3

Joseph retreated, praying wordlessly as one of the rustics exhaled a death-wail. His Roman attacker need only turn to kill a defenseless man—him. As he retreated, Andronikos hissed in Greek, "Iosif, hurry!"

He shoved Joseph and Stephanos between the pillars within Solomon's Porch and stood between them and the soldier who straightened and turned, bloodied sword readied. Kore was also sheltered between the pillars, but he stepped toward the fray. Joseph dragged him back. "Kore! What can you do? Be still!"

Kore protested, "They're invading the inner courts. They'll defile the sanctuary!"

Maintaining his grip on the younger man, Joseph muttered, "Pray for the safety of all within. For now, let's go. Run for the gate!"

Andronikos herded them together, particularly nudging Stephanos, who looked stunned, dazed to stillness. "Go! Run before more soldiers are sent from the fortress! We'll surely die then."

They fled as if they, not the Romans, were the corrupting intruders.

Joseph cast a final anguished glance at the fallen rustic, who lay dead amid a pool of spreading blood, and then he raced with his friends toward the eastern gate, praying as he fled.

***

Passover. Seated among the women amid their second night of feasting, Elisheba lifted her fragile red-glazed cup and glanced along the low, richly laden tables, seeking her husband. Joseph, elegant in gold and crimson robes, was reclining to his father's right in the large lamp-lit reception room. His cousin Malchos sat to his left. Usually, Joseph relished such gatherings. Place him amid other men of learning and wit and he would set them all to laughing until Elisheba could think of nothing else but pelting him with questions the instant they returned to her bedchamber.

Here was the trial of being Elisheba, daughter of Barzel. Despite her wealth, she was as all women, silenced and isolated by traditions that ensured her deprivation of new ideas and spirited thoughts.

At least, when they were alone together, Joseph could be cajoled into sharing with her most of what had been discussed with the men. Indeed, if she didn't cajole him for details, he'd be disappointed. "Beloved," Joseph would ask, his dark eyes wide, his expression all drama, piteously appealing, "why are you so quiet? Don't you love me?"

Tonight, however, Joseph didn't appear to be enjoying the rich food or the men's conversation. Instead, he picked at his meal, looking distracted. Ill.

Elisheba understood his distress.

Even now his eyes reflected pain, as if still seeing pools of Galilean blood staining the white courts of the Lord's House. For according to reports, it was a band of Galileans who'd fallen in the holy courts this morning, with several innocents amid the blood of their own sacrifices before the altar itself.

"It was evil," Joseph had told Elisheba when he returned. "How can the Almighty Lord endure such an unholy slaughter in His House?"

She shivered now, considering what the Lord might answer.

The instant their ceremonies and meal were finished, Joseph rose from the table and headed toward their private rooms. As he walked, he pressed one hand to his side, his complexion as pale as his friend Kore's.

Elisheba hastily excused herself from the other women and followed her husband. Clearly, his distress involved more than the deaths of those poor men in the Lord's House. Joseph was truly ill.

She caught up with him just beyond the formal courtyard, at the entrance to her bedchamber. Before she could say a word, Joseph doubled over, seized by pain. As the spasm passed, he looked up at her, the image of a healthy young man shocked by true agony. He whispered, "Something...must end this..."

Elisheba slid an arm around his waist and then staggered as he leaned heavily against her. "Joseph," she warned, "I won't permit you to argue. I'm sending for a physician."

He swallowed and nodded, pausing again, his beloved face drawn. "Yes. A man could die of such pain."

***

Elisheba kneeled beside her cushioned bed and clasped her husband's fevered hand. Joseph stirred, wincing while Pallu's own Greek physician, beardless and dispassionate in a stately white tunic and mantle, prodded Joseph's belly, then checked his eyes and pulse. Elisheba, too, studied her husband's dark, sunken eyes. No inviting sparkle encouraged her that he was recovering. Joseph's previous physician had retreated last night, muttering prayers like incantations as Joseph wrestled his mounting fever.

Lord, Lord, let my husband smile! Heal him....

Joseph closed his eyes.

Straightening, the physician spoke, not to Elisheba but to Joseph's parents who were standing a safe distance apart in the doorway. "His pulse is rapid. When was his last meal?"

Lord Pallu answered, clipping his Greek as neatly as his gray beard. "At our feast, night before last. He was ill afterward."

"And the pains eased yesterday?"

"Yes," Pallu agreed. "Before midday."

The physician frowned as if displeased. "Any flux of the bowels?"

Joseph's mother, Levia, widened her lovely kohl-darkened eyes at Elisheba, questioning her silently. Elisheba nodded. "Yes, when he first became ill. Nothing since. The previous physician's remedies did little to ease my husband's pain."

Useless man, that physician—she'd nearly lost her temper with his throat-clearings and mumbled opinions. Not to mention his senseless incantations and herbs bought at great cost.

The current physician studied her, then Joseph again, as if debating his conclusion. Finally, he sighed. "I won't charge you a fee; there is nothing I can do. Perhaps a few days and his own youth and natural strength may be his best treatment. Encourage him to consume liquids." He beckoned his attendant slave with the slightest crook of a finger. The small man edged forward, offering his master a wooden box as full of compartments and curiosities as Levia's Egyptian cosmetic chest.

Sliding open a drawer, the physician removed a linen bag and gave it to Elisheba. The bag was light, its contents rustling dryly as she clutched it. The physician said, "You need to reduce his fever. Brew a large pinch of this in a cup of boiling water. Make him drink the entire cupful, no matter how long it takes. He is in your care."

Nodding with polite but distinct finality, the physician departed. Obviously he wouldn't welcome another summons if Joseph worsened. Elisheba knelt beside her husband, biting down tears. How could the physician simply abandon Joseph?

Pallu, however, seemed hopeful. "Good! He will be better soon." He spoke to Elisheba graciously, reverting to his usual Aramaic. "You'll want to tend him yourself, I know. We'll keep everyone away from you for a few days to avoid the fever. Call out if you need anything."

Though she also kept her distance, Levia looked more worried than her husband. She told Elisheba, "I'll keep Benjamin with his cousins. If they tire him out, he won't fret for you."

Benjamin. Elisheba ached to see her son. He certainly knew something was wrong. He'd not seen his father since Passover, and until now, he'd played with his father every day. But it would be foolish to let Benjamin visit Joseph now and risk illness. "Kiss him for us," she begged Levia.

Joseph squeezed Elisheba's hand, muttering agreement, "Yes. Tell him…I'm thinking of him."

The chill from her husband's fingers made Elisheba glance down, and her breath caught. Joseph's fingertips were now blue-tinged. Surely the physician had noticed.

Levia's composed aristocrat demeanor softened. She encouraged her firstborn, "Joseph, don't worry. Benjamin will be fine. Just rest and get well quickly."

Joseph sighed agreement.

"His fingertips are blue," Elisheba told her mother-in-law, her heart thudding as she spoke.

Levia pursed her lips. "I'll send one of the servants with more coverlets and some hot broth. Keep him warm, Elisheba, and send me word of his condition this evening."

When his mother left, Joseph looked up at Elisheba, concern shadowing his handsome fever-flushed face and haunting his brown eyes.

Denying her own fears, Elisheba kissed his hot, whiskered cheek, her sheer veils cascading around them both in fragile, insubstantial waves.

***

Throughout the day, Joseph felt Elisheba tending him, gently rubbing his cold hands with oil, cooling his hot face with damp cloths, and offering him liquid he couldn't drink.

Rest, he thought to her, shivering with the fever, too nauseated to speak. He worried about Elisheba. Perhaps she was with child again. What if she caught this fever? She needed to rest. Later, when he was recovered, he would buy her a new gown. A ring. Anything his love wanted. She deserved everything.

Elisheba was whispering to him now. He tried to listen. Stephanos … Kore … Andronikos … asking for you … praying for you … worried.

His friends. Soon, they would travel to Capernaum together. He would make Elisheba rest while he played with Benjamin along the rocky shores of Galilee. They would find the Rabbi Yeshua … who was more than a prophet … and listen … listen …

Joseph's thoughts slid away into darkness.

He awoke, struggling to breathe, his flesh hot then cold. He shifted, lightheaded though he'd not stirred from bed. Sweat pooled around him and he trembled, fighting off the dimness.

I'm dying.

He wrestled the thought hard, focusing on the sunset-red glow that lit their hushed bedchamber. Elisheba sat up beside him, disheveled as if she had been napping. With the warmth of her body gone, his own body shook so violently that his muscles spasmed painfully, making him gasp. "Ah!"

"Joseph?" Elisheba huddled against him now, her voice rising in fear. "What should I do?"

One thought cut through all. Joseph exhaled the words, slurring. "Y'shua … Carry me … to him." He must be healed. Elisheba and Benyamin needed him.

She gaped, and then rolled out of the bed. Her movements flustered, she draped more coverlets over him and kissed his cheek in parting agreement. "Yes, yes! I love you!"

Unable to turn his head to watch Elisheba run from the room, Joseph closed his eyes, shaken by tremors, trying to form prayers within the encroaching darkness.

***

Dragging her crushed linen robes together, Elisheba ran from the rooms she shared with Joseph, through the slab-paved central courtyard, and up the stairs to her in-laws' private rooms. She had to be calm. Joseph was worse. So much worse! Panting, biting down her sobs, she pounded on Levia's antechamber door until her knuckles hurt against the wood.

Levia opened the door, her dark hair and light robes all unbound. Seeing Elisheba, she backed away, keeping her distance, gasping, "Oh! What's wrong?"

Pallu emerged from their bedchamber, clad in a long tunic and a mantle, and holding a silver cup. The instant he saw his daughter-in-law, he froze. "Joseph—"

Elisheba kneeled, too shaky to stand. "He's worse, my lord. Much worse. He …"

"How is that possible?" Pallu's eyes widened beneath his thick-furrowed brows. "The physician said he would recover."

Elisheba shook her head. "He's not recovering. Please, lord, hear me." Gathering her courage, she continued. "He sent me to ask—and I know you *don't* want to hear this—but he wants to be taken to the Rabbi Yeshua. The Healer."

Levia put a hand to her slender throat. "You mean the Galilean?"

Before Elisheba could nod, Pallu cried, "That fanatic-magician who created a riot in the Gentile's Court last year? I never did recover all the silver he dumped off my men's tables! Does Joseph know what he's asking? The fever's sent him mad!"

Fanatic-magician. Elisheba's hopes faded to a wavering spark. The Rabbi Yeshua *she'd* seen and heard was calm, welcoming. An extraordinary man. But naturally Pallu and Levia saw him differently. Forcing down her agitation, she persevered. "Joseph believes he can be healed if we'd just take him to—"

"No!" Pallu glared at Elisheba, twitching as if he wanted to grab her and give her a ferocious shake. "The man's a fraud and it's dangerous to associate with him!" Pallu hesitated, his color faded. "Are you saying that my son is dying?"

Was Joseph dying? No. Elisheba rocked forward, palms chilled against the tiled floor. No. He must not die. Controlling herself, she looked up at Pallu. Without his help, she could do nothing. "Please, lord, grant your son's request—for his sake, because you love him."

Her father-in-law tossed his cup clanging onto the floor and rushed past her, his flowing apparel creating a draft in his wake. The very fact that he'd come so near Elisheba while she was possibly contagious revealed his distress. Pallu, a Sadducee, lived for each day with no hope of anything beyond this life. For him, the soul died with the body. Therefore, he would never honor a prophet who proclaimed joy within eternal life—such ideas were childish daydreams.

As Levia rushed outside after Lord Pallu, Elisheba scrambled to her feet. Whatever they thought of the Rabbi Yeshua, they *had* to listen. Clutching her robes, she dashed after them down the stairs and through the courtyard.

She caught up with them at the door of her bedchamber. Pallu and Levia were actually clinging to each other as they stared into the chamber at Joseph. When they realized she was near, they backed away to let her pass. Elisheba had no need to ask if Joseph was still alive. His breath wheezed so hard in his throat that she inhaled as if she could breathe for him. A futile thought. And yet—

"There's still time!" she cried, not caring that she had raised her voice to her proud, high-born in-laws. "Please. *Please!* Let me fulfill his request and take him to the Rabbi."

"He never said those words," Pallu choked. "My son would never disgrace me with such foolishness. It was your own insane request."

Elisheba stared at him. He'd deemed her a liar? Why did he doubt her? Joseph needed his father's help. "I'm not lying, lord. He was still able to speak when I left him, as he might yet. Please!"

His voice almost as hoarse as Joseph's fraught breaths, Pallu said, "Save your words. They're useless. Useless …"

Tears slid down Levia's face and she called to the servants. "Bring lamps! Hurry!"

Pallu ran a hand over his face and slumped down in the doorway, alternately restraining himself, then sobbing aloud. His shoulders shook and tears slid down his smooth cheeks, merging with his close-shaven, silvering beard.

Elisheba saw Pallu's intent. A death vigil. How could she bear this, knowing they had one last hope? She couldn't. But she had to. She was helpless against Pallu's absolute refusal. Outwardly, she complied, kneeling beside Joseph, kissing his hot face, holding his cold hand as she wept.

Inside she screamed, pleading to the Almighty Lord.

Chapter 4

Ashes. In the quiet bedchamber, Elisheba stared at the dark powder of ashes sifting from her hair onto Joseph's calm, cold, blue-mottled face. Dazed with fatigue, she rinsed away the ashes and gently dried his face again. He must be clean.

This ritual cleansing would be her last act of love for Joseph, solitary until his childhood manservant, Eran, entered the room, carrying clean linen strips.

Thin, silver-haired, slowed with grief, Eran bound Joseph's wrists together, then his ankles. Unfurling another linen strip in his veined hands, he said brokenly, "Young Mistress ... allow me."

She stepped back, permitting Eran to bind the linen beneath Joseph's chin encircling his dear face. Elisheba stared, blankness taking hold. She'd wake up soon. This must be a terrible dream. Joseph was alive. All his brightness, his love and joy of life could not be sealed away forever in a tomb.

"Elisheba?"

Hearing her mother's voice, Elisheba looked to the doorway. There, Daliyah hesitated, olive-skinned, barefoot, and clad in sackcloth, her soft brown eyes brimming.

Weakened by her mother's tears, Elisheba felt her own tears stinging her eyes and tightening her throat, the pain making Joseph's death too real.

No, I don't want to do this! Joseph...please, don't be dead!

As she sobbed, Eran crept from the room. Daliyah set down a basket, crossed the room, and enfolded Elisheba in a protective hug. "Little one, you should have sent for me. Have you any symptoms?"

She patted Elisheba's face and forehead, evidently checking her for signs of the fever. Seeming reassured, Daliyah looked down at Joseph and cried, then finally managed, "He looks so peaceful ... Oh, my dear boy! How can we bear to lose him?"

We didn't have to lose him.

The words almost crossed Elisheba's lips. She bit them down with her tears. Elisheba knew her mother loved her and would listen sympathetically, but her mother shared Lord Pallu's beliefs. Elisheba also knew she couldn't speak ill of Pallu and Levia in their own house. She remained bound to them for Benjamin's sake. Instead, when she was able to talk, she said, "Ama, thank you for coming, but you've made yourself unclean. I've ... been tending Joseph, with the fever."

"I'm here as I should be." Daliyah straightened, wiping her eyes, covering her grief with an attitude of busyness. "Later, we'll bathe and you'll rest. Look." She retrieved her basket. "Joanna sent this."

Joanna, Andronikos' mother, had befriended Joseph when he was a little boy. Elisheba, too, had visited Joanna's perfume shop as a child. The perfume shop had been the first tie binding Joseph's friendship with Andronikos, and her own marriage to Joseph. Now, to share her grief, Joanna had sent an alabaster vial of anointing oil.

Reluctantly, Elisheba broke the seal, opening the vial. Rich, earthen, balsam-like fragrance filled the bedchamber, almost stunning her. This was no mere flower-scented oil. Joanna had sent the most costly ointment of all—spikenard. Worth months' of wages in silver.

"How can I accept this?" she asked, imploring her mother's advice.

Daliyah's dark eyes reddened, filling again. Tenderly, she said, "You know how much Joanna loved Joseph, and you. Don't deny her this sacrifice. Andronikos will want to honor Joseph. They were like brothers. You can thank them later."

Obedient, Elisheba anointed her husband's cold forehead with the precious roseate spikenard and her tears. But, surely, she would never endure spikenard's scent again.

***

Benjamin clung to his grandfather's neck as Lord Pallu carried him toward stone steps cut into the earth. There, at the bottom of the steps, he glimpsed a small white doorway and a huge round wreath-carved stone, big as a door. Strange men were carrying his Abba—wrapped tight in pale cloth—through the white doorway, into darkness.

"Here we all end," Pallu said quietly, setting Benjamin on the top step. "We all die. Then there is nothing."

Benjamin tried to think of nothing. But his thoughts rushed on, upset by the hired mourners now wailing horribly all around him. And his mother, his Ama, was crying too, her hair and face smudged with ashes and tears. He didn't want her to be crying. It meant that she was afraid. If she was afraid, then everything was very bad.

Tears burning his eyes, Benjamin watched as the strange men finally emerged from the doorway without his Abba. He blinked as they rolled the heavy wreath-carved stone over the shadowed entrance, trapping his father inside. Were they going to leave him in there, asleep and tied up?

The men brushed their hands clean, climbed up the steps, and walked past Benjamin. Yes, they were leaving his father tied up and hidden in that dark place. Worse, Lord Pallu tapped his shoulder. "Come, my son. Let's go."

"Abba!" Benjamin called hopefully toward the stone-sealed entrance. "Let's go."

"Benjamin!" Pallu sounded stern. Angry. "He is *dead*. He won't come home with you."

"He will!"

Clambering down the steps, Benjamin slapped his hands on the huge stone, shoving it with all his might, willing it to move. "Abba, wake up. Let's go!"

The stone stayed. His hands scraped, hurting against the stone as he shoved it again. Benjamin sobbed. "Move. *Move!* Please, move …!"

His grandfather came down the steps and swiped an arm around Benjamin's waist, lifting him off his feet. "He is dead. He will never wake up again. Come now."

Benjamin kicked at air, struggling to reach for the stone. "No! G-get him out!"

Lord Pallu set him down at the top of the steps and took his hand. Benjamin wrenched free and flung himself on the ground, refusing to go. Lord Pallu raised his voice. "He cannot come out—ever. You must understand this."

"He can come out! I *need* him out!"

At a distance, Ama kneeled, calling to him. "Little one, please follow Lord Pallu. We must go home."

"No, Ama!" he insisted, so angry he screamed through his tears. They were playing a mean game, and he wanted them to stop. "Get Abba out now!"

Others approached—his father's friends: Stephanos, Kore, and Andronikos. They would help him. He scrambled to his feet, passing his grandfather as he charged toward the three men. "Get Abba out! I don't want him in there!"

But Andronikos didn't obey. Instead, he bent and lifted Benjamin high in his arms, holding him tight. Quietly, as if sharing a secret, he said, "You'll see your Abba again someday. But you must allow him to rest now."

"Not in there!" Benjamin argued fiercely.

Stephanos placed a hand on Benjamin's shoulder, kind but serious. "Listen, Benjamin. Abba wants to rest. And he wants you to go eat."

"And play," Kore added, poking his pale face in front of Benjamin's.

They sounded so sure. And no one else would help him. Weakening, he pleaded, "But I d-don't want Abba in there."

"Neither do we, but there he must stay." Stephanos smiled, but his dark eyes remained sad, not lying at all. "Come to me. I'll carry you home," he offered.

"No, you won't," Andronikos argued quietly, tightening his hold on Benjamin and ducking away. "I'll carry him."

"You two don't deserve to carry Joseph's son." Kore tugged at Benjamin's arm, starting a hushed game. "*I* will take him."

Their arguing made Benjamin feel safe. He could almost forget about his Abba being tied up and hidden in the cold, dark room inside the ground. Almost.

***

Elisheba sat on the mosaic floor in Pallu and Levia's elaborately plastered and marble-frescoed reception room. Her mother and Joanna sat with her, while Levia and her friends clustered a safe distance apart, all barefoot, wearing coarse garments instead of soft linen and jewels, and adorned with ashes instead of veils.

Levia was still sobbing—her swollen eyelids red, devoid of kohl, her nose raw, her whole demeanor so crushed and dazed that Elisheba hurt for her.

She couldn't blame Levia for Joseph's death. Pallu ruled her.

But how could it serve the Lord to remove the most devout man in this family? And the sweetest, most tender and loving husband …

If she remembered any more, she would die right now, killed by grief.

"Here." Offering Elisheba a cup, Joanna smiled, her golden-brown eyes gentled with sadness. "Joseph would want you to eat."

Elisheba hesitated, whispering in Greek. "Should I touch anything? What about the possibility of spreading Joseph's fever? Perhaps I should leave."

Joanna shook her head, her silver-streaked hair catching and reflecting light despite her crowning haze of ashes. "No one else in your family is sick. Your mother and I are certain you won't be ill. Unless you decide to starve yourself. Come now."

As she sipped the bitter drink, Elisheba noticed her father, Barzel. Slight and black-bearded, Barzel was seated on the floor, talking quietly to Pallu, as if trying to persuade him to agree to something. But Lord Pallu remained grim and stone-faced, watching Stephanos, Benjamin, Andronikos, and Kore, who sat together unobtrusively in a corner of the imposing room.

Evidently noticing Elisheba's gaze, her mother hugged her. Daliyah whispered, "Your father is asking Pallu to allow you to rejoin our household next month. You and Benjamin. Would you like that, my baby?"

"Yes, Ama," Elisheba murmured, too distressed to concentrate on her mother's words. Pallu seemed ready to snatch Benjamin from Joseph's friends.

How could Lord Pallu not appreciate these three young men and their concern for Benjamin? Her son needed to hear about his father as he had been in life—warm and vital, full of joy. Not merely Pallu's flat-spoken, "He is dead."

Y'shua ... carry me ... to him.

Remembering her husband's final words, Elisheba longed to claw at Pallu. Joseph could have lived. But Pallu had refused his final request. Wouldn't any parent—even a Sadducee—have snatched at the slightest, most foolish hope to save a precious child?

"It takes strength to mourn," her mother said, almost crying again. "Won't you eat something now? There are so many gifts of food here."

She offered Elisheba a dish of red lentils—herdsmen's food. A serving of mourning symbols promising that the future still held life. Elisheba held the warm bowl, unable to eat. How could a future exist without Joseph?

Looking away from the lentils, Elisheba noticed Pallu pointing at her, while whispering at Barzel, leaning toward him accusingly. Barzel was leaning away from Pallu, clearly aghast.

Was Pallu condemning Elisheba to her own father?

Her certainty strengthened as Barzel looked at her, his rounded face a study of hurt and betrayal. She could almost hear him asking, "How could you? My only child, how could you wound me so?"

A slap would have been easier to accept. Now her father would forever regard her as an embarrassment—an easily led fool. And there was nothing she could say to defend herself. Indeed, her defense of the Rabbi Yeshua would only deepen Barzel's mortification. Elisheba looked down at the lentils again, defiance making her clench the bowl until her knuckles appeared bloodless with strain.

She should have taken Joseph to the Rabbi without asking permission, never mind the scandal. In the hills of Galilee, she'd seen miracles born of the Rabbi's touch upon others. Joseph would have lived. Yes, and yes again!

She endured the rituals of grief in wounded silence.

***

In a corner of Lord Pallu's formal reception room, Andronikos offered some lentils and bread to Benjamin. The little boy sat beside him, peaceful for now, eating his food. During this fragment of calm, Andronikos glanced around the elegant room and noticed that his mother was the only woman, excepting Daliyah, who dared to sit with Elisheba to comfort her. How ironic. Under normal circumstance, he and his mother would have been less than auspicious guests. But Joseph's death and perhaps his family's gift of the spikenard ointment had temporarily lowered the noble Pallu's ideals.

Or perhaps not. Andronikos frowned. Why was Lord Pallu glaring at him, and Stephanos, and Kore? As if they were lepers who'd intruded upon the purity of his Sadducee household.

How could the man, lord or not, be so uncivil?

Andronikos watched Lord Pallu turn an equally cold look upon the grief-stricken Elisheba, then gesture toward her father as if furious. Did

Lord Pallu blame Elisheba for Joseph's death? Andronikos seethed at the thought.

Stephanos, ever sensitive to others, leaned into their circle and whispered, "Have we offended Lord Pallu?"

"It seems so," Andronikos muttered, resisting his unrighteous longing to thrash that boor Lord Pallu.

Stephanos winced. "Perhaps we should apologize and excuse ourselves. Later we'll find out what we've done to insult him."

"No." Kore leaned into their conversation, his thin face indignant as he ever was when faced with injustice. "Are we cowards? Let's just ask him why he's angry with us."

Looking around, fidgeting, Stephanos argued beneath his breath, "Not now, Kore. That would make us look like fools. We've only been welcomed here for Joseph's sake. We're nothing to Lord Pallu; he'd throw us out."

"Then we should ask the servants," Kore persisted, scratching at his sackcloth tunic. "Servants know everything."

Andronikos shook his head at his friend. Trust Kore to recommend gossip. "Don't you say a word to the servants or anyone. We will be dignified and leave courteously for the sake of Joseph's good name." And Elisheba's.

"Juice," Benjamin blurted out, looking up at the young men hopefully, lentils smudged red-brown on his chin like a badly grown beard. "I need juice."

"Go ask your Ama," Kore suggested.

Before Andronikos could stop him, Benjamin stood and trotted toward Elisheba. But the Lady Levia called to him, obviously fearing that Elisheba was infected by Joseph's fever.

Benjamin looked as if he wanted to argue, until Levia offered him a cup. Thirst won. The little boy sat beside his grandmother and even allowed his face to be wiped by a servant in order to receive a drink. Elisheba watched all this, her soft dark eyes reflecting such pain that Andronikos hurt for her sake. Joseph would be furious to see his wife thus isolated and scorned.

Andronikos had never felt so insignificant, so unable to help Joseph's wife and son.

Ever obsessive, Kore said, "I still say we should ask the servants why Lord Pallu is so offended with us. If we're going to be brought up on charges for some reason …"

As Stephanos gripped Kore's cloak in alarm, restraining him, Andronikos stood. "If he does bring charges against us for some foolish reason, we'll answer publicly. We've done nothing wrong. Nor will we. Let's excuse ourselves and go."

***

Born of the eternal, they descended as commanded, circling just beyond the boundaries of flesh to their designated prey.

Though its body is small, all souls are the same size.

Take this one's courage and crush it. Whisper into him such terrors of the night that he becomes a trembling thing, unable to describe his panic. Bind his soul with fear.

Fear must lead him away from It.
Fear. Perfect fear.

***

Things moved in the darkness just beyond the lamplight, of that Benjamin was certain. And whispers that he could almost hear made him jump. Made him choke for breath as he huddled on his pallet near his sleeping cousins and their maidservants. He couldn't—wouldn't—reveal his fright to his cousins, Malkah and Zimiyrah. They were girls. They would tease him. Benjamin wished they were boys. He could be braver then. But now, surrounded by nighttime sounds, Benjamin shivered. Was he being watched?

Eran would have understood. But Benjamin couldn't stay with Eran, or with his Ama, because the maidservants said Ama and Eran were "exposed to the fever."

Because of that fever, everything was bad, and he was alone.

Abba would have helped him. Nothing ever whispered at Abba or moved in the darkness when Abba was nearby. But Abba was gone.

Feeling the closeness of the watchful things and remembering his father shut in the cold darkness, Benjamin pulled his blanket over his head and cried.

***

Elisheba opened her eyes in the night, her sleep broken by a sudden oppression quite separate from her grief. Panic descended upon her, thick as a cloak, making her clutch the coverlets to her chin as all the hairs prickled on her scalp and arms.

Was someone in her room? Benjamin?

"Who's there?" she whispered into the stillness, darting glances into the shadowed corners, fully expecting a reply.

Silence answered. And the only movement she glimpsed was the soft flicker of the carved stoneware lamp, its solitary flame glowing steadily as it drew upon the wick, consuming her nighttime ration of oil. *Almighty Lord, save me from my foolish fears.*

Praying, she slipped from beneath the coverlets and crept through her room to the courtyard door. Opening it softly, she peered outside, listening hard. Nothing. Not even the distant echo of a faraway voice beyond the walls.

Elisheba stood there until an icy breath of air descended upon her bare face and throat. Closing the door softly, she barred it and returned to her cushions, staring into the endless night, chilled.

Chapter 5

Scrupulously cleansed, her hair combed free of any loose strays, Elisheba set her slender oil jar into the wall-shelf of Levia's secluded ritual bathing pool. The enclosing room was beautiful, adorned with red and gray tiles, an arched stone ceiling, small, high sunlit windows, and whitewashed steps that invited the participant downward into the pool. A delicate trickle of fresh living water also spattered from a pipe into the pool, avowing its purity.

Removing her robe, Elisheba descended the steps, shivering as her toes met the cold, crystalline water. She must accept this ritual immersion, body and soul.

Outwardly, her body needed purification from her unwelcomed monthly flow. Inwardly her heart needed cleansing because more than four weeks of grieving and isolation hadn't removed her anger against Lord Pallu.

He never spoke to her. And he'd kept her hidden for the full thirty days of formal mourning as if he believed she would prance through Jerusalem like a harlot, flirting with all the young men. Worse, he'd refused to let her take Benjamin to visit her parents, evidently not trusting Elisheba to supervise her son properly. All because of her "offensive" behavior while Joseph was dying.

Truly, she had to calm herself now and be restored to rightness with the Lord in these waters. "Oh, Lord, forgive me. Pardon all my offenses. Cleanse my heart as my flesh is cleansed. Blessed are You, oh Lord ..."

Still praying, she stepped into the small, deep pool, ducking, holding her breath as the water closed over her head. She stayed beneath the surface as long as she could, to ensure that she was completely overcome by the ritual water. Finished, she stood, gasping for air as she surfaced from the pool.

According to all the laws, she was now ritually pure. Still, her heart contracted in anguish for Joseph and in rage against Pallu. How could he fail to snatch at any hope to save Joseph, knowing death was so near? In a similar position, she would have done *anything* for Benjamin!

Anything? She could almost hear her conscience whispering the question. She cringed inwardly. She must forgive Pallu. Otherwise, how could she live in his house, eating his food? It was unpardonable of her.

She wasn't the only mourner in this household. Lord Pallu simply acted according to his beliefs. He had lost his only son—and he did love Joseph.

Elisheba wrung the excess water from her hair, tugged on her robes, and reached for her oil jar as she'd done countless times before. She would anoint herself with scented oil and then stand before a brazier of smoldering incense until the fragrance permeated her hair, her garments, and her skin. Then she would go to her own rooms and Joseph would be there, slim and so handsome that he would steal her breath away. He would kiss her, embrace her, and murmur his desire, rejoicing that their monthly time of separation was ended.

He will never kiss me again.

She sat on the uppermost step and cried.

***

Stephanos followed Kore into the perfume shop, suppressing a mocking huff as Kore yelled his habitual greeting to Andronikos. "You! Merchant, do you sell gum?"

"If you actually bought it, sir, I'd be amazed," Andronikos responded dryly. He glanced up at them and nodded to Stephanos, but then he continued to measure ashes into a cauldron with a scoop. Without his usual words of blessing and welcome.

Disturbingly unlike himself.

Stephanos looked around. "Where's your mother and the little ones?"

"At the market. Loukas has outgrown his sandals and Maria broke her comb." Andronikos usually brightened when talking about his younger siblings. But not today.

"You're in a bad mood." Stephanos leaned against the work table, prepared to listen. Every aspect of human nature interested him, just as every ideology intrigued him, be it Hebrew, Roman, Samaritan, Greek, or any other. Andronikos, however, was no willing subject for study today.

Instead, he muttered, "I'm in a hurry. I want to get my work done before we leave."

His sourness was caused by more than the work, Stephanos decided, noting Andronikos' too-intense focus on the ashes.

Less understanding, Kore leaned against another of the work tables, eyeing a dish of cinnamon quills. "Are we sure it's safe to go to Capernaum?"

Stephanos leaned over and pushed the cinnamon out of Kore's reach. "Yes. We've arranged for armed guides. And I've heard of no more rebellions or deaths."

Not since Joseph's death.

The realization pierced Stephanos like a spear, grief spreading through him yet again. Joseph should be planning this trip with them and enjoying their banter as he'd always done. How could he be dead? It seemed too unjust. If the Lord … Stephanos paused. Who was he, plain Stephanos, to question the Almighty?

Resisting profane thoughts, he watched Andronikos work.

Andronikos finally shoved the ash-dusted scoop back into its stone container then straightened. When he remained silent, Stephanos asked cautiously, "Have you heard anything more about what we've done to offend Lord Pallu?"

"I've been told that Lord Pallu considers us a bad influence." Andronikos looked Stephanos straight in the eyes. "He wants us to stay away from his household."

"Fearing we might corrupt Joseph's son?" Kore guessed, looking mutinous.

"No doubt." Andronikos reached for a basin and water pitcher. Stephanos took the pitcher and poured, allowing Andronikos to rinse the ashes from his hands.

Still subdued, Andronikos continued. "My mother spoke to Daliyah yesterday. Lord Pallu has isolated Elisheba for offending him. It seems that when Joseph was dying, Elisheba asked Pallu's permission to take Joseph to Master Iesous."

"That explains everything." Stephanos set down the pitcher, frowning toward the clouded water in the basin, not seeing it as much as their potential for trouble with Pallu.

Kore lurched away from the table, disgust etched over his narrow features. "So there's nothing we can do for Benjamin or Elisheba?"

Stephanos settled him with a quiet reminder. "Elisheba is under Lord Pallu's authority until he releases her. But Benjamin, being Joseph's only son, will always belong to Pallu, and Elisheba won't leave her son unless she must."

Andronikos nodded, silently measuring fragrant olive oil from a massive jug into a stoneware bowl.

"Ashes and oil," Kore noticed aloud. "You're making soap?"

"Obviously." Andronikos continued measuring.

"It always amazes me that you make soap from filthy ashes," Kore mused.

"Filthy?" Andronikos stopped measuring long enough to protest. "It's burnt saltwort. You don't get cleaner than that."

"You'd better go find the biggest piece of gum in the jar and chew instead of talking," Stephanos advised Kore.

"Gladly," Kore teased. "If the gum-gatherers didn't leave goat hair on it."

"Say anything else and I'll dump you into the street," Andronikos warned.

Hoping to prevent a scene, Stephanos waved a hasty attention-getting hand at him. "Will you be ready to leave tomorrow morning?"

"I said I would. So I will." Appearing bleakly amused, Andronikos added, "Mother can manage without me for a few weeks. She always tells me exactly how well she and the little ones can handle things. And I'll welcome the change."

"So will I," Stephanos murmured. Three weeks of hiking and talking and listening to Master Iesous would give them all a fresh perspective. Lord Pallu might be calmer when they returned. And perhaps all the walking would wring enough spiritual vinegar from Kore that his parents would actually welcome him home.

Kore returned from poking around in the stoneware gum jar, his face skewed to one side as he pretended to pull a long hair from between his lips. Andronikos shot him a grim half-smile and went back to work.

***

Alerted by a soft tap, Elisheba sat up amid her coverlets and cushions and looked toward her bedchamber door. Joseph's little sisters stood in the doorway. Malkah, eleven, slender and pretty as a flower stalk, hesitated as if worried about disturbing

Elisheba. But Zimiyrah, seven and buoyant with a froth of dark curls, burst out impatiently, "We *can* come in to visit, can't we?"

Zimiyrah's dancing eagerness and Malkah's distress struck Elisheba with an almost physical impact. What a wretched sister-in-law she'd been, neglecting Joseph's sisters during their mourning. Truly, in her own defense, the girls and Benjamin had been kept away from her until now to protect them from the threat of fever. But Elisheba could have sent one of the servants to them with a loving message. Remorseful, she held out a hand. "Yes, please come in. I've missed you."

Malkah slipped inside, looking around wistfully, as if hoping to see Joseph. Zimiyrah kissed Elisheba's cheek then frowned at her heap of cushions and thick mats. "Where's your bed?"

"Gone," Elisheba murmured. "Perhaps I'll get another later." She hoped her explanation was enough. The truth would upset the girls. Lord Pallu had ordered the bed and its bedding burned after Joseph's death. He'd deemed it infected, which had been a dark blessing. Except for her days of separation each month, Elisheba had never slept in her marriage bed without Joseph. She would have had nightmares sleeping in it without him now.

"Can I play with your rings?" Zimiyrah asked, nodding toward Elisheba's carved clothing chest where she also stored her jewels.

"Of course. Just don't break anything." But why worry if anything broke? She'd never care to wear jewels again.

Malkah sat with Elisheba, silent, leaning against her. Elisheba gave the girl a hug. "Don't you want to go play?"

Shaking her head, Malkah whispered, "No, thank you."

She was missing her brother, of course. Not daring to let herself dwell on thoughts of Joseph, Elisheba hugged Malkah closer, smoothing her soft dark hair.

They sat together, quietly watching Zimiyrah work the chest's iron clasp until Benjamin charged into the room, followed by Levia. Benjamin pitched himself into Elisheba's arms and clung to her. "Ama!"

How warm he was! How sweet. And heavy. "My baby! Mercy, I think you've grown! And you don't know how much I've missed you!"

"They wouldn't let me see you," he complained. "I asked every day."

"He did," Malkah whispered to Elisheba. "And he cried almost every night."

Resting her cheek on Benjamin's curls, Elisheba held him gratefully. No need to ask him why he'd cried every night. Why stir up new grief?

Levia sighed and scolded the girls. "I sent for you two but none of the servants could find you. The next time you run off, tell someone where you're going."

"*You* said we could visit Elisheba today," Zimiyrah argued pertly as she lifted the clothing chest lid.

"I didn't say 'immediately,' and don't answer me like that, Zimiyrah. You sounded like a rude market woman." Levia settled beside Elisheba and gave Malkah and Benjamin commanding nudges. "Go play."

Malkah obeyed, drooping a little, as if play wasn't what she wanted.

And Benjamin trudged over to Zimiyrah, who had finally opened the clothing chest. Ever dutiful, Malkah held the clothing chest lid while the two younger children dug inside, the chest's cedar and spice scent drifting through the air.

"Are you sure they can't hurt anything?" Levia asked Elisheba.

"They're usually careful."

"You let them take advantage, Elisheba. You know you do."

"I know," Elisheba confessed, watching Zimiyrah happily entwining herself in a long crimson sash, while Benjamin dragged out a blue veil, covering himself as if it were a prayer shawl—a tallit. "But I enjoy their company."

Now, she looked at her beautiful mother-in-law. How Levia could put on her kohl and a soft violet robe and pin her hair up with jewels not even five weeks after Joseph's death? It felt like a betrayal, as if Joseph had never lived.

"I wanted to warn you," Levia said beneath her breath. "My lord will speak to you tonight after the children go to sleep. Just ask his forgiveness and listen to him, as you should. Then he will permit you to visit your parents."

"Thank you for advising me," Elisheba murmured, hurt that she had to request Lord Pallu's forgiveness for wanting to save her husband's life.

Offended because Pallu had refused.

"So you aren't bearing another child?" Levia kept her gaze fixed on Malkah, who had finally given in to play and was donning a pair of delicate gold bracelets that Joseph had given Elisheba after Benjamin's birth.

Another child? Elisheba shook her head, the hurt expanding, becoming an unseen gash of a wound within her. "No."

Despite all her prayers and days of waiting and longing, she would never bear Joseph another child. She suspected she'd had another miscarriage instead. As her sight blurred with tears, Elisheba felt Levia hugging her.

"I had hoped you would ... just one more child," Levia mourned. "We could have named him Joseph."

Elisheba turned her face from Benjamin and her young sisters-in-law, not wanting to upset them with her tears. "I'll n-never recover. I can't."

"You will." Levia smoothed Elisheba's hair. "For Benjamin's sake, you will recover. We both will. Now, pay attention. When we send for you tonight, be sure your hair is combed and braided and covered. And wear a fresh tunic and mantle. Don't upset my lord Pallu if you can help it. He's still grieving."

Mute, Elisheba nodded. Yes. She understood grief.

Trying to console herself, she wiped her eyes and watched her small son. Benjamin marched through her chamber still wearing her veil as a prayer shawl—his father's boy.

***

In their lamp-lit reception room, Lord Pallu motioned for Elisheba to sit on a couch opposite Levia and himself. "I realize you loved my son," he began, courteous.

Love! Elisheba corrected him inwardly, almost a-tremble with her own ferocity. *I still love your son.*

"And I understand you weren't thinking clearly that night." Pallu looked at her sharply from beneath his thick eyebrows, obviously expecting her to agree.

Elisheba nodded, folding her hands in her lap. Yes, for the most part, Lord Pallu's statement was true. She hadn't been thinking clearly that night. She'd been terrified. Yet, even now, she knew the Rabbi Yeshua could have saved Joseph.

"But," Pallu continued, "I expect you to forget all that foolishness you suggested. Had I known that your little excursions to Beth-Shan and Galilee last year would give you such misguided beliefs, I would have forbidden your going. Also," Pallu added, his voice deepening, "I want no more mention of that renegade-Yeshua-magician in my house."

Elisheba felt the threat within those words. Pallu was lord and master here. No one would prevent him from removing Benjamin from her care, citing her "misguided beliefs." That, paired with Joseph's death, would be enough sorrow to send her straight to her own tomb. Lowering her gaze, she pleaded, "Forgive me, lord, for offending you."

"Certainly I forgive you." Pallu's severity eased. "Still, you must face your father. I spoke to him in the Holy Courts today. He intends to question you tomorrow."

Elisheba's spirit sank. Her father intended to question her tomorrow, and Barzel was as much a Sadducee as Pallu. How could she tell Father that her beliefs had changed without upsetting him?

"You are ... how old? Nineteen?" Pallu asked.

"Yes, lord." Elisheba straightened, caught by surprise.

"You are still young and lovely," Pallu said, as if these were suddenly awful traits. "Wherever you go, I expect you to conduct yourself with perfect discretion. Your behavior will be a reflection upon the honor of my name. Do you understand me?"

"Yes, lord."

"And you will avoid those young men—Stephanos, Andronikos, and their sort."

Their sort? Elisheba restrained her furious protest, biting it down almost hard enough to draw blood. She had to behave. For Benjamin. Another worry caught her.

Meek as possible, she raised her head, glancing at Levia in silent appeal before asking, "Might I go to Joanna's shop and thank her?"

"Joanna?" Pallu stared at Elisheba, blank-faced.

Levia interrupted hurriedly. "Joanna is Andronikos' mother *and* the perfumer who sent the spikenard ointment as a gift for Joseph's burial. We haven't thanked her for it. Elisheba is good to remember that we owe her a debt of gratitude."

Pallu frowned, as if mentally weighing the cost of good manners toward a miscreant's mother against the price of spikenard. "Naturally, Elisheba must express our thanks to Joanna for her generous gift."

"And she can buy a few things for me while she's there." Levia's dark eyes brightened and danced like Joseph's in a good humor. "Joanna creates my perfumes and oils."

"That would also be proper," Lord Pallu agreed. But Elisheba saw his frown deepen. No doubt he was subtracting the cost of Levia's perfumes from the large inheritance Levia had brought him in marriage.

When he didn't protest, Elisheba sighed her relief. "With your permission, lord, I'll go to Joanna's shop tomorrow after I've visited my parents." She hesitated, clearing her throat. "May I take Benjamin with me? My parents would love to see him."

"Oh, yes," Levia said, distracted, obviously pondering what Elisheba should buy tomorrow. "I'm sure the excursion will do Benjamin good. He needs a day outside."

"But you will both return tomorrow night," Pallu commanded, taking control of the conversation again. "Before dusk."

"Yes, thank you, lord." Elisheba bowed her head politely and excused herself for the night.

Outside in the chilly lamp-lit courtyard, the aged manservant Eran waited, holding Benjamin, who was supposed to be asleep. Traces of tears gleamed on Benjamin's cheeks in the low golden light. Elisheba hurried to take him, asking, "What's wrong?"

Passing Benjamin to her, Eran whispered, "Forgive me, young Mistress, but he awoke in a nightmare and wouldn't be comforted until I promised to take him to you."

"Thank you, Eran." Elisheba settled her son on her hip, rubbing Benjamin's back as he buried his face in her neck. Worried by Benjamin's clinging stillness, Elisheba said, "I'll keep him tonight, Eran. You go rest."

Eran sighed out a prayer. "May the Lord Most High bless you both with peace."

"And you," Elisheba murmured, rocking Benjamin, feeling him hiccough. He must have been crying hard. "My boy, I'm sorry. Can you tell me about your bad dream?"

Benjamin shook his head, refusing to look at her or to speak.

***

He couldn't explain. He didn't want to remember.

But if he had a sword, then he'd be brave. And his dreams wouldn't turn bad.

Abba would remain Abba, and not change to … Shivering, Benjamin kept his eyes wide open so he wouldn't dream. But then he saw the shadows moving, and he pulled the edge of his Ama's veil over his eyes.

Chapter 6

Seated within the swaying, blue-curtained litter, Elisheba tightened her grip on Benjamin's wide linen sash. He leaned toward the curtains, yanking them open, his nightmares apparently forgotten as he cried, "Ama, look! Swords!"

"Close the curtain, Benjamin," Elisheba said, glimpsing two soldiers in rich red and bronze, walking by chance alongside her litter. One soldier slid Elisheba an appraising look that sent horror washing over her. "Benjamin, do as I said. Close the curtain. *Now*."

He obeyed too vigorously, throwing himself off balance, making Elisheba strain to pull him upright. He looked up at her, begging, "Ama, can I have a sword?"

"No. Not until you're grown—when you're taller than Lord Pallu."

Benjamin flopped into the cushions and groaned. "Taller than Abba Pallu?"

Elisheba cringed. When had he started calling Pallu *Abba*? The word struck her like a dart. Was Benjamin forgetting his own father so quickly?

"But why can't I have a sword?"

"Benjamin, a real sword would be too heavy for you to lift."

He stared ahead, bleak. She suspected he would argue. Instead, he whispered, "I wish he didn't change."

"Who?"

"Abba." Benjamin sounded endlessly hurt. "I need him to stay the same."

Elisheba leaned forward. "What do you mean ... that you wish Abba didn't change?"

His small chin puckered and he ducked away, refusing to speak.

As he fought his grief, Elisheba pulled her son close again, hugging him, smoothing his curls. Laughter and jubilant voices echoed in celebration from a nearby house while her litter was carried through Jerusalem's Upper City. Elisheba ached to hear the celebrants' unknown joy. "You made your Abba very happy, Benjamin. Remember that. He loves you."

Loves. Surely Joseph loved his son even now, at rest in his tomb. How could love not be eternal?

Benjamin remained quiet, except for an occasional sniffle. At last, a shadow darkened the curtains about them, changing swiftly into sunlight again. They had just passed beneath an archway near her father's home. Sitting up now, Benjamin said, "I smell food."

Elisheba inhaled the aromas of garlic, onions, herbs, and oil, roasting together with meat. If Daliyah was cooking, then Elisheba must definitely visit Joanna's perfume shop today. She and Benjamin would have to anoint themselves with sweet oil and chew some cleansing herbs or gum. Otherwise, Levia would complain about the garlic and onion odors tonight.

As soon as she felt the litter being lowered and set firmly on the ground, Elisheba released her son. Eran had gone ahead of them and was already hailing Benjamin kindly in Greek from beyond the litter's curtains. "Come out, little Master!"

Benjamin brightened and scooted from the litter, some of his usual cheer returning. Elisheba smiled up at the gentle servant. "Thank you, Eran."

Immediately, Eran looked distressed, glancing toward his fellow slaves, Pallu's blue-clad litter-bearers. And particularly at Sethi, her father's sleek-bearded, pompously correct gateman, who was a freedman. Low-voiced, Eran said, "Please don't thank me, young Mistress. There's no need. I am a mere slave."

"You are more than that." Indeed, Eran had never been a slave as far as Joseph was concerned.

"Elisheba!" Robes and veils fluttering, Daliyah rushed into the courtyard as Elisheba entered the gate. "My girl …" She hugged Elisheba, redolent of sandalwood and garlic, delighted as if they hadn't visited for a year.

"Ama." Elisheba sighed, resting in her mother's embrace, unable to say more. Despite knowing that she must face her father today, she was grateful to be here. This house was like balm to her aching soul.

Her parents were respectably wealthy, but their home was smaller and older than Pallu and Levia's, and more welcoming. Unlike Pallu's stately formal mansion, the rooms in Barzel's house terraced cozily around a rustic courtyard paved with irregularly shaped slabs. And the maidservants were unashamedly leaning out the kitchen doorway—an informality never allowed in the House of Pallu.

"Where's Abba?" Elisheba drew back, still holding her mother's hands.

Daliyah's smile turned rueful. "He's upstairs, waiting for you."

"Then I'd best go talk with him."

Swords and sorrow forgotten, Benjamin capered around Daliyah, tugging at her gown, begging, "Please, can I have some almonds, please-please?"

"You know you can." Daliyah bent and snatched her grandson into her arms, hugging him fiercely. "Give me a kiss first!" Benjamin obeyed and then laughed while Daliyah shooed him off toward the kitchen. As he disappeared, Daliyah caught Elisheba's sleeve. "Be sure you explain things to your father. Don't quarrel."

"I won't, Ama. You know I honor him."

After kissing her mother's soft cheek, Elisheba crossed the courtyard and slowly climbed the limestone steps to her parent's secluded chamber. At the top, she paused. The door was open. *Lord, be with me,* she prayed. *Let Abba understand.*

"Abba?" She tapped on the door and stepped inside. Her father sat in a woven chair near the ornate lattice window, slivers of sunlight falling on his shoulders and trimmed dark hair. Seeing Elisheba, he hastily set his cup aside.

"Come in." He motioned for Elisheba to sit on a nearby footstool.

She obeyed, eyeing his cup uncertainly. He was drinking his palm wine too early in the day. Was she the reason? When she summoned the courage to look her father in the face, she saw his agitation. Clearing his throat then smoothing his beard, Barzel began abruptly. "Do you know how I felt, Elisheba? Hearing Lord Pallu tell me that I've raised a reprobate daughter and sent her—*you*—to his unsuspecting household?"

Heat suffused Elisheba's face. Lord Pallu's accusation against her father was no surprise, yet Father's mortification was still fresh after all these weeks. Had he been so deeply humiliated? She hadn't realized. Crushed to speechless shame, Elisheba knotted her fingers together and waited. Barzel took another drink and finally asked what he had evidently been dreading. "Did you allow those men—those pretend prophets—to baptize you?"

He sounded as if "those men," John the Immerser and the Rabbi Yeshua, were criminals for causing her and Joseph to think of spiritual matters and to evaluate their lives.

Humbled but no longer ashamed, Elisheba looked her father in the eyes. "Yes, Abba. I followed Joseph into the water last year, just before the prophet was arrested."

Barzel stared at her, owl-eyed. "What were you thinking—you and Joseph?"

"We were thinking of our son," Elisheba defended softly. "Loving Benjamin as we do, we longed for more than just living for each day. And for more than wealth and power. We wanted to understand the eternal as—"

"As that 'Immerser' now understands eternity? Without his head? Elisheba!"

Elisheba winced at the unexpected reminder of the Prophet John's brutal death.

More gently, Barzel asked, "Didn't you consider that you might be drowning your future in Pallu's household by going down into that water?"

"Joseph feared his father would be angry," Elisheba admitted. "But Joseph was a good son. Dutiful and respectful. How could Lord Pallu condemn him for submitting to the Almighty Lord?"

As her father shook his head in disbelief, Elisheba pleaded, "Abba, haven't you ever felt that there was something amazing, just beyond your own understanding? Something you could almost grasp in your thoughts—so wondrous that you *must* comprehend it?"

"It's Joseph's friends, those Greek-taught boys," Barzel declared. "They corrupted your thoughts and persuaded you and Joseph to listen to those misguided Galileans."

"The decision was ours, Abba." Sighing, she asked, "What use is there to being alive if nothing is eternal? Why bother obeying laws or taking sacrifices to Jerusalem's Holy House if the Lord doesn't care for His people?"

"Society needs laws, and we obey our commandments as our fathers did before us," Barzel argued, clearly overcome by his impatience with spiritual matters. "But it doesn't need this Pharisaical 'we shall live forever' insanity! Even so, I believe it's your grief for Joseph talking."

"Abba—"

"Hush!" Her father leaned forward now, more serious than Elisheba had ever seen him. "Hush your foolishness and listen to me! I am sorry Joseph is dead. I was always grateful to him because I knew you were protected by his love. But now, you must protect yourself and your son. For my sake and your Ama's sake!"

His dark eyes softening, Barzel admonished Elisheba. "You are all I have, you and Benjamin. When I am nothing but dust, you will continue life for me."

"Abba, please, don't speak of such a thing!" Her stomach twisted hard with pain. She didn't want to consider his death. Ever. She was suffering enough after losing Joseph. Worse, she hadn't moved her father's beliefs a jot. He truly believed he'd become nothing but dust, his nonexistent soul vanquished with his last breath.

As she mourned, Barzel smiled at her sadly. "Let's not discuss this further, my baby. Give your grief time to work. I'm sure you'll see these matters differently in a few years. Just guard your tongue and obey Pallu. He has more men in his debt than I do, and most likely they'll champion him through any legalities concerning our rights to Benjamin. How will we survive it if he takes Benjamin from us, eh?"

"I won't."

"*We* won't," Barzel corrected, standing. "Now, where is my boy?"

***

Wealth was deserved only by those who truly worked for it, Joanna believed. And she worked hard now, crushing dried cassia in a mortar, it's fragrance rising to tickle her nostrils like strong cinnamon. If Andronikos had been here, he would have reduced the stuff to powder in no time, with no complaint.

He's a good son, she told herself, trying and failing to reduce her pride in her firstborn. She could usually trust him to behave. And to use his brains.

But was she wise to allow him to march off to Galilee after that Master Iesous? She still didn't know what to think of Andronikos following the man and listening to his teachings. Even so, she must allow her son to reason out all his thoughts and settle his mind now, while he was young and—

"Mother," Loukas called plaintively from across the workroom, "isn't this enough?"

Joanna frowned at her eleven-year-old son. Loukas might resemble Andronikos but he certainly didn't work like him. He was supposed to be starting the pomade, placing rose petals on trays of purified white fat, which would absorb the rose scent. Working on her own trays opposite him, his sister, Maria, shook her glossy dark head, primly fourteen.

Joanna rapped sternly on her stone work table. "Loukas, you need twice as many petals on that tray! Get busy."

Voices lifted outside, and the shop's doorway darkened. A late customer. And not just any customer ... "Elisheba!"

"Joanna." The young woman met her with a sweet-sad smile and a hug.

But Benjamin peered about the shop, his lower lip pathetic. "Where's Neekos?"

The child was as difficult to resist as his father. Joanna smiled at Benjamin, smitten. Noticing his worried look, she hastily reassured him. "Andronikos is on a journey with Stephanos and Kore. They'll return in a few weeks."

"They're not asleep?" Benjamin pleaded, fear edging his voice.

"Oh, no, no, no!" Mercy, the poor boy was remembering his father "sleeping" in the family tomb. "I promise you a piece of gum, they're not sleeping."

"I'll get the gum!" Loukas cried, snatching the chance to leave his work. Maria huffed, silently mimicked his words, and went on working self-righteously, but Joanna didn't scold Loukas. Poor Benjamin needed the distraction.

As Benjamin followed Loukas like a lamb to the stoneware jar, Joanna turned again to Elisheba, recognizing the half-numb, wounded demeanor Joanna herself had experienced after the death of her own husband, Zebedaios. Only the children and the business had kept Joanna sane during those terrible months of grief.

Elisheba sighed. "Thank you, Joanna. I'll pay for the gum."

"You will not," Joanna said stoutly. "Joseph's son can have a piece of gum."

"I also wanted to thank you for the spikenard." Elisheba's voice trembled over the words. "I … I wish I had thanked you sooner. I'm sorry."

The girl looked ready to melt into a puddle. Joanna steadied her and gave her another hug. "It was a blessing to us that we could give you the ointment. Joseph was a jewel. Such a delightful teaser! And the best of friends to Andronikos."

Not a snob, unlike most of the other highborn Sadducee whelps. And Elisheba was equally charming and unaffected. Which was why Joseph had fallen in love with her. And why she had also turned Andronikos' head at one time.

Joanna had scolded Andronikos then. "Sadducee with Sadducee, Pharisee with Pharisee, and Libertine with Libertine!"

It was one of the few times Andronikos had made a face of rebellion when she reproved him. And she understood his defiance. How it hurt to be reminded that Libertine Jews such as themselves were scorned by others, just because they or their parents had been born elsewhere. Oh, the Jerusalem-born "betters" were so smug and so wrong!

Elisheba dabbed her eyes. "Joanna, if everyone was as kind and thoughtful as you ..." She seemed afraid to finish her sentence. Instead, she removed a coin purse from her sash and straightened. "The Lady Levia wanted me to buy a few things. She needs some hair oils and bdellium, please. And the wonderful incense you make with the cinnamon."

Joanna hurried to collect the necessary ingredients, sighing to herself. If only Elisheba could have been an ordinary Greek-Jew of their own kindred. Joanna would have gladly encouraged Andronikos to marry her.

Impossible of course. She set the thought aside, opened her box of dark, fragrant bdellium resins and went to work.

**

Stephanos allowed his thoughts to drift as they marched along behind their guides and fellow travelers on the hot, dusty road toward Galilee.

Walking for so long was actually restful mentally. With nothing more taxing than to follow a well-trodden road and their weathered comrades, Stephanos found time to contemplate—

He nearly halted as Kore tapped his shoulder.

"We should sneak off from the others and go see Tiberias," Kore suggested, his eyes brightening with the thought of mischief.

"Tiberias?" Stephanos threw his younger friend a suspicious glance. "That pig-eating city? I feel unclean just thinking about it."

"He's turning Gentile on us, I knew it," Andronikos said from behind them. Stephanos threw his friend a glance. Andronikos remained straight-faced as he coaxed their dawdling, gear-laden donkey to follow, but his eyes betrayed amusement.

Kore thumped his walking staff hard into the road, grumbling. "Just one little suggestion for a brief adventure and you're acting like two old Pharisees."

"Pharisees?" Andronikos protested, "Oh, now, that's too brutal a comparison!"

Playing to the idea, Stephanos tottered against his own walking staff, quavering. "Listen, young Kore, be satisfied! It's enough of an adventure that we'll stay in Scythopolis tonight. That pagan city'll gray my hair by morning, may the Lord send all their gods' temples to dust!"

Scythopolis—Beth-Shan, Joseph had always called it—*was* heavily pagan, but it had a respectable Jewish district where they could stay the night. Stephanos felt comfortable there. The city of Tiberias, however, was thoroughly Gentile and would be completely unacceptable. He hoped Kore would give in peacefully.

Grimacing, Kore shrugged. "I was just hoping to visit different places this time."

"Well, wherever you go, nothing can compare to Jerusalem," Andronikos told him. "Except that your parents are in Jerusalem and you'd get caught if you tried to sneak into the theater or the horse races."

Kore pivoted around to eye Andronikos. "I don't bet on horse races."

But he didn't deny wanting to visit a theater, Stephanos noted. Abandoning his old-Pharisee posture, he said, "That's the dilemma, Kore. You just want to get into trouble without your parents knowing."

"It's not trouble if we're only looking," Kore argued, sounding far too certain as he resumed walking forward.

Unconvinced, Stephanos shook his head. "Looking gives you too many ideas."

Kore narrowed his eyes. "Are you taking money from my parents to guard me?"

"No," Stephanos countered. "But perhaps I should. You worry me enough."

"Speaking of Pharisees ..." Andronikos nodded ahead at their traveling companions. "We shouldn't walk too fast. We're catching up to them."

Their three hired guides, all properly bearded, somberly garbed, and heavily armed men, were silently watching and listening to the others in their party—a small band of Pharisees, the two eldest on donkeys, three others on foot. All five were talking, hands gesturing wildly as if each Pharisee had a point to make that was more important than anything the others might say. The five had ignored Stephanos, Andronikos, and Kore after preliminary introductions, obviously considering them unsuitable company.

"We can't have that, can we?" Kore snorted. "Why, we might actually *speak* to them. You'd think we're lepers or something! The dogs. I've even smiled and nearly bowed to them, but they haven't said a word to us since leaving Jericho yesterday. They're ruining our journey."

"If a ruined journey is the worst that happens, then we shouldn't complain," Stephanos said quietly. "Who would have thought at the beginning of last year that both Joseph and the Baptist John would be dead before our return to Galilee?"

Sharing his suddenly bleak mood, Andronikos and Kore went silent.

***

Andronikos looked up at the brilliant blue sky, remembering last year. They had eagerly ventured into Galilee with these same guides, as well as Joseph and Elisheba and their servant, Eran. And

Benjamin, who had enlivened them all, chattering happily at anyone who would listen to him—while they carried him, of course.

Joseph, meanwhile, had been grateful to be outside Jerusalem. For Joseph—initially at least—hearing the Baptist John had been secondary to temporarily escaping Lord Pallu's deceitful business practices and personal indiscretions. "I feel guilty just knowing everything he's done," Joseph had confided as they walked along this same road. "Sometimes, in the Holy Courts, I can't look my father in the eyes."

Listening to him, Andronikos had pitied his friend and finally understood why Joseph was so eager to slip outside his family's privileged circle. He hadn't trusted many of the Sadducees, least of all his own father. "Why do I long for a sense of honor?" Joseph had asked, genuinely perplexed. "My father has none, so I shouldn't care."

It was because you felt the Lord's Spirit, Andronikos told his now-absent friend. And because Joseph loved his wife and son—may the Almighty Lord protect them.

Grieved, Andronikos pondered their future as it would be without Joseph, with Lord Pallu training the bright, sociable Benjamin. *Be like your father,* Andronikos encouraged the little boy. *Not like Lord Pallu.*

He wouldn't think of Elisheba.

***

"I'm going to persuade my father to shift our business interests from money-changing and lending to something equally lucrative," Joseph had told Stephanos upon their return from Galilee last year. Joseph had been so eager, so sure. "No matter how long it takes, I'll convince him."

Stephanos hadn't realized the extent of Joseph's despair over Pallu's moral failings, his sanctioning of financial usury and bribing authorities for legal favors. Not to mention instructing his own men in the Court of Nations to coerce inexperienced foreign-born Jews to unwittingly pay more than was fair to exchange their foreign silver for the Tyrian Shekel, the only silver accepted in the House of the Lord.

But his friend's spirit had been renewed after being baptized and later hearing and observing the Rabbi Yeshua healing lepers, even causing the paralyzed to walk.

"He's so much more than a prophet; surely he's the *Mashiyakh*!" Joseph had insisted. "If only I could listen to him the next time he comes to Jerusalem and preaches in the Holy Courts. But my father would notice and question me, and I'm not ready to confront him yet."

Sighing, he'd pleaded, "Stephanos, you must listen to the Rabbi when he visits Jerusalem and tell me what he says. And next year, we'll return to Galilee."

But Joseph hadn't returned. Nor did the Baptist John. Surely the Lord, in His wisdom, had a reason.

Stephanos lifted his gaze to the warm sky, trying to imagine seeing beyond it into heaven—to comprehend the Lord and His will. The effort was more than his mortal mind could encompass. Futile.

And it was equally futile to contemplate the earth and its depths in his search for understanding. He feared he would see nothing but dust and find nothing but despair. *Stop,* he scolded himself, *or you'll go insane.*

Joseph's death and the Prophet's execution had shaken him badly. Their deaths and Stephanos' recognition of his own mortality haunted his thoughts amid bouts of despair.

Lord, at times I feel I'm walking in darkness, in the land of the shadow of death. Show me the light of Your will during this journey.

***

Unseen, they walked with their quarry, fixated upon this one's wariness of death. Even as it prayed it was easily beset by weakness. Easily subdued by its own fears.

How slowly all flesh moved! Ponderous, sodden clay! Flesh was unable to see or comprehend more than one, perhaps two things at a time within their own dirt-birthed realm. Flesh was so easy to wound and goad to panic.

So unworthy of His Almighty regard.

***

Scythopolis, a mingling of black basalt homes and shops and white limestone Gentile temples, with grander white temples being outlined and constructed, rested amid green slopes in the heart of the region known as Decapolis.

Self-important citizens bustled along the paved streets, calling to each other in Greek and cutting sharply across the travelers' paths. Irritated, Kore complained to Stephanos. "I'm sure we only think we exist because these people don't see us at all!"

To Stephanos' relief, Kore seemed unimpressed by the pagan temples, while Andronikos ignored the temples altogether, determinedly leading the wearied donkey toward the modest inn they remembered at the northwestern section of the city. They were all as tired and dusty as the poor donkey. Stephanos looked forward to scrubbing his hands and feet, eating, and crawling onto his bedroll for some sleep.

Andronikos glanced back over his shoulder at Stephanos.

"The innkeeper's name was Timaios, wasn't it?"

"That sounds right," Kore interposed. "I hope he has some food for us."

"I hope he has room for us all." Stephanos cast a wary look at their guides as three of the Pharisees ducked inside the inn's low stone-arched doorway.

"I wish we could lodge somewhere else." Kore frowned at the remaining two. "I've had enough of those old men. I've been polite, but now I'm finished."

Unwilling to create a scene, Stephanos murmured, "Let's not be hasty, Kore. And don't provoke them."

But the remaining two caught sight of Kore's scowl and glared. When Andronikos went inside to monitor the bargaining for rooms, the two Pharisees guarding the donkeys threw the young men criticizing looks. Stephanos smiled politely. One

Pharisee answered with a tight nod. The other turned away.

Andronikos emerged from the inn, seeming pleased. "We're blessed! Our party claimed their last rooms, and I smell food cooking." He tugged the donkey's harness from Stephanos' grasp. "Why don't you two haul our gear inside and wash for the evening meal? I'll take this poor creature to their stable and settle him for the night."

"I was hoping we'd have to find another place," Kore muttered. But he followed Stephanos inside the dark inn, lugging their bedrolls and gear.

Stephanos mutely acknowledged the flushed, balding innkeeper, who was still dealing with the three Pharisees in his main room. The guides had obviously abandoned them as soon as they could politely excuse themselves.

"It's too high a price." The grayest Pharisee was shaking his head, as his two shawl-draped followers nodded solemnly. "It's almost robbery!"

Their host said, "I can assure you that the rooms are clean, and the water and food are also pure. And you've the synagogue only a few steps away." With admirable self-control, he suggested, "If you wish to reduce your costs, however, you can pay for just one large room and share with your guides and fellow travelers. I'll give you back a portion of your money."

"Robbery!" the Pharisee huffed. But he turned away from the innkeeper, obviously considering their bargaining done. Seeing Stephanos and Kore, he gave them a narrow, quizzing glance.

Stephanos offered them the same courteous smile he had given their comrades outside. Nodding formally, the eldest Pharisee approached, speaking in Aramaic. "You and your friends are young scoundrels!"

"Forgive us, good sir; we meant no offense," Stephanos murmured.

"You must be teachers, all of you," Kore said.

Alarm jolted through Stephanos as a physical shock. Kore had always argued with his teachers. Stephanos gripped the back of Kore's tunic and hissed, "Restrain yourself!"

Kore muttered, "Fine, I'll be quiet."

The Pharisee lifted his gray-bearded chin proudly. "We are indeed teachers. And since you've recognized us, you must be students... somewhere. *Libertines*, perhaps?"

"We are of the Synagogue of the Freedmen," Stephanos agreed, stifling his resentment. How condescending of the man—of all these men. It had taken only three days for them to speak to Stephanos and his friends, to learn who they were.

A third Pharisee leaned into the conversation, his nostrils flaring so wide that dark hairs protruded, thick and spiky. "Why are you seeking the Rabbi Yeshua?"

"To hear him speak. The Rabbi has clarified many questions for us."

"And he has created many for us!" the eldest Pharisee snapped. "Now, young men, we will tell you, many have come to Jerusalem claiming that this Rabbi Yeshua is the *Mashiyakh*. As teachers of the law, with our high connections, it is our duty to observe this Rabbi and determine if these claims might or might not be true, lest our faithful ones be led astray."

"We trust you will not interfere with our work," the third Pharisee added, his nostrils flaring again as he frowned at Kore in particular.

"But since when is honoring the law work?" Kore protested too politely, smiling.

"Forgive us, good teachers," Stephanos interjected before the Pharisees could decide they'd been insulted. "We must settle our gear and wash before evening prayers."

"Truly, I love the law," Kore said, bland-faced. "It will be a pleasure, sirs, to merely observe and stay out of your ways."

"He meant no good by that, I'm sure!" one of the younger Pharisees cried.

Clearly offended, the eldest Pharisee shouted in parting, "Here's fine advice, young men! Return to Jerusalem, get married, and devote yourselves to the Lord's House. Become useful in His sight. Return to the ways of your fathers and be made pure."

"Forgive us," Stephanos pleaded again, to Kore's wry-faced disgust. Passing the innkeeper, Stephanos said, "I think we'll eat in our room tonight."

"Of course." The innkeeper nodded toward a doorway, looking anxious as if Stephanos couldn't remove Kore quickly enough. "I will send someone with your food. Call for me if you need anything else, sir. I am Timaios."

"Thank you, Timaios." As they went into their small, stark room, Stephanos grumbled at Kore. "I should have asked him for ropes to tie your mouth shut."

Kore grinned. "Thank you, but I can find my own ropes."

True. Stephanos had almost forgotten that Kore's father was a rope-maker. Probably tested his knots on his son. "Please, Kore, don't say anything to those Pharisees tomorrow. If they attack us, we won't be able to fight them all off."

"They did look angry, didn't they?" Kore mused pleasantly. "No matter. I still say they need to be thrashed. Our guides must be sick of them too."

"Almighty Lord, please help us."

Chapter 7

"Are you Roman sympathizers?" one of the Pharisees demanded the next day, swiftly matching steps with them along the road. Stephanos studied the man, who was pole-thin and twitching visibly in his eagerness to confront the "Libertines."

"No, we're not Roman sympathizers." Andronikos cast a stern glance at Kore before the youth could speak or set a hand threateningly on his short-sword.

As if certain they were wrongdoers either way, the Pharisee persisted. "Then you must be hoping to urge this Rabbi Yeshua to lead a rebellion."

Stephanos sighed and spoke in Aramaic, deeming it safer. "Good Sir, you are a son of Abraham. We are also sons of Abraham, and we seek the Almighty Lord's will. But, as for the Romans, didn't the Lord tell the Prophet Yesaiah that He will contend with those who contend with us? We believe He will do as He says."

The Pharisee looked disappointed by his devout-student answer. He took leave of them, quietly returning to his comrades.

Kore grinned. "I still say one good wallop with the flat of a sword …"

**

In a tiny community near Gennesaret, along the calm, sparkling sea, they heard that the Master Iesous had been visiting in the area, preaching and healing the sick, while slowly traveling northward.

"But," a sun-weathered fisherman cautioned as he sold Andronikos some salted fish, "many have advised the Rabbi Yeshua to leave Capernaum to escape Herod's spies. We've heard assassins are looking for him."

Aware of the fisherman's sudden squinting look, as if judging them as possible assassins, Stephanos said in Aramaic, "May the Lord protect the Rabbi. He's done nothing wrong."

"Now, I wouldn't say he's done nothing wrong," the fisherman argued, sitting on a coarse mat to mend a net. Obviously he expected them to sit and listen to him while they ate and waited for their traveling companions to catch up with them.

Andronikos tied the donkey, and they courteously settled down in the sunlight, though Stephanos wished for shade. Continuing as one eager to discuss something that had been disturbing him, the fisherman said, "Listen. Last time I was in Capernaum, the Rabbi Yeshua said that he is 'living bread' and we must eat his flesh and drink his blood to gain eternal life."

"Eat his flesh and drink his blood?" Kore looked squeamish, while Andronikos flinched.

Drink his blood? Stephanos' thoughts stumbled. But even as his Jewish heart recoiled from the unclean thought of consuming blood, his Greek-trained mind turned the idea over and over, studying it. *How? Why? There's a meaning hidden here ...*

"See?" The fisherman nodded wisely. "You three look the very way I felt. Who wants to enter any kingdom by drinking blood? Ha!" Bitter, he added, "King of Bread or not, the Rabbi offended most of his followers. They've all gone, along with a big chunk of trade. I had to salt more of my catch this week than I've done in months."

Stephanos couldn't tell what made the fisherman more upset: the thought of drinking blood, or having to salt-preserve his catch because the Rabbi Yeshua's erstwhile followers had left the region.

While the younger men ate their fish, hard bread, and dried olives, the fisherman rambled on. "Did you know he fed five thousand of us at one time with bread and fish? Amazing! But it didn't save him from being rejected. Drinking his blood indeed!"

How could Master Iesous possibly feed five thousand followers at one time? Stephanos pondered the story, his thoughts distractedly reverting to Greek. Surely this fisherman was exaggerating. The Teacher lived humbly and couldn't have afforded to purchase such a feast.

"There are our fellow travelers," Andronikos announced, standing. The three guides and five Pharisees were approaching, all of them clearly ready to drop into the shade near the lapping sea for some rest and food. "Be warned, sir. They love to quarrel about prices."

"If they don't like my prices, they can just walk on ahead." The fisherman squinted toward the Pharisees as if bracing for a battle.

"Let's find a stream or a well," Stephanos muttered to his friends. His mouth dried at the thought of another confrontation. And their meal had consisted of more salt than fish, leaving him parched.

Andronikos nodded and grasped the donkey's halter. "Yes, this poor beast needs water."

***

"We've no reason to come here," Kore announced as they followed their guides into Capernaum's town square. The place was, of course, rustic compared to Jerusalem. Cypress trees shaded the black basalt stone houses, the small shops, olive presses, and a dark rough-hewn synagogue, while boats glided here and there in the nearby sea, their sun-bleached sails billowing in the breeze.

Joseph and Elisheba had insisted Capernaum was restful. Kore, however, considered it dull. "If Master Iesous has gone mad, then we shouldn't waste our time."

"We can't leave without seeking some explanation for the fisherman's story," Andronikos told Kore. "And it would be foolish of us to depart without the others."

"Tonight is Sabbaton," Stephanos reminded them in Greek, turning their attention to the afternoon sun. After sunset, long walks would be forbidden. "Let's ask around then buy some food and a corner to sleep in for the night. Tomorrow we can observe our day of rest and listen to the Master Iesous at the synagogue. If he's there."

***

Sunlight shone through the synagogue's small windows, illuminating its dark basalt interior, gleaming against Master Iesous' prayer shawl as he translated the words of the Prophet Isaiah from Hebrew aloud to Aramaic. " ... Listen, hear me and eat what is good, and your soul will enjoy the richest foods. Pay heed and come to me. Hear me, that your soul will live!"

Listening, Stephanos relaxed on his bench against the wall. Master Iesous was not insane. Truly, he was referring to matters of the spirit when he said they must eat his flesh and drink his blood. Wasn't this reading today proof? The fisherman had misunderstood.

Clear-eyed and concise, his voice rich with joy in the holy words, Master Iesous continued. "And *I* will make an everlasting covenant with you, my enduring love promised to David."

He sounded like a king, ready to seal a bargain. An everlasting covenant.

But wasn't this the Lord's covenant? How could Master Iesous make a divine and eternal bargain sound like his own to give? Unless... Unless he was truly the Lord, Himself, offering His Kingdom now. Stephanos hesitated, pondering. *What do I believe about you?*

The five Pharisees, too, were watching Iesous from amid the crowd as they had all day. They also eyed Master Iesous' followers, displeased by something. Stephanos saw them whispering to each other, shaking their shawl-draped heads.

Seated beside Stephanos, Andronikos spoke softly. "There'll be a confrontation."

"I want to hear it," Kore said.

As the meeting ended, Master Iesous' disciples clustered around him, talking eagerly. All twelve were so similar to him—brown-skinned, rugged, dark-eyed and dark haired, wearing plain robes and prayer shawls—making it difficult to distinguish them from each other.

When Master Iesous spoke or looked someone in the eyes, he was beyond all other men. And yet when Iesous finished speaking, he simply blended in with his followers and departed amid the crowd.

As Stephanos expected, however, the five Jerusalem Pharisees didn't blend into the crowd. Predictable as night following day, they marched after Master Iesous from the synagogue into the roughly paved open yard.

Stephanos followed Andronikos through the crowd, with Kore eagerly jostling past their wary guides to witness the confrontation. Even as they reached Master Iesous, Stephanos heard the eldest Pharisee's indignant voice. "Why don't your disciples live according to the ways of their fathers, instead of eating their food with unclean hands?"

Iesous stiffened and turned, raising an eyebrow, shaking his dark-curled head severely—the expression of a father undeceived by an errant child. Stephanos almost squirmed, glad the look wasn't aimed at him.

In a carrying voice that hid nothing, Master Iesous said, "Isaiah was right when he prophesied about you *hypocrites* ..."

His tone inferred that the Pharisees were common actors, making them gasp and blink, shocked into silence.

Beside Stephanos, Kore grinned approval as Master Iesous continued. "It is written, 'These people honor me with their mouths, but their hearts are separated from me. They worship me in emptiness; their ways are nothing but rules taught by men.'"

The eldest Pharisee opened his mouth to protest, but Iesous fixed him with another hard look. "*You* have abandoned the commands of the Almighty Lord and are clinging to the traditions of men."

The thinnest, most zealous Pharisee cried, "That is untrue!"

Iesous frowned and studied the zealous one as if paring the man's soul to its core. "You have a wonderful way of rejecting the commands of the Lord in order to protect your own traditions. For Moses said, 'Honor your father and your mother.' And 'Whoever curses his father or mother must be put to death.' But you say that if a man tells his father or mother, 'Whatever support money you might have received from me has become a gift devoted to God,' then *you* never again let him provide anything for his father or mother. This is how you reject the word of God with your traditions that you've passed down."

The thinnest Pharisee lowered his gaze uneasily, making Stephanos wonder how many aged people the man had dispossessed for the sake of the Holy Treasury—and his share in the profits. How easy it must be to excuse greed by cloaking it with rich gifts to a sacred cause.

Facing the eldest Pharisee now, Iesous added, "And *you* do many things like this." The eldest Pharisee shifted from foot to foot, like a guilty man fearing his sins were about to be recited. His companions retreated, their mouths rebelliously down-turned.

Iesous shook his head again and then raised his voice, drawing the crowd's attention. "Listen to me, all of you, and understand. Nothing outside a man makes him unclean by entering him. Instead, it's what a man thinks and says that makes him unclean."

Hearing the Master upend many of their most basic customs with those few words, the ordinary citizens of Capernaum stared at him, open-mouthed and unblinking. Until their rustic Pharisee teachers glared at Iesous and began to herd their people away as if the Master's words would corrupt them. Watching them go, Stephanos winced inwardly.

Master Iesous and his followers wouldn't be welcome here much longer.

Still clearly disgusted, Iesous strode into a nearby house. But his disciples watched the Pharisees, who stalked from the open meeting area in offended silence. Turning, one of the disciples addressed Stephanos, Andronikos, and Kore sharply in Galilean-accented Greek. "Weren't you with them?"

"Yes," Kore said. "And it was worth the whole journey to see them insulted."

"But that's not why we came," Stephanos told the man. "I am Stephanos, this is Andronikos, and the outspoken one is Kore."

"I am Matthaios—Matthew." With a wry smile, the disciple added, "You're swimming against the current, you know. Most are leaving us."

"We've heard stories on our journey here," Andronikos agreed, his hushed voice betraying his doubts.

"Yes, I'm sure you did," Matthew grumbled, lowering his prayer shawl to his shoulders. "The crowds rush to eat the Master's bread when it's free, and they leave just as quickly when he gives them too much to think about. Thank you for coming anyway."

"By the way," Stephanos said, detaining the disciple an instant longer, "what did Master Iesous truly mean today, with his reading 'eat what is good'?"

Matthew shook his head. "I can't answer that. He makes complicated thoughts simple and simple thoughts complicated. Perhaps after we talk with him ..."

By now, the other disciples were filing into their Master's house and Matthew seemed eager to join them. Stephanos retreated politely, allowing him to leave.

While they walked back to their small lodging room, with the bored Kore wandering after, Andronikos spoke his thoughts aloud. "Do you think

Master Iesous believes that most of our traditions should be abolished?"

"It sounds as if he does." Stephanos frowned, trying to sift through the jumble of new questions and doubts filling his thoughts.

Abolish traditions. Disrupt the rituals in the Holy House. Proclaim that the Kingdom of the Lord is near. Utter anarchy. The Pharisees, the Sadducees, and the Romans would certainly attack Master Iesous if he dared to suggest such things. And he would be defeated. Likely killed, taking others with him. *What do I believe?*

***

Even now He saw those Pharisees cursing Him from within their own self-created fires of hatred ... their souls raging, searing amid Ghehennah's eternal flames.

As flesh, Yeshua recoiled, shutting His hard eyes against the image.

With Him amid their thoughts, also perceiving the fallen ones, Spirit grieved.

Chapter 8

"Benjamin!" Elisheba lowered her mending and frowned across the bright courtyard at her son as his new leather kick-ball—a gift from his grandfather Barzel—tumbled to the stone pavings at his feet. "Ignore your toy and pay attention to Eran."

Guiltily, Benjamin tucked his hands together at his waist, looking wretched as Eran scolded in Greek, "Because you're distracted, young Master, we'll go through this twice. Now, to form the *Tau*, think of a tree ..."

While Eran coaxed Benjamin through the lesson, their heads bent over a parchment on a low table, Elisheba worked small firm stitches, lengthening little Zimiyrah's favorite red gown with a wide, decoratively striped band. She concentrated upon the shining bronze needle, welcoming the work. But even now, Joseph crept into her thoughts with every stitch, every piercing of the needle through fabric.

She'd never realized how much of her time she'd devoted to Joseph, maintaining his clothes, persuading the cook to add his favorite meals to the menus, adorning herself for his pleasure. And making their rooms such a calming haven that he schemed for excuses to join her there—all to her own delight.

Now she was grasping for work—any work—as she tried to cope with losing Joseph. What a blessing that Benjamin still needed her, though Eran and the other servants often took charge of him.

As Lord Pallu expected them to do in order to lessen her "misguided" influence.

"Mistress?" A shadow fell across Elisheba's work. Levia's maidservant, Thamar, stood solidly between Elisheba and the sunlight, her blunt face apologetic. "The Lady Levia sends for you."

Elisheba set the gown aside and stood, trying to suppress a stab of alarm. She hadn't seen Levia yet this morning. And she had looked ill last night. "Is she feeling worse, Thamar?"

"Oh, the same," Thamar whispered, lowering her braid-coifed head furtively. "We just can't do anything to please her."

"We" included Elisheba's former maidservant, Leah, who had somehow become Levia's servant over the course of time. If Thamar and Leah had, between them, failed to soothe Levia, Elisheba doubted she could do any better. Reluctantly, she crossed the courtyard, climbed the pale stairs. Reaching the upper rooms, she tapped on Levia's ante-chamber door, the action raising memories, fresh and cruel.

Y'shua .... Take me to Him.

Elisheba lowered her hand, trembling. *Lord, when does this wound inside stop bleeding?*

Leah opened the door and grimaced, crossing her big brown eyes wildly at Elisheba as if to say, "You deal with her. I give up!"

Any other time, Elisheba would have been amused. Now, she wanted to sit on the floor and wail. Unable to speak, she motioned Leah outside and closed the door. Alone now, she leaned against the cool plastered ante-chamber wall, hugging herself tight. Trying to force the pain away long enough to move—just to breathe.

"Elisheba?" Levia called from the bedchamber, sounding forlorn, congested as if she'd been crying. "Are you there?"

Elisheba calmed herself and entered the bedchamber. "I ... I'm here."

"Are they gone?" Levia demanded, sniffling moistly, curled up within blue and gold cushions on the wide bed.

"Yes. No one else is here—just me."

Elisheba stared at all the garments strewn over the furniture and floor like a riot of pastel curtains blown apart in a storm. Nearby on a stonework table, Levia's large gilded Egyptian cosmetic chest looked rummaged, its tiny drawers half-opened, delicate ivory pots and hairpins littering the tabletop. A tray of cold food was shoved into a corner of the bed, clearly rejected, and an incense burner had been overturned, its cold ashes smudged on the tiles as if someone had started to clean them but failed to finish the job.

Amid this chaos, Levia began to cry, looking exhausted without her usual touches of cosmetics. Was she grieving for Joseph?

Sympathizing, her own grief still so raw that she ached, Elisheba kneeled close to her mother-in-law. "What can I do for you?"

"Nothing. I cannot talk to the servants. Or anyone else." Levia dabbed her eyes and face with the edge of her linen sleeve, then sat up, still sniffling. "He's unfaithful to me, you know."

Lord Pallu? Elisheba gaped at her lovely mother-in-law's bluntness. But why be shocked? Hadn't Joseph hinted at this possibility?

"And," Levia continued between sobs, "he's only going to become worse these next few months. I'm with child again. I can't endure this! I'm going to become so big and ugly. And food tastes so awful, but the incense smells worse!" She flung an accusing look at her overturned incense burner. "Thamar lit that stuff and I was sure I'd vomit. I had to put it out. Don't we have some mild herbs to scent my chamber? Oh, my head aches!"

"I'll get you a cool cloth for your head," Elisheba murmured, reaching for some of the scattered garments. "And I'll see about some sweet herbs."

"And get me some hair oil that's not so heavily scented. It makes me ill. Also, don't we have any fresh fruit?"

"I'll send Leah to the market for everything that's in season," Elisheba said, folding a particularly delicate pomegranate-pink tunic.

Tearful again, Levia moaned. "You watch. The wider I become, the longer my husband will stay out at night. In fact, as soon as I tell him I'm with child, he'll stray like a dog. When my wedding contract was written, I should have added that he can't have another wife. Then I could divorce him!"

Divorce. Elisheba stopped folding the tunic. She'd never heard Pallu or Levia utter the word before. Joseph would have been as horrified as she was.

"I've shocked you." Levia picked morbidly at a gold-edged pillow. "But who else can I talk to? You won't tell anyone, will you?"

"No." Elisheba kept her voice gentle, but her thoughts whirled. If Pallu and Levia divorced, then Elisheba and Benjamin would have to return to her father's household, where they should be. But that was the only brightness she saw. A divorce would cause an unholy scandal. Malkah and Zimiyrah would be devastated. And Levia's unborn child might be suspected as one conceived in adultery. But perhaps Levia was simply overwhelmed by her pregnancy and talking wildly. Elisheba had to settle her down.

Kneeling beside the bed again, she spoke soothingly. "I'm sorry you're so unhappy. But certainly Lord Pallu will be overjoyed when you have another son. He's going to honor you. And," she added encouragingly, "think how sweet this little one must be. He will have your eyes and we'll be infatuated with him."

As Levia smiled reluctantly, Elisheba continued. "If you don't mind, I'm going to send word to my mother, though you know she'll visit you and make a fuss."

Elisheba would make sure Daliyah fussed. Levia would enjoy it thoroughly. She was already sitting up and patting her hair at the thought of company.

"Oh, if you must tell her, then do so. But put down that tunic and tell Thamar to come clean up this mess. And you must go buy me some more hair oil and perfume. I feel so wretched. I wish I could eat."

"Rest a little," Elisheba commanded gently, as if Levia were a child herself. "I'll bring you a cool cloth, and some fresh bread and fruit."

"He *is* going to stray," Levia mourned, scrunching a pillow between her slender hands. "But don't tell anyone I said so. I'll deny it!"

"I'll say nothing," Elisheba promised. She left the chamber, feeling as if she'd taken Levia's headache with her. This was going to be a difficult pregnancy.

Levia was bearing another child. Elisheba stopped inside the ante-chamber door again to control herself, to pray for dignity. And to deal with her envy and hurt. This was her new task. To soothe Levia throughout this pregnancy and to help keep this household intact. For an instant, Elisheba paused. Actually … here was a potential blessing. If Levia bore a son, then that son would become Lord Pallu's heir. Perhaps then Lord Pallu would relinquish Benjamin to Elisheba with no restrictions. A blessing indeed.

"Let it be so!" Her shoulders squared, she descended to the courtyard just in time to see Benjamin nudging a toe toward the leather kick-ball. Elisheba sighed. "I leave for just a little while and you return to mischief."

"All's well, young Mistress," Eran assured her, rolling up their parchments. "I believe this lesson is finished for the day. "Tomorrow, young Master, you'll work with numbers instead."

"Numbers make my mind confused," Benjamin complained.

Elisheba smiled. "Which is why you must study them until your mind clears. Now, however, we are going to Joanna's shop."

Benjamin whooped, scrambling up from his cushion as Eran laughed.

***

Joanna's shop smelled wonderful as always, rich with spices and herbs. Beguiled by the fragrance, Elisheba led Benjamin inside the sun-brightened workroom. As she expected, Joanna was there in a plain work gown, her hair subdued beneath a linen wrap, her kind face blooming with the heat and the still-warm ointment she was stirring.

"It smells wonderful in here," Elisheba announced in Greek, inhaling deeply to emphasize her words.

Joanna glanced up, recognized her, and beamed at the compliment to her work. But she sighed self-deprecatingly. "I've almost let this heat too long; it's dreadful to ruin ointment."

"I'll eat it anyway," Benjamin offered, eagerly standing on tiptoe, peering over the top of the worktable.

"Of course you will, brave soul, but this isn't for eating." Joanna smiled, opened the stoneware gum jar, and nudged two clear lemon-hued droplets of resin toward him. "Test this instead while I prepare your Ama's order."

"Thank you!" Benjamin tucked the kick-ball beneath his arm and then popped the two bits of resin into his mouth. Just as he'd chomped down on the gum, Andronikos entered the shop, drawing Elisheba's gaze.

Joseph's best friend was more sun-darkened than ever, hauling an enormous crate on his shoulder. His siblings, Maria and Loukas, followed him, lugging a second crate between them, which they set down the instant they entered the shop. Andronikos raised one dark eyebrow at them and stepped around the crate. "Move this away from the entrance, you two. We don't want to pay physicians to plaster up any of our customers' cuts and bruises." He nodded to his mother and said, "The remainder will be delivered to us; I brought what we needed immediately."

Elisheba averted her gaze. It was unseemly of her to stare at any man, even Andronikos, though she was eager to pelt him with questions. Obviously, he'd returned from Capernaum. Had he found the Rabbi Yeshua? What was said? Did Andronikos still agree with Rabbi's teachings?

Benjamin saw Andronikos and nearly choked. Recovering, he charged across the shop, yelling despite the gum. "Neekos, I have a new kick-ball!"

Maria kneeled beside the crate, silent and pretty, clearly more worried about unpacking the alabaster vials within. But Loukas looked interested.

"Is it a good kick-ball?" Andronikos asked. "How far can you send it?"

"I don't know. Ama wouldn't let me test it. I had to tend lessons instead."

Andronikos laughed, setting down his crate. "Your Ama is wise; you'll do well if you listen to her. What else have you been doing?"

Clearly delighted to be the center of attention, Benjamin shifted the gum wad into his cheek and chattered, looking happier than he had in days.

Watching, Elisheba mourned. Joseph should have returned from Capernaum with Andronikos to hear his son. But amid this pang of grief, she was glad to see Andronikos again. He was so good to take time with Benjamin.

She caught herself, again, staring at Andronikos. And Joanna was watching her stare. Almost squirming, though her stare had been quite innocent, Elisheba said in Greek, "I'm pleased to see he's returned safely. Joseph was so eager to go with them and hear Master Iesous again."

"They returned yesterday," Joanna told her softly. "But my son isn't talking so much about the Master Iesous this time. I wonder what happened." Businesslike, she asked, "Is the Lady Levia ordering more perfume?"

"Yes, but something very mild, please. And some hair oil and incense, not too strongly scented."

Joanna's eyebrows lifted and she smiled. "Say no more. The last time the Lady Levia sent me such a request, she was bearing her youngest. Mild sweet oil it is then. I'll put some into one of our new vials." Raising her voice, she hinted, "As soon as my sons help their sister to unpack those crates!"

"We're busy with a customer," Andronikos said. Mock-stern, he leaned down to Benjamin and held out one bronzed hand. "You must pay me for that gum, sir."

"Just pretend to give him a coin," Loukas urged.

Joy lighting his wide dark eyes, Benjamin swiped a nonexistent coin into Andronikos' hand, then laughed heartily while Andronikos pretended to weigh a coin and stash it in a box.

Elisheba couldn't help laughing as well. It was a relief to genuinely laugh, to feel pure joy for just an instant. "Joanna, please sell me some more of that gum."

***

As Elisheba gathered her purchases and left the shop with Benjamin, Joanna glanced over at her firstborn. Andronikos was watching the young woman leave, his expression unmistakable. He still cared for her. After all this time! And Elisheba had looked at him too. Such a match would be scandalous—completely unacceptable.

Brooding, Joanna resealed the remaining gum in its stoneware jar. *I'm going to find you a wife,* Joanna silently pledged to her firstborn. *You must forget Elisheba.*

Two women came in then, swathed in elegant veils, rings, and embroidered gowns, comfortably wealthy and eager to indulge themselves with perfumes. Joanna smiled, welcoming them and urging her family to their work.

***

"You disobeyed my orders and took my grandson—my heir—to that place again!" Pallu snapped, confronting Elisheba openly in the courtyard before the evening meal. "Don't deny it. Benjamin told me where he got that gum. I won't have his thoughts tainted by those people! Have I not made my will clear?"

Taken aback, Elisheba stammered, "I ... I forgot, lord, truly. I was only fulfilling the Lady Levia's requests. She can tell you so." Aware that the distressed Benjamin and the servants were watching, Elisheba babbled on. "I won't go there again; I give you my word. I'll send Leah or Eran. Please, pardon my—"

Pallu shook his head, cutting off her apology. "One more offense and I'll throw you out. You'll return to your father without a single coin and without Benjamin. We'll see who has more rights then. You won't see him again until he's grown. Do you hear me?"

"Yes, lord. Forgive me." She trembled helplessly, mortified by the tears welling in her eyes. His rage was so unjust. And he'd shamed her before Benjamin and the servants. Worse, the servants would testify against her before witnesses if Pallu commanded it.

Was that his intention? To deliberately create witnesses to use against her in the future? At least her Ama hadn't still been here to observe this scene. Daliyah would have been furious. She might have provoked Lord Pallu enough to carry through with his threat to send her away, keeping Benjamin as his own.

Elisheba closed her eyes and bowed her head. She must behave perfectly from now on. But could she? Not likely.

Particularly if Lord Pallu was determined to be rid of her.

The instant Pallu departed, storming up the stairs into his private rooms, Benjamin ran to Elisheba, clinging to her as if in mute apology.

Feeling his small body shiver, she hugged him close. How vile of Lord Pallu to shame her and instill such fear in her son. "Benjamin, don't worry. All's well—you'll see."

She prayed it was the truth. But in her heart of hearts, she knew better. Lord Pallu intended to take her son and leave her with nothing.

She must overcome this. She must fight Lord Pallu for Benjamin, and for her own reputation.

But how?

Blessed are You, O Lord my God, King of the universe. Turn your face toward me! Bless me and my son and save us from despair!

Chapter 9

Evil circled and hissed at Benjamin, so quick and strong that he knew even a sword couldn't chase iit away. Hate reached for him with its claws, its face changing from a monster to Abba, wanting to cut him apart. "No!"

Ama couldn't help him; Abba Pallu had thrown her into a pit and Benjamin would never see her again. He awoke crying until he realized Eran was rocking him and whispering prayers for him and for Ama.

But not for Abba.

Unable to be brave, Benjamin huddled against Eran and sobbed.

***

"Why did you tie this fabric over your window?" Levia fingered the blue veil covering Elisheba's lathe-worked bedchamber window.

"To hide my view of the street. I don't want to see anyone," Elisheba looked up from her sewing lesson with Malkah and Zimiyrah. "Actually, I've had it up there for weeks." Furthermore, if her lattice window was covered, then Lord Pallu couldn't accuse her of flirting with men down in the street.

"But it casts such a shadow in here," Levia complained. "Though I suppose the cold weather will be upon us soon and we'll be covering the windows anyway." Levia turned from the window, smoothing her green gown, showing her advancing pregnancy.

Two weeks earlier, in spiritual preparation for the autumn High Holy Days, particularly the Day of Atonement, Elisheba had confessed her envy to Levia and begged her forgiveness. Levia had forgiven her kindly, but Elisheba sensed the older woman's satisfaction at being envied.

Smiling, Levia eased herself down to sit on the puffy red cushions and coverlets beside Elisheba, Malkah, and Zimiyrah. The two little girls seemed intent upon their stitchery, though Elisheba knew her young sisters-in-law were drinking in the whole conversation. As Levia plumped up one of the cushions and leaned an elbow on it, she said, "You know, of course, that we'll have our feast tomorrow night."

"Yes," Elisheba agreed politely. Pallu and Levia always hosted a delicious, well-attended meal during the Feast of the Tabernacles. "But I am hoping you will excuse me from the feast this year."

"We've invited your parents," Levia coaxed. "They've been worried about you and so have I. You've been too low-spirited recently. Won't you allow yourself to enjoy this one evening? Wear a pretty gown and let Leah arrange your hair. I insist! We've invited only a few relatives, so it's not as if we'd dishonor our year of mourning."

Truly? By all appearances, Levia and Lord Pallu had ended their year of mourning months ago.

Immediately, Elisheba scolded herself. How could she fairly judge anyone else's sorrow for Joseph?

For Benjamin's sake, she sighed. "If that's what you wish, I'll attend."

"Can we attend too?" Zimiyrah pleaded while Malkah leaned forward eagerly.

Levia smiled and lifted a strand of hair off Malkah's slender cheek, swirling it upward as if imagining her daughter in an adult hairstyle. "Certainly. It's only family."

Malkah and Zimiyrah dropped their needles and tangled white threads. Laughing, they clapped their hands until Levia hushed them fondly.

***

Wearing a blue gown and robe threaded with gold, her veiled hair swept high in a gold-tipped spray of pins, with long tendrils curling dark against her forehead and throat, Elisheba wandered into the torch-lit courtyard.

Pallu and Levia's gathering of "a few relatives" for the Feast of the Tabernacles was as elaborate as anything they'd ever hosted. Their traditional "booth," which should have been modest, was a massive, open-air structure filling a large portion of the courtyard. Pale gauzy fabric trailed down two sides of the booth, while the remainder was lavishly fretted of willow branches, myrtle, and palms, decorated with vines, fruits, and herbs. Thick mats and bright cushions were spread within the booth, and low stone tables were positioned in the center, prepared for their food. At least twenty richly-garbed adults lingered here and there around the oversized booth, laughing, talking, and sipping wine from slender stoneware cups.

The only children here tonight were Malkah, Zimiyrah, and Benjamin, already sitting impatiently near the women's table, staring at the ornate lamps in its center. Seeing Elisheba, Malkah stood and turned delightedly like a dancer, showing off her long gold-twined braid, which was crowned with a delicate gilded-silver circlet befitting Lord Pallu's eldest daughter. "What do you think?" she demanded, facing Elisheba again, her eyes sparkling in the lamplight.

"You look perfect," Elisheba told her. "So near-adult that I feel ancient."

Not to be left out, Zimiyrah scrambled to her feet and grabbed Elisheba's hand, pleading, "Can I have a citron?"

"I want one too," Malkah said, pointing to a fruit-embellished garland dangling above their heads. Even Benjamin brightened at the thought.

Elisheba smiled. "Do you know why they've hung the citrons way up there?" When the children shook their heads unhappily, Elisheba said, "Because the Lady Levia knew you would steal them if they weren't out of your reach, and you won't like the taste."

"I would. I'm so hungry," Zimiyrah whimpered, her elbows on the table now, her head in her hands, a tragic figure.

"You'll eat soon," Elisheba promised, patting Zimiyrah's back, then reclining on the cushions beside her. The children scooted closer, Zimiyrah fidgeting, Malkah playing with her gold-threaded braid, Benjamin lapsing into his now-usual silence. Elisheba studied her small son, worried by his gloom and the shadows beneath his eyes. Eran said he was still having nightmares several times a week. *Lord, protect my son.*

"Elisheba!" Daliyah sat next to her before Elisheba could stand. "My baby, oh how wonderful to see you looking so well. Your father will be most pleased."

As they hugged each other, Levia approached, dazzling in violet and gold, her veiled hair secured with pearl-garnished pins and a fragile gold diadem. She settled beside Elisheba delicately, shaking out her veils while she complimented Elisheba. "My, I've forgotten how beautiful you are when you take time with your appearance. Everyone has. Look! My husband's family can't help admiring you."

She cast a meaningful look toward Pallu and his cousin Eliezer, who was a heftier, more richly garbed version of Pallu. The two older men were studying her and murmuring to Eliezer's son, Malchos.

Thin and fastidious in a bright yellow tunic and mantle, with a beard so sculpted that it looked painted along his jaw, Malchos watched Elisheba, his thick eyebrows raised, his expression ... avid.

Feeling perused like goods in a market, Elisheba glanced away from Malchos. She held no grudge against the young man. Indeed, she'd never so much as spoken to him. But he was staring too ardently for her comfort. Furthermore, he had more pomade on his hair than she had on hers. And, kindred or not, Joseph had never been a close friend with his cousin.

"No one exists for Malchos," Joseph had said years ago. Now, Elisheba wished she had asked her husband to explain his cryptic, dismissive comment.

Levia nudged Elisheba slyly. "What do you think of him?"

"He's nothing like Joseph," Elisheba murmured.

Lowering her voice, Daliyah said, "No man will ever be like Joseph."

Elisheba stared at her, appalled. "Ama, are you trying to marry me off again? So soon?"

"No, not so soon," Daliyah protested gently, as Levia smiled agreement. "But it doesn't hurt to have a plan, does it? And Malchos is one of Joseph's relatives, so everyone will be pleased. Furthermore, I've heard he's clever with money. He would protect your inheritance, and Benjamin's. Consider him, for Benjamin's sake. In a year, perhaps."

"Does Abba agree with you?" If Abba agreed, then his word was law to her. She'd have no choice but to marry Malchos.

Daliyah patted Elisheba's hand. "Naturally, we've discussed your future. But you know your father won't make such a decision until he absolutely must. Malchos is only a possibility, though a serious one. Lord Pallu suggested him."

And Lord Pallu expected to be obeyed.

Elisheba brushed her fingers over her son's curls, keeping her movement gentle despite her growing rage. Here she was, still in mourning, yet her father-in-law was already planning her next marriage.

Clearly, Lord Pallu wanted to control her and Benjamin permanently, even if it was only through a relative—Malchos. Why? And yet, she should have guessed that Lord Pallu and Levia would barter her off this evening. Jerusalem's wealthiest, most influential citizens conducted the majority of their business negotiations during frequent and lavish meals such as this. Even so ... Malchos.

She would not—must not—voice her outrage.

When Elisheba remained silent, her mother-in-law Levia said, "It's not that we're eager to be rid of you, Elisheba, or that your grief for Joseph is anywhere near finished, but ..." Her voice broke off. She dabbed at her eyes and began again. "I know how you loved Joseph; I was always delighted for you both. But now Pallu and your father are concerned for your future. And you must consider Benjamin's future too."

I do little else.

Warming to the subject of Elisheba's potential remarriage, Levia whispered, "Just consider this. Malchos has his own lands and so much silver he'd hardly know if you'd spent his wealth or your own. And he would never mistreat Benjamin. Particularly if he becomes infatuated with you, as Joseph was."

Benjamin sighed loudly, evidently listening and displeased by their conversation. "Ama, when do we eat?"

"We eat now," Levia answered, before Elisheba could speak. "But remember your manners, Benjamin, and stay with your Ama." Turning to Malkah and Zimiyrah, she said, "You stay with Elisheba too. And behave or you'll have to leave immediately and go to your chamber and sleep."

While Levia warned the girls, the servants brought out trays of thin, crisp, cumin-scented bread, fish fried with leeks and olives, roasted nuts, spiced sauces covering tender bits of chicken, cinnamon dusted dates, vessels of new wine, and tipsy-looking figs so saturated with honeyed glaze that they almost looked translucent. And Benjamin's favorite—

"Eggs!" Benjamin leaned toward a dish of puffy, gold-crusted eggs. Elisheba hastily restrained him.

"Shh, or you won't get a single bite." He hushed as if he meant to be so well-behaved she would let him eat the entire dish of eggs.

Levia left them for her own cushioned place among the other women nearby. But after the formality of prayers, Daliyah stayed to visit, sharing Elisheba's meal.

When Benjamin was settled with his eggs and Malkah and Zimiyrah were whispering over their bread, chicken, and figs, Elisheba whispered, "Ama, do you really want me to marry Malchos, or did you say that to please the Lady Levia and Lord Pallu?"

"To please them, of course," Daliyah murmured. "But Malchos isn't your only choice, I'm sure. Now, forget him. Let's try the fish. And serve me some bread and almonds."

"Thank you, Ama." At least her parents would speak on her behalf if Lord Pallu tried to force her into remarriage. Smiling, Elisheba tended the children and ate her own food, listening to others talk as they always did during these gatherings. *Lovely evening. Delicious food. Pallu's courtesy. Money to be made from worshipers streaming in to visit Jerusalem this week...*

Malchos' father, Eliezer, became particularly loud after his third cup of aged wine, calling out, "Has that Galilean lout shown up yet?"

"Their *Master* Iesous?" Malchos sniffed, scooping a tidy bit of chicken onto a crisp piece of bread. "We'd have heard by now, don't you agree? He's never subtle."

"But he's obviously clever enough to realize that He must stay away." Pallu jotted a cinnamon date at the air, emphasizing his words. "I attended the last meeting, you know. They're going to arrest Him if He shows His face this week."

The last meeting of the Sanhedrin, Elisheba realized. Pallu loved having members of the leading council in his debt, as a number of them were.

"I must add," Pallu said, pausing to chewed his date, "if that fraud-prophet is led off in chains, I hope I'm there to see it, for all the silver He cost me last year."

Another cousin, Philetos, spoke now, fingering his dark beard, which was trimmed virtually out of existence. "They'll have to be smart about arresting the man. The common people love Him."

Eliezer snorted. "Of course the common people *love* Him, good Philetos. They'd love anyone who promises them the chance to keep their own money from the Romans and from the Lord's House. That's what life's all about, isn't it?"

"I don't care how much the commoners keep or don't keep as long as they pay the rents I'm owed." Malchos grinned and lifted his wine cup in praise of the idea. The other men laughed and lifted their cups to drink with him.

Throughout this conversation, Elisheba was aware of her father reclining quietly in his place at the men's table, watching her reaction to this conversation. *Yes, Abba,* she told him silently, picking at her fish. *I still believe the Rabbi Yeshua is righteous, and a healer, and a prophet—everything a man of the Lord should be. Unlike those priests being held by Pallu's purse-strings.*

The Rabbi Yeshua should be leading worship in the Holy House, rather than those bribe-loving men from the priestly families of Phiabi, Anan, and Kathros. They—

Daliyah poked Elisheba's back, making her jump. "What?"

"Get that frown off your face," her mother whispered.

Had Pallu noticed? Elisheba gave her mother a quick smile. "Yes, please forgive me."

"You're looking too fretful," Daliyah scolded. "You need to get out more."

"With you?"

Her mother chuckled. "Who better? Let's go somewhere tomorrow."

"Could we visit the Holy Courts?" Elisheba almost surprised herself with the question. Corrupt priests or not, the Lord's House was the most beautiful place in Jerusalem. And she still felt the Almighty Lord's presence there. "It will be safe, won't it? Since the Rabbi Yeshua's not coming?" Though she wished He would.

"Of course," Daliyah agreed, her dark eyes shining with inspiration. "Then we can go down to the market afterward and select some fabrics for new gowns. I'll have your father ask Lord Pallu, while you settle the children for the night."

***

In her bedchamber, Elisheba helped the children arrange their mats, cushions, and thick coverlets into a nest-like sleeping area. They were all happy, giggling and smacking each other with the cushions until she stopped them.

"Lord Pallu won't be pleased if you give each other bloody noses," she chided. "And I'll send you right back to your own rooms."

Benjamin immediately sat down. But Zimiyrah piped up, "Why don't you have a bed yet?"

"Because I don't need one," Elisheba answered with unfelt calm. "My cushions are comfortable enough."

More to the point, why would Lord Pallu repay her for her marriage bed when a new husband could provide one for her? She tried to imagine being married to Malchos. That proud, self-indulgent man, touching her …

Her imagination failed, and she felt squeamish. Malchos would never understand her.

Nor would he ever provide her with a bed. Ugh! She would not accept him.

Even as she resisted the proposed marriage, her breath caught in panic at the idea of quarreling with Pallu and Levia. How could she tell them no? Pallu would take Benjamin from her.

Scared, she knelt and kissed her son, hugging him so tight that he squealed. "Ah, I can't breathe!"

"Neither can I," she whispered.

***

What must I do? Elisheba begged the Lord, pressing a hand to her veiled face as she leaned against a cold white marble column in the Women's Court. *If only I could stand before You and plead my case, for these greedy people don't care about my fears.*

Benjamin tugged her free hand hard, making her look down at him from beneath the edges of her veil. He gave an imploring grimace, his little-boy patience worn thin. And Ama was watching, fingers subtly tapping as if she'd been waiting for Elisheba to finish her prayers so they could begin their shopping excursion. Sighing her regrets, Elisheba nodded and followed her mother quietly from the Women's Court.

But as they departed through the southern gate and passed around the carved stone balustrade to the Gentile's Court, Elisheba continued to pray, her soul wrenched by worry. *Malchos will not love my Benjamin, O Lord! Nor can he love what I have become in Your sight as a follower of the Rabbi. Almighty Lord, I beg You ...*

Benjamin pulled her along seeming eager to escape the Holy Courts, to follow Daliyah to the marketplace. Afraid that she might lose him amid the crowd, Elisheba bent, warning, "Don't let go of my hand, Benjamin."

"I won't let go," Benjamin promised, looking up at her. "I—"

Someone crossed their path, causing Benjamin to collide with a coarse-clad, prayer-shawl-draped man. Elisheba glanced at the man involuntarily, expecting him to stare past her as if she didn't exist. Or worse, to acknowledge her presence with an infuriated glare.

Instead, He actually grinned at Benjamin from beneath His concealing prayer shawl, His tallit, as if amused by the little boy's misstep. He steadied Benjamin, who seemed dazed, then He looked at Elisheba, His eyes full of compassion. He ...

She blinked, her thoughts scattering into fragments of recognition. Rabbi Yeshua. Master Iesous ... watching as if He understood the cries of her heart. As if perceiving her thoughts, her very soul ... and then offering His unspoken encouragement.

How was this possible?

She trembled, reduced almost to weepiness by His concern. But the instant passed, and He moved on in silence like any other devout worshiper hidden beneath His tallit.

Did someone see? Had one of Lord Pallu's servants noticed her trading looks with the "renegade" Rabbi? In a quiet panic, she hurried to catch up with her mother, who was departing from the Lord's House. Benjamin lagged behind until Elisheba finally scooped him up into her arms.

Still staring over her shoulder at Rabbi Yeshua, Benjamin demanded, "Who is He?"

"Shh!" *Lord, don't let me lose my son forever because of one misstep!* Yet amid her fear, she remembered the Rabbi's smile, His compassion, and she took courage as she fled.

***

He considered the young widow and her son, knowing the troubles they must pass through within their time-bound lives. But Spirit exulted at what He saw in them. Within the brilliance of endless light. And joy.

Almost laughing aloud, Yeshua strode toward His yet undiscerning disciples—allowing Himself to be seen now, while Spirit called those who hungered in darkness.

Come to Me in My Father's court!

Chapter 10

Caught by Master Iesous' intensity, Stephanos lingered in the crowded, windswept Gentiles Court.

Facing his enemies near the gold-crested marble porticos, Master Iesous raised his voice to be heard by everyone. "In your law it is written that the testimony of two men is credible. Therefore, I am one man, testifying for Myself. My other witness is My Father who sent Me."

Kore yanked at Stephanos' elbow, but Stephanos ignored him. How often did they have the chance to listen to fresh ideas? And yet ... Did the Teacher understand that He risked His life and His disciples' lives by coming here? For the guards of the Lord's House were loitering nearby, also listening and liable to arrest Iesous at any time. However, they didn't move to seize Him. And the Master showed no fear, calmly defending His right to testify before them.

How could He dare? Stephanos recoiled inwardly. He himself would never have such courage.

An elder Pharisee, proud in his long heavily tasseled garments, challenged Iesous in a strong, carrying voice. "Where *is* Your Father?"

By his tone, the Pharisee implied that the Teacher's unknown Father was a wicked man to raise such a reprobate Son as Master Iesous, who claimed to be more than He obviously was: a simple Galilean fisherman.

Iesous leveled a look at the Pharisee. "You do not know Me, or my Father. If You knew Me, you would also know Him."

The Pharisee smirked exaggeratedly to his companions as if to say, "A decent man would declare his father's name instantly. This man is hiding something." They agreed with subtly echoed sneers and nods, implying Master Iesous was baseborn.

Ignoring them, Master Iesous changed the subject, warning the crowd and the curious guards. "I am going away, and you will look for Me and die in your sins. Where I am going, you cannot come."

"What?" Kore muttered to Stephanos. "Is he going to kill himself, saying, 'Where I'm going, you cannot come'?"

"Shh!" he hissed to Kore. "He's not talking about death. Any man can go down to Sheol." A shiver ran through Stephanos even as he spoke. He had to force himself to remain still and listen to the Master.

"You are from below. I am from above," Iesous emphasized, looking again at the Pharisees. "You are of this world. I am not. *This* is why I told you that you will die in your sins, for if you do not believe that I am who I claim to be, then you will truly die in your sins."

"Who are you?" one of the Pharisees snapped back, scornfully reminding everyone that this miscreant hadn't the nerve—or good reputation—to speak his father's name.

"Just what I have been claiming from the beginning," Iesous said, quiet but clear. "I could condemn you for many things—and I could teach you much. But the One who sent me is Truth, and I say only what I hear from Him."

"Aw," Kore complained beneath his breath, "he's talking riddles again. Let's go!"

He tugged at Stephanos' cloak, pulling him away. And indeed it was time for them to leave. Their families were expecting them for this last, greatest night of the feast. Still, Stephanos turned, looking back over his shoulder as Master Iesous continued. "When you have lifted up the Son of Man, then you will know that I am *He*—as I claim—and that I do nothing on my own but say exactly what the Father has taught me...."

Stephanos halted. Son of Man. Was Master Iesous truly the Christos—the Anointed? Joseph had called him *Mashiyakh*. Joseph had believed.

As I ... might. Fear coiled in his belly, ready to strike. Stephanos sucked in a breath and walked onward to the tunnel leading down to the gate.

"I don't appreciate being teased by riddles that no one bothers to explain," Kore grumbled as they worked their way down the uneven steps, past the priests' guards, to the public courtyard below the Holy House.

"If you believe, then you understand," Stephanos told him, while veering within his own thoughts from understanding to fear.

"You're talking riddles like Master Iesous. Quit!"

"I'd prefer to quit too." Quitting was safer.

As they threaded their way through the most ancient streets of the city, a profound chill swept Stephanos amid the breeze. He glanced over his shoulder at the Lord's House, agitated to his very soul. Everything he had once believed, he now questioned. And he longed to doubt the emerging answers.

Why was he so tormented by this?

Because if he believed Master Iesous was the Christos, then his life was endangered.

And if he decided to not believe … he would be lying to himself. Ultimately, his soul would wither away.

And the Lord's House, which he loved, would become less to him than a gold-crowned, white marble tomb. Death would greet him there.

A deeper chill slid over Stephanos with a sensing, as if Sheol's eternal pit opened beneath him. He rushed after Kore through Jerusalem's timeless streets, pounding down long-terraced steps of stone, trying to escape.

***

Adonai perceived His adversary—light forever darkened—treading shadow-like through the crowd, slinking down the steps of Father's House, and through His city. Whispering lies. Sneering. Casting unseen darts of fear and doubt.

To dupe the wolves and scatter the lambs.
Craving chaos to obliterate what Father loved. What Spirit desired.

What I, formed as man, will save by sacrifice.
His flesh trembled as if already flayed.
He had only to speak one word and His torment would be past. Temptation beckoned him ... No.

He set the thought aside.
Drink the cup at its proper time.
For Love.

Chapter 11

"You should have heard Him," Stephanos said, so quiet that Andronikos had to lean nearer, listening as they ate beneath the palm-roofed shelter of a crowded, modest tabernacle shared by their families. "Today, in the Lord's House, He spoke, yet again, as if He's the Son of our Almighty Lord."

"That's what I am afraid of," Andronikos admitted beneath his breath. "But how can we truly decide?"

"I don't want to decide." Stephanos pushed his food away, brooding. "I need time to think."

"Too much thinking will make you insane."

"Not thinking enough will make us dead."

"Only if Kore is involved," Andronikos muttered, dry as dust.

Reluctantly, Stephanos grinned. "You're right. Somehow, he's going to accidentally kill us both. But since he's not here tonight, I suppose we'll survive until morning."

As they laughed together, Andronikos reached for a piece of fresh bread and glanced around, checking on his siblings. Loukas reclined alone, eating everything within his reach, while Maria sat quietly amid the chattering women, doubtless enjoying their gossip. But his mother noticed him from her place among women and she lifted one dark eyebrow, smiling purposefully.

She'd probably remembered another very respectable Greek-born girl he should consider as his wife. *No,* he told her silently, practicing for when he must finally say the word aloud. He didn't want to upset her, or quarrel. But he wasn't ready to marry.

Not yet.

***

Seated in cushions before an ornate stone table in the courtyard of Pallu's cousin Eliezer, Elisheba ate in silence, listening as the men talked. They were becoming louder as the evening wore on, their words echoing upward to the palm-and-garland-draped shelter above their heads.

"Those fool-guards should have arrested Him!" Pallu fumed. "You should have seen the looks on their stupid faces, as if He'd dazzled them." Tipping his head, he mimicked the guards' shamed expressions, their befuddled words. "'But no one has ever said such wonderful things.' They sounded like weak-willed women!"

"What did Caiaphas say to them?" Eliezer demanded in Greek, talking through the remains of a fruit pastry, some of its edges crumbling and dropping from his mouth as he spoke.

"What could he say?" Pallu shook his head at the mention of their High Priest. "The fraud-prophet was gone for the day. And today, again, the same thing—the guards didn't touch him. I want to see that Man *beaten* for His crimes. When I think of all the silver I've lost to that fraud's theatrics—"

"Caiaphas should have had the guards beaten." Malchos sniffed as he helped himself to some honeyed fruit.

"As High Priest, he needs their loyalty," Pallu reminded the young man, mincing his Greek with exactitude as if counting coins. "Treat your guards badly and they'll serve your enemy instead."

Malchos laughed. "I buy loyalty from my guards and my enemies. Caiaphas goes about this all wrong."

Listening, Elisheba chafed at his arrogance. Malchos would make a superb high priest.

A delicate nudge to her back made Elisheba turn. Levia reclined beside her now, her dark eyes dancing as if to say, *Malchos can buy whatever he wants. Isn't it wonderful?*

Elisheba glanced at the young man again, trying to see anything wonderful there.

He caught her glance and smiled subtly. She could almost hear his thoughts. *Admit it. I'm clever. Admire me.* As brief as her glance was, she saw his expression deepen, becoming desire, promising pursuit. She looked down at her now-unappealing food, the spice-scented bread and tender roasted lamb glazed in a wine sauce. The sauce was congealed. Overcooked.

"He's watching you," Levia whispered, her beautiful face lit with mischievous delight. "My Lord Pallu will be so pleased."

Elisheba took refuge from discussing Malchos by telling Levia the truth. "Your expression just now was so like Joseph's. Oh, how I miss his smile!"

Levia's smile faded and her eyes closed in a pained grimace. "I'm trying to help you, Elisheba, and you *kill* me."

Sensing that her mother-in-law wasn't angry, Elisheba dared a light, comforting hug. "You are the one who had such a handsome son. How can you blame me if I can't forget him?"

Levia drooped, looking wistful. "He was beautiful, wasn't he?"

"In every way." So let that be an end to this discussion of Malchos.

"Even so," Pallu was saying to Eliezer, his loud voice interrupting Elisheba's thoughts, "we cannot have some rustic magician swaying the crowds to believe that He's their '*Mashiyakh*.'" Pallu looked offended at merely having to say that ridiculous word, *Mashiyakh*. "Can you imagine what would happen if He inspires a rebellion?"

"The Romans would commence a butchery," Eliezer agreed. Belching moistly, deeply, he added, "They'd remove us from power—and from our properties."

Malchos sat straight up, frowning. "Then let's persuade Caiaphas. He must convince his guards to apprehend that false Mashiyakh and his followers and cut them off. Better the Galileans than us."

Listening, Elisheba almost shrank down into her cushions. How could she possibly marry Malchos? He would divorce her and denounce her the instant he perceived her faith in the Rabbi Yeshua.

More important, she had to find some way to warn Joseph's friends. Stephanos. Andronikos. Kore.

Would they be counted as followers of their Master? She could almost hear Pallu or Malchos accusing them, causing their imprisonment.

Joseph would want her to warn his friends. But a note would be unwise. Traceable.

Elisheba gnawed the inside of her lower lip, plotting.

***

Eran paused in the street before the perfume shop, the shifting autumn sunlight and a breath of air bringing a fragrance to him. Of sun-warmed wood mingled with a precise tang of spices that made him clutch one hand to his heart, struggling for reality.

How was it possible that memories, buried for years, could be brought to agonizing life by inhaling just one hint of scent?

His precious Abigail, slipping beyond this existence ... These same wood-spice fragrances were wafting from the robes of that last physician who'd told him she would die. After all of Eran's silver was gone, weighed out to save her. Equally crushing, they had no surviving children to remind him of the lilt of Abigail's voice, the sparkle of her eyes in laughter. *My sweet girl. Even now, if I recall your laughter, I will weep.*

Nothing had seemed alive for him in the years after her death. Until his small Master Joseph redeemed his years of impoverished servitude with an unexpectedly joyous friendship. A life-loving child had taught him to smile again. And if he remembered Master Joseph further, that too would cause him to weep.

Lord of Heaven and Earth, let my little Master Benjamin survive me!

Recovering, he hesitated just inside the shop's doorway, watching the young merchant Andronikos measuring out spices for an equal weight in silver as a severe, well-dressed man eyed the scales suspiciously.

Obviously familiar with the older man's habits, Andronikos spoke blandly, covering a smile. "I'll let you look at the scales until you decide we're even, Iakobos. Tell me if you become thirsty while you're watching."

Iakobos gave Andronikos a stern look from beneath his grizzled brows. "I'll take a drink and we'll call the scale even."

They chuckled together as if enjoying a longstanding joke. Andronikos poured Iakobos a modest cup of new wine and, as the older man drank, the younger man tipped the spices neatly from the scale into an alabaster box. "May the Almighty Lord bless all your ways," he told Iakobos.

After the man left carrying his box, Andronikos grinned. "Eran, good teacher! Please, come have something to drink. It's a blessing to see you." After locking away the silver, he handed Eran a small, clean cup. As Andronikos poured the dark new wine, he asked, "When are you coming to work for me, sir? Loukas needs your help with his writing, you know."

"Nothing would please me more, sir." Eran returned his grin. "But I already have a young master, and he rules me kindly."

"Benjamin will be a good student and a fine man, just like his father." Somber now, Andronikos asked, "How is he?"

Sipping at the sweet, unfermented wine, Eran sighed. "Terrors haunt his sleep. He wakes trembling and crying, yet he won't speak of his fears. How I pray for him! And particularly, I pray that he and his mother will again find joy."

Having mentioned the Lady Elisheba, Eran glanced around the shop. They were alone, but not for long, he was sure. "I am sent to warn you, my friend, to be cautious. There are plots against our Master Iesous *and* His disciples, so warn everyone to be wary. Those in the highest places are speaking of His death—and of sending His followers after Him. Certain people might consider you and your friends to be among those followers."

"I'm grateful for the warning." Andronikos covered the stoneware wine flask and then stared down at the stone table intently as if it could speak wisdom to him.

"Do you no longer follow the Master?" More than anything, Eran wanted to discuss the Teacher, to ask Andronikos for the latest miraculous happenings, to debate all the ideas Master Iesous had prompted within him. Not to be swayed by fear.

Meeting his gaze, Andronikos said flatly, "I still believe and trust the Master. But I wish our thoughts of heavenly matters weren't so bound by earthly concerns like death threats. Not to mention the need to protect our loved ones." He stirred a stoneware pitcher of warm golden oil, studying it hard. Frustration tightened his movements. And the sharp wood-and-spice scent lifted around them, exuded by the spiced oil.

Eran pushed down the memories wrought by the rising fragrance and asked, "Is that anointing oil?"

The young merchant's tension eased with a smile. "It's not sacred oil made by the honored priestly House of Kathos, but it will do."

Your oil is untainted by bribes. Eran masked a frown. Why should corrupted priests made oil for the Lord's House when good men like Andronikos were more fitted to the sacred duty? Yet, the priests could boast of their rights by heritage, by blood. Whereas Andronikos ... they'd shower him with scorn. Sighing, Eran placed his emptied cup on a small table nearby. "I must go. May the Almighty Lord bless you."

"And you, my friend. Is there anything I can prepare for you? Balm? Ointment?"

Other customers entered the shop now. A family—grim husband, harried wife, six jostling and visibly irritated children. Eran smiled and said clearly, "Your balsam ointment, please. It is the best in Jerusalem."

Packing ointment from a stone tub into a small terra cotta pot, Andronikos murmured, "Please thank *her* for the warning. Did she send you?"

"She did. At great risk, I might add."

Andronikos nodded. "Thank you both. I'll tell the others. You've confirmed what we feared."

Protect them, Eran prayed. He paid from his small hoard of copper and left the shop. The wood-spice-oil scent lingered in his garments.

Death haunted his memories in its fragrance.

***

When the squabbling young family departed with their purchases of incense and rosewater, Andronikos stirred the pitcher of oil, breathing in the aromas of frankincense and cassia. He could almost imagine being in a forest amid these scents, hiding within the trees. No politics. No death threats.

So Elisheba had warned him. Interesting. But he shouldn't suppose that just because she had remembered him …

His mother entered the shop from their courtyard door, wiping her wet hands on a clean linen towel. "You've been busy. I heard all those voices."

"I pray the perfumes lighten their moods." Andronikos focused on pouring the oil into alabaster vials, pushing away all thoughts of Elisheba.

Joanna inhaled and silently praised the oil by offering no suggestions for its improvement. "Maria and I will have food ready when you're finished," she told him, removing the coins from their money box, silver and copper ringing thinly in her hands.

Listening, Andronikos hid a wry smile. "Have plenty of food ready. I'm hungry."

He watched his mother go out back to the courtyard. Someday, he would ask where she was hiding all their silver. She hadn't thought of telling him. In her mind, he was still her child and she still controlled the shop. But he didn't begrudge her control. She was a good businesswoman. Careful, frugal, and admirably sensible. He'd learned so much just watching her.

Even so, they must have a business talk soon. He hoped they would both remain calm.

***

Lord Pallu's voice echoed up to the cedar beams of the reception room. "Send the children away." Fixing Elisheba with an acute look, he said, "You stay."

Elisheba's heart thudded. He'd found out that she asked Eran to warn Andronikos and the others.

She would lose Benjamin. She was going to be sent back to her father's home in disgrace. And Eran would be punished for honoring her request. Gulping, she prayed.

Nearby, Levia shifted uncomfortably, pressing her hands to her full-rounded belly. Elisheba could see the unborn child kicking, vigorously alive.

Elisheba looked away. Forcing herself to breathe, to remain composed.

As Malkah and Zimiyrah hastily finished the last bits of their food, Benjamin scooted over to Elisheba, his brown eyes wide with fear, silently imploring her to let him stay. *Be calm*, she warned herself. Benjamin must remember that she was dignified when Lord Pallu sent her away.

Leaning down, Elisheba wiped her son's hands, checked his tender face, then hugged and kissed him, whispering, "I love you—more than *everything*! Be my good boy and go quietly with your cousins."

Pallu waited, tapping his smooth, impatient fingers on the polished stone tabletop. When the children and servants were gone and the door closed, he frowned at Elisheba. "Why are you so defiant?"

Elisheba gripped her hands together hard in her lap. She must argue now. Plead her cause and protect Eran.

Pallu leaned across the table, accusing, "I go out of my way to secure your future with an honorable, wealthy man—a son of my own brother—and you behave as if he's filth!"

This was about Malchos. Elisheba almost went limp with relief. Eran was safe at least.

"You listen to me, girl!" Pallu snapped. "And listen carefully because I won't repeat myself. Malchos is your best choice for a husband, and you know it. Now…"

Realizing that he was delivering an ultimatum, Elisheba watched his imposing, hard-willed face.

"You are going to tell your father that you desire to marry Malchos."

Desire? No! Her tongue would rot with the lie.

"Don't you dare give me such a look!"

"Forgive me, lord." Elisheba struggled to soften her defiant expression. "It's just that I've never desired any man but your son."

She saw Pallu's eyes flicker, his hands clench. Evidently Joseph's memory still pained him. He **had** loved Joseph.

If only he could have overcome his hatred of the Rabbi Yeshua.

Averting his gaze, Pallu said, "Nevertheless, Malchos wishes to marry you. And this arrangement will benefit us all. I expect you to tell your father that you agree. That you desire this marriage." His voice hardened again. "I will be present when you tell him. Malchos, too, will be here, so you say exactly what I've told you."

Malchos would be here. Her stomach squeezed sickeningly as she imagined their meeting. Malchos. Pallu. Her father—and perhaps her mother and Levia. And a lie that would probably choke her.

Abba, I desire to marry Malchos. Ha!

But wasn't this better than losing Benjamin?

"You may go," Pallu muttered, dismissing her with a jerk of his chin. "And not a word to the servants."

"Yes, lord."

She departed, aware of Levia's unhappy expression and of her low question to Pallu. "Will you be leaving again tonight, my lord?"

Elisheba trudged into the courtyard and lifted her face to the sunset sky, breathing deep with relief. And trying to summon her wits.

Yes, she would agree to the marriage. For Benjamin's sake. The fear of losing him had been too close tonight. She would rather marry Malchos and accept the consequences, such as the regrettably scandalous divorce that would soon follow.

This marriage would purchase a little more time with her son. Unless... Could she possibly shift this miserable situation to her advantage?

Malchos. Just the thought of his primped, smiling, overly groomed self approaching her, kissing her, touching her ... Elisheba shuddered.

Joseph! She cried to him in her thoughts. *I don't want this! I don't want to be without you anymore!* She paused, composing herself with a prayer. *Now, Lord, ruler of the universe, what should I do?*

A soft gust of wind caught her sheer veils, caressing them against her throat. She rested in the coolness, thinking hard.

Yes, she would agree. But didn't she have rights? Indeed, she did, and she would use every last right to her own advantage.

Seizing hope, she walked toward her rooms, her steps lighter, her mind speeding ahead, fueled by inspiration.

Benjamin scampered toward her from the shadowed doorway of Eran's small room. As Eran looked on, Elisheba bent and caught her son beneath his arms, kissing him as he shrieked. "Laugh," she teased, jostling him playfully. "This is a good night, and I want to hear you laugh!"

Giving in, Benjamin laughed, hugging her neck. Refreshed by her son's delight, she smiled over his shoulder at Eran, reassuring the gentle old man in silence.

Surely the Lord was with them.

***

The dark-fire hatred tried to reach for him as he drifted toward sleep. But it didn't catch him. Not yet.

Benjamin opened his eyes for another drowsy peek. Eran sat on a bedroll nearby, praying. And Ama had laughed. He felt safe.

Even the monsters might stay away.

Chapter 12

"Look at that bow-legged little Pharisee." Kore eyed the newest member of their synagogue, drawing Stephanos' gaze to Sha'uwl, a thirteen-year-old Cilician emigrant. Short and ungainly though he was, the youth had wasted no time in making a place for himself among the men. He was standing in the stone-paved public area with the elders now, listening to the older men with flattering intensity, asking their opinions on points of the law. And he wore his long-fringed tallit as if he'd been practicing with the garment for years.

"Leave him alone, Kore, please," Stephanos warned. "Someone has to listen to all the teachers and elders. If you don't, it might as well be him."

"He's got nothing else to look forward to," Kore said, loudly enough to be heard by too many people. "What girl would marry such a pompous know-it-all?"

"Lower your voice! I'm sure people are asking the same question about you."

"I'm perfectly willing to talk about your being married," an amused voice said behind them.

Father. Stephanos turned, showing respect as his benevolent father, Isaak, deserved. But he longed to kick Kore. He hadn't yet found a young woman who might tolerate his love of study and his spiritual wrestlings, much less try to understand them.

"Listen." Isaak put a thin arm around Stephanos, steering him away from Kore, his dark eyes crinkled with delight. "You know we've done well with the painted stonewares this past year. Next year will certainly be better. Now, I'm sure you'll say that you're too young to marry and you want to continue your studies, but we should plan for ..."

Father was serious. Over his shoulder, Stephanos shot Kore a frosty look, promising retribution.

Kore grinned.

***

Every bite of food was sand in Elisheba's mouth, each swallow torturously dry. Her dining companions were watching her so closely. Pallu and Levia pleased, Malchos smiling and covetous, her parents obviously concerned. She ate little and drank less, but managed to be pleasant.

At last, when they were satiated, picking at bits of food from Levia's prized red plates, sopping the last of rich golden sauces with their bread, Pallu cleared his throat. "Barzel, have you heard your daughter's joyous news?" Prodding Elisheba with a cordial look, he said, "Tell your father."

Feeling her color rise hotly, Elisheba glanced over at Malchos, who was staring at her as if he imagined already possessing her. She turned to her father, forcing herself to speak quietly. "Abba, I desire to marry Malchos." For Benjamin's sake.

Lowering her gaze, she added a limitation. "After Passover. After ... Joseph's second burial." When Joseph's bones would be removed from the stone bed in Lord Pallu's family tomb and placed in a stone box—an ossuary—to rest forever inside one of the tomb's dark shelves. She ached to think of that darkness.

"That would be a proper time," her father agreed, aiming a doubtful look at Pallu. "It will give us ample opportunity to discuss the marriage contract."

"What do you suggest as terms?" Malchos leaned forward, clearly eager to bargain. "I will put an oath in writing that I can provide your daughter with a generous settlement, if it's ever required. In return—"

"In return, I will be certain my daughter never lacks for anything," Barzel interrupted, stern but polite. "I want her and Benjamin to be protected. But we'll discuss our terms another evening, Malchos, when we've both had time to consider these matters."

"Please, might I request one more condition?" Elisheba turned to her father. He looked so tense she feared he would snap like an over-tightened lyre string. When he nodded stiffly, she said, "I will regard my next husband as a treasure and, of course, I will always be faithful to him. I ask that he regard me in the same way and never take another wife. Only me."

Her words, gently spoken, brought perfect silence to the table. As she'd hoped, Malchos raised his groomed eyebrows, clearly shocked that she wanted to deny him other wives though he could afford them. Pallu flushed. Levia played fretfully with an edge of her sheer veil. But Daliyah smiled almost to herself and Barzel relaxed visibly.

"My daughter is truly mine," he said. "I was going to require this same phrase in the contract. But for a different reason: I don't want her properties or silver entangled with those of yet another family—namely those of a second wife to Malchos."

"Is this necessary?" Pallu demanded. "She's being insecure. And Malchos will treat her honorably."

"Certainly I will," Malchos assured Barzel. "You have no reason to worry."

Then why don't I trust you? Elisheba asked Malchos silently. *Reject this contract. Now.*

"Nevertheless," Barzel leaned back, lifting his bearded chin, and narrowing his eyes at Malchos, "I do worry. She is my only child. She and Benjamin are my heirs. This particular condition is not negotiable."

"Then I'll consider your request." Malchos toyed with a slender red glazed cup, watching it instead of Barzel.

Elisheba hid a smile. Without a doubt Malchos would halt all talk of the marriage. But legally she was within her rights to ask for this phrase in the contract. And Barzel's demand would be given precedence in these negotiations.

To her satisfaction, Pallu abruptly shifted the conversation to some loans he'd made recently. He boasted, praising himself. "The interest I'll make in return is well worth the wait."

"What of the risk?" Barzel asked, at ease once again. "What did you take for surety?"

As they talked, Elisheba picked at her food, her appetite returning. They'd drag the negotiations out with promises, pleas, and a thousand tiny legalities. Most likely she wouldn't marry him.

Before departing at evening's end, Malchos approached her boldly. Leaning down, his breath warm against her cheek, making her shiver, he whispered in her ear, "Such a high price you set upon yourself! If I accept, I expect you to prove you're worth treasuring."

Not the reaction she'd wanted.

Covering her dismay, she watched him leave, his heavy-sweet perfume of myrrh lingering in the room after he was gone.

***

"What made you request such a thing?" Pallu demanded, so close that he was breathing in Elisheba's face—an older reflection of Malchos. "Did you conspire with your father beforehand? Did you?"

"No, lord." Elisheba shrank back as much as she dared. "I've only asked for a promise of the same love and regard I enjoyed with your son."

"You don't know that Joseph would have kept you as his only wife," Pallu argued. "You gave him only one son, and he would have become bored with you eventually."

How cruel of him to taunt her for having only one living child! Surely he remembered her grief over past miscarriages. And how untrue to speak as if all men became bored with their wives. Her father loved her mother dearly, and most men were esteemed for having only one wife. Moreover, didn't Lord Pallu consider what he was saying in front of his own wife, who would give birth in mere weeks?

Levia was listening, her lovely face tensed as she reclined on her couch, picking the edge of her veil to shreds. Elisheba winced at her mother-in-law's hurt.

"Please forgive me, lord," she answered softly, "but Joseph and I never tired of each other, and it was my husband's preference to be faithful."

"That's your opinion."

"It's what Joseph vowed to me," Elisheba persisted. "I never saw him admire another woman."

Pallu exhaled, looking as if he wished he could argue and taunt her with instances he had witnessed of Joseph's infidelities. Instead, he asked, "What did Malchos say when he was departing?"

"He said that if he accepts our terms, he expects me to prove I'm worth treasuring."

His back to Levia, Pallu gave Elisheba a gleaming, nasty-minded look. "Of course. I'm pleased to hear that he's still considering the matter." Raising his hand in a gesture of dismissal, he added, "But remember that unless you want your time in my household to end badly, with you departing alone, don't say or do anything else to jeopardize our negotiations."

Elisheba nodded and then inclined her head in farewell. She'd done all she could to discourage Malchos for now. If compelled, she would take another, stealthier step to rid herself of Malchos, hopefully without seeming to be involved.

Outside in the cool night air, she studied the vast, opulently starred sky. Why was Lord Pallu so eager for this marriage to take place? What would motivate him?

Money? Had he made such unwise choices with his silver that he couldn't relinquish control of the properties given to her when she married Joseph? Perhaps.

Confronting Lord Pallu might be too great a risk. Yet she must learn the truth.

***

"Didn't I tell you?" Levia demanded in a whisper, clutching Elisheba's arm as they crossed the winter-chilled courtyard, the morning deceptively golden. "He's been straying like a dog! Do you think he will come home tonight? No! He's probably married some spoiled little creature and is afraid to tell me. I can't endure it!" Moaning, her breath rising in a soft vapor, she added, "You were so wise negotiating your contract to keep yourself as Malchos' only wife."

"Nothing's been signed yet," Elisheba murmured.

"But it will be, I assure you. Pallu talked privately to Malchos' father last week. Malchos is wild to have you. That's why he's joining us more often for meals."

Thank you for telling me. Now I'm going to be sick.

As they approached the stairs, Levia paused, panting, gripping Elisheba's arm hard. "Wait. I must catch my breath."

"If these are true pains ... " Elisheba hesitated. "They're not too early, are they?"

"Look how fat I am! Of course they're not too early, but they're not true pains."

Then why was Levia practically crushing her arm with a sudden death-grip?

When Levia nodded that she was ready, Elisheba accompanied her up the stairs. Entering Levia's glowing, richly tiled ante-chamber, Elisheba beckoned her former maid, Leah. "Send for the midwife."

Obedient, Leah covered her dark-braided head with a thick veil and moved toward the door until Levia stopped her. "Wait." Her belligerence made Leah hesitate, and Elisheba braced herself as Levia argued. "Elisheba, we don't know if these are true pains. You're trying to hurry things."

"Let me fret over you," Elisheba pleaded. "I just want you to be safe." Motioning to Leah emphatically, she whispered, "Go!"

Levia started to call Leah back, but then she froze, sucking in a breath, closing her eyes hard. Elisheba held her, willing the older woman strength. A torrent of birth water poured from Levia's robes down onto the floor. Levia shrieked. "Oh, no!"

"Let's go into your chamber," Elisheba urged, tugging her along, willing her to accept that her time was here. "You need some dry clothes. I'll help you get ready."

Levia's huge eyes betrayed her frantic longing to escape the encroaching pains. Becoming weepy, she babbled between tormented gasps as Elisheba helped her change into fresh garments.

"You know I've signed my will. If I die, you'll have my pearl earrings."

"I'd rather have you live," Elisheba promised. She removed Levia's soaked garments, dropped a light tunic over the laboring woman's head, then guided her to a temporary bed of thick-padded mats and cushions.

She knelt beside Levia, praying that her mother-in-law's labor would be swift. Praying Levia and the child would survive. Praying the midwife would arrive in time to catch the child. Soon, another pain closed upon her, and Levia screamed. "Ah, no! It's killing me!"

Thamar dashed inside the room, terrified.

"Don't you dare leave us," Elisheba threatened the flustered maidservant.

Thamar hesitated, wringing her hands. "But what if I do something wrong? Lord Pallu will take revenge on me."

"He'd take revenge if you do nothing. Just get some cloths and kneel behind the Lady Levia to support her. And pray."

Time slid by and still the midwife didn't arrive. Pain poured upon pain, hard and fast, making Levia wail, begging for her misery to end. And causing her to bear down so fiercely that Elisheba admitted the truth to herself. She must catch the child who might deliver her from Pallu's household.

Chapter 13

Swathed in her winter robes, Elisheba sat on a chilly stone bench in the courtyard, keeping watch over her tiny brother-in-law, the well-swaddled Nathan, tucked in his basket beside her, sound asleep. Precious lamb. He looked so much like Joseph.

She had all but begged Levia to let her take care of Nathan while Levia was preparing for this evening. Now, Elisheba lifted the newborn gratefully, inhaling his just-cleaned scent. Oblivious to her adoration, Nathan slept in her arms, sucking in his lower lip.

"Ama?" Benjamin scooted from his room, freshly scrubbed, wearing his favorite red robe and blue sash, ready for the celebration. Earlier today, Levia had gone up to the Lord's House and offered the priests silver, a lamb, and gifts, ending her forty days of ritual impurity. Tonight, Lord Pallu was hosting a "quiet" feast to honor his son's birth and Levia's safe recovery.

Obviously eager to attend the promised feast, Benjamin sped through the courtyard to Elisheba, halting with a bounce that threatened the baby's basket. "Is he still sleeping? I want him to smile."

"Seeing you smile makes me just as happy." Elisheba leaned over to kiss his soft neck and to let him admire Nathan. "No bad dreams last night?"

Benjamin scrunched up his face, as if offended. "No, those don't catch me anymore. Eran and I pray them to stay away."

"Oh?" Before she could cajole for more details, Malchos emerged from the entry hall, robed in yellow and crimson, with gold rings flashing on his hands, his hair gleaming with oil, his servants following discreetly.

Seeing Elisheba, he lifted his dark eyebrows and smiled, speaking in his accustomed Greek. "How pleasing it is to see you so ... domestic." Uninvited, he removed the baby's basket from beside Elisheba and dropped it at her feet, then settled himself into the basket's place. "It's good that you enjoy children; one of us must. I consider them dull until they've grown."

He smiled at Benjamin, as if expecting the little boy to be glad that Malchos found him dull. Benjamin looked down at the courtyard's paving stones, his small jaw tight.

"Shy?" Malchos asked him, condescending to speak Aramaic. "You must become used to me. I will marry your Ama soon."

"Once the contract is settled," Elisheba reminded Malchos, smiling through her irritation. She couldn't like this man. However, she must try. Though if divorce followed soon after, accompanied by a scandal, he wouldn't be much of a father to Benjamin. Why should she concern herself?

Leaning closer, surrounding her with an unseen cloud of thick-spiced fragrance, Malchos whispered, "If I could speak to you alone, I'm certain we could negotiate our terms."

She wanted to negotiate a clause forbidding him to kiss her as he seemed near to doing. And his whisper insinuated a physical rather than verbal negotiation. Lowering her eyes, she murmured, "I'm protecting your good name by ensuring my excellent reputation. I cannot do that if I'm secretly 'negotiating' with you in Lord Pallu's house or elsewhere."

The young man laughed, apparently interpreting her refusal as a joke, or worse, a flirtation. "Yes, but I'm already persuaded you are excellent in every way."

He sounded as if he'd heard some secret details about her. Was someone in this household discussing her with him? Lord Pallu? The idea made her squirm and blush. She focused on little Nathan, warm in her arms, and on Benjamin, who patted her knee impatiently.

"Ama, can we go inside now?"

Elisheba wanted to kiss her son for giving her the ideal excuse to leave. Standing, cuddling Nathan, she offered Malchos a smile. "Forgive me, please, but I should take the little ones inside. It's too cold to keep the baby here for very long."

"You are the judge of those matters," he said, lordly as if they were already married and within his own household. "I'll take you to the reception room."

He stood and wrapped an arm about her, too familiar as they left the courtyard. Caressing her waist, Malchos said, "Your father is planning to attend the celebrations, is he not?"

"Oh...yes, he's attending," Elisheba agreed, badly distracted. Joseph had been the last man to touch her this way. Why must Malchos be the next man to embrace her? She should have realized that he was the sort who wouldn't accept a polite hint. She should have stayed in the open courtyard. Foolish of her! Why hadn't she considered that he would accompany her and touch her?

Her stomach tightening, she quickened her pace, but Malchos matched her steps smoothly. "Good. I will talk with him again about our negotiations."

Girlish squeals echoed greetings as they entered the jewel-rich, lamp-lit reception room. Robes flaring with their movements, Malkah and Zimiyrah dashed toward Elisheba. "There you are! Is he awake? Nathan, Nathan! Open your eyes!"

To Elisheba's secret relief, Malchos released her, stepping away from the eager children, but still watching. As if she were already his wife.

***

"After Passover, after Joseph's second burial, we'll formalize your betrothal," Daliyah told Elisheba softly, reclining beside her near the table. "Malchos has agreed you will be his only wife."

He agreed? Elisheba glanced toward Malchos, who was laughing and joking with the other men now that they'd eaten. She had been so certain he would deny her request to be his only wife. But now this marriage would happen. After Passover. Weeks away. Yet not far enough. *Oh, Joseph, why did you have to die?*

She had to force down the grief. Had to speak quietly. Had to slow the negotiations once more with her next planned legal hurdle. "Ama, thank you. Has Abba inquired about the properties and money I brought to this family when I married Joseph? It would comfort me to know they are making some profit for Benjamin's future. If only we could ask Lord Pallu to sign them back to Abba until this marriage takes place."

Daliyah stared at her now, surprised. She frowned and then whispered, "What are you saying? Do you have doubts about Lord Pallu's handling of your properties?"

Refusing to state her suspicions outright, Elisheba murmured, "I've heard nothing of my properties or my money. I'm just curious."

"I'm certain you've no reason to fear, my baby. When you married Joseph, your father received documents proving that Lord Pallu had placed your properties and money under the care of a steward they both trust. And Lord Pallu will simply give their management to Malchos. But then ..." Daliyah's defense trailed off, and she straightened on her couch, frowning.

Elisheba watched her mother's inward struggle playing out over her soft face—the hope that Lord Pallu had dealt honorably with Elisheba battling against the suspicion that Lord Pallu had misused income from her dowry. "I've no doubt everything's accounted for. But I'll mention this to your father."

Was she right to do this? Elisheba clenched the edge of her mantle in one fist. Would questioning Lord Pallu's integrity with money cost her Benjamin?

She tried to reassure herself, watching Benjamin and the girls clustered around the proud Levia with the other gold-adorned, laughing ladies, all doting upon the wide-awake, hiccoughing baby Nathan.

***

"I hear that you follow the Galilean Teacher, Iesous." Young Sha'uwl of Cilicia stepped in front of Andronikos, Stephanos, and Kore amid the synagogue's cold stone-columned meeting area.

"Yes, we have," Stephanos drew his cloak together, trying not to frown. The youth was blocking their path to their seats, pugnacious enough to deserve the insults Kore would snap out if Stephanos didn't shift the conversation. Hurriedly, Stephanos asked, "What do your teachers say of Him?"

At once, Kore clamped his mouth shut, rolled his gaze upward, and turned away. For him, there had been unexpected adventure in following the Baptizer and Master Iesous. They spoke the truth and allowed the consequences to fall as they might upon unwary or hostile questioners. Kore found great enjoyment in their blunt honesty. But there was no fun in listening to this self-important youth expounding on his opinions.

"My teacher, Gamaliel, suggests moderation with your Master Iesous. But our elders say the man is a danger, that He will lead a revolt against Rome and fail." Sha'uwl emphasized his opinion by lifting his short chin. "I know He will fail. I am a Roman citizen, and—"

Kore huffed, giving the youth a dagger-look over his shoulder. "That little boast won't earn you any favors here, with your elders, or with us!"

Sha'uwl bristled in offense. "Seeking favor was not my intention. Do you think I'm such a fool? No! My whole point is that your Master Iesous is insane and faithless. I've heard our elders in the Holy Courts saying that the Man derides our sacred traditions, and if—"

"But do you really know the truth?" Andronikos asked, carefully polite. "By your own admission, all you've learned is hearsay. Yet you're condemning Him and us."

"You *are* defending Him."

The young man looked furious enough to draw a sword. Stephanos watched, nauseated. A memory returned, of Master Iesous defending himself in the Holy Courts this past autumn, His enemies closing in, eager to destroy Him. *You do not know Me.* Provoked by alarm to defend himself, Stephanos snapped at the young scholar. "Forget the rumors! Pay attention to your Master Gamaliel and abandon your stupid arrogance. Otherwise, you'll learn nothing."

Sha'uwl glared up at him, jerked his long-fringed tallit higher over his tousled hair, and stomped off without another word.

While Kore chuckled, Andronikos turned to Stephanos, wide-eyed. "That was amazing and completely unlike you. What's wrong? Are you ill?"

"No." Unless this feeling of Death itself reaching for his soul counted as illness.

He must be going insane.

"Let's go gather for prayers," Andronikos urged quietly.

Stephanos followed him, beset by inexplicable tremors. Why? Why had he lost his temper?

***

They acted in unseen swiftness—gloating, provoking the sluggish weak-witted creatures of dust. Stabbing one's pride with another's impatience.

Searing one's resentment.

Tending the other's dread.

Confronting enemy with potential enemy.

And exulting at their near-mastery of the cowering one's spirit.

The weakest was even now sensing their continual nearness, though unable to see their reality. Flesh dimmed all that was vital and worthy of existence.

Flesh obscured the eternal.

***

"Why have we been summoned?" Pallu asked quietly, meeting Eliezer and numerous other men, most members of the Sanhedrin, at entry of the high priest's palace.

"Who knows?" Eliezer muttered, his voice harsh within the ornately frescoed entry. "It's most likely something to do with our business in the Holy Courts."

It was more likely something to do with the priests wanting more silver. Pallu suppressed a grimace.

They joined a subdued line of fellow Sadducees, chief priests, and to Pallu's disgust, pompous, heavily robed Pharisees. Servants were kneeling before the doorway, well-trained and silent, placing small stools and stone foot basins before them, then untying Pallu and Eliezer's shoes and sandals.

Sitting on a stool, Pallu placed one bare foot and then the other on the stone footrest within the basin. A servant rinsed his already-clean soles, his heels, and even up to his ankles with warmed, perfumed water. It was a point of pride for Pallu that the used water was un-darkened and that the linen towels revealed no traces of dirt when his feet were dried. No one could fault his fastidiousness.

Avowed ritually clean, Pallu followed the other men into Caiaphas' lavish courtyard. Handsome rosette mosaics and a pristine pool opened to the magnificently sculpted stone skylight, provoking Pallu's envy, while gold-corded curtains framed deeply cushioned couches, tempting him to sit and rest. But the men continued onward into Caiaphas' reception area, his open court. There, the air was already filled with the indistinct whisperings of numerous voices and the mingled rich fragrances of spices and anointing oils used by Jerusalem's wealthiest men.

Caiaphas and his father-in-law, the former high priest Annas, entered the room now, all showy dignity in gold embroidered blue and white robes, signet rings, their silver-streaked beards well-oiled and groomed, their bare feet manicured. Annas affected cold smoothness, but Caiaphas' eyes were dark and hard beneath black, suspicion-raised eyebrows. Lifting one hand, he greeted his guests and they sat on various stone benches and chairs, though many of the Pharisees clustered together as if to proclaim, "We do not belong here, and for this we are grateful."

Pallu almost smirked. What torture it must be to live as a Pharisee.

Now, casting a reproachful look at several unassuming, plainly garbed men standing nearby, Caiaphas intoned, "Say to them what you have told us."

Moistening his lips, smoothing his beard, the leader of the unassuming group said in Greek, "We, with our own eyes, saw and testify...that the Galilean they call Master Iesous ... has brought a man to life again. Lazaros, a well-known citizen of Bethany, was four days dead. Yet the Master called out to him and Lazaros emerged from his tomb—still bound in his burial cloths."

He's mad, Pallu told himself as whispers lifted sharply throughout the reception room. Surely they were all mad! The dead do not come to life again.

"And you still say that Master Iesous cannot be the Anointed One?" another man asked everyone, quiet but firm. Nikodemos. Pallu sneered just listening to the overlearned fool. The man was a known supporter of that magician-rabbi Yeshua.

Undeterred, Nikodemos continued. "How can we deny him, with all the miracles he's performed openly in the Holy House and throughout the land? And now to raise one from the dead—after four days! No one, not even the prophets of old, has ever performed such a miracle."

"We saw Lazaros dead," another somber-faced witness added, testifying as those around him nodded. "His skin was mottled and blue. And even as they were tying him for the tomb, his limbs were turning rigid in death."

Impossible. This was a deception, Pallu decided. But the witnesses looked sincere, convinced they'd seen something remarkable.

"What must we do?" one of the Pharisees called out from a corner. "There's no doubt the Man does miracles."

"Well," Pallu snapped, unable to keep the sarcasm from his voice, "let's leave Him alone then! The entire nation will follow after Him, and the Romans will send an army to kill us and ransack our country." Disgusted with them all, he added, "You should have arrested that fraud weeks ago when He was here for the Feast of Dedication."

"Exactly," Eliezer snorted, then nodded vigorous approval.

"Why should they have arrested Him?" Nikodemos lifted his hands toward Pallu and Eliezer in a sweeping plea. "We cannot condemn an innocent man. Particularly not without an honorable trial."

"And the Master Iesous is not guilty," the lead witness added.

As the other witnesses from Bethany yelled their agreement, Caiaphas cried out, "You fools!

Idiots! It is better to let this one man die for us. Why should our entire nation perish?"

Ignoring the protests of the witnesses and Nikodemos, who turned away in despair, Caiaphas continued. "Let it be announced that any man who sees this Master Iesous, Rabbi Yeshua, must immediately report His presence so that we can arrest Him."

The revered teacher Gamaliel interceded now, his clear, kindly voice soothing everyone like healing balm. "Arresting the Rabbi will provoke the riot you're trying to prevent."

Caiaphas glared at him, but paused, obviously finding merit in the warning.

Gamaliel stood his ground, calm and silent, benignly stroking his grizzled beard.

"We shouldn't arrest the man during Passover then," one of the Pharisees decided aloud, earning a scowl from the still-powerful former high priest, Annas. The Pharisee coughed, shaking out his tasseled robes. "At least, let's not arrest Him openly."

"The Master shouldn't be arrested at all," the lead witness argued, moving forward. "If you had been there—if you'd seen—"

"Seen what?" Pallu cried. "A dead man brought to life again? Rubbish!"

"Exactly!" Eliezer yelled, the other Sadducees echoing him, bounding to their feet in condemnation of this Pharisaical foolishness. Unintimidated, the Pharisees matched them, accusation for shouted accusation.

But even as Pallu enjoyed the commotion he'd created, an errant thought whispered, *What if it's true?* He eyed the witnesses from Bethany. They seemed to believe in what they'd seen, sincerely enough to defy Caiaphas, the priests, and every man here who conducted business in the Holy Courts.

What if it's true? The thought nagged again. If Joseph could have been saved ...

He remembered Elisheba, weeping, begging just before Joseph's death. *Please, grant your son's request...because you love him.... There's still time.*

Pallu shoved back the memory ferociously. No one could have saved Joseph.

No one.

He'd made the right decision, refusing to be swayed by a weak-minded girl.

A lesser man would have beaten her.

Chapter 14

"Where have you been for the last two days?" Pallu's cousin Eliezer fretfully plucked at Pallu's sleeve, drawing him into the shade of a pillar amid the confusion of the Gentile's Court in the House of the Lord. "Look!" He pushed his bearded chin toward a near-riotous crowd milling through the tower-protected eastern gate, adjacent to the southern gate Pallu had entered.

"We've sent word to the priests that the Galilean is approaching with a mob of commoners. Yesterday, they all but proclaimed Him their king."

Pallu sneered. "Their *Mashiyakh*, Rabbi Yeshua, is coming to save us by pretending to bring the dead to life again."

But what if it's true? The thought whispered yet again. Shoving the ridiculous notion aside, Pallu said, "Where is He? I don't see Him."

It was impossible to track anyone with all the worshipers pouring into the Holy Courts. Sudden cries of rage and yowls of laughter drew Pallu's attention toward a whip-wielding rustic, who was opening makeshift enclosures and vigorously herding all the cattle and yearling lambs toward the eastern gate. The animals charged off as if sensing their lives were spared, while their merchant-owners screamed in protest, rushing after their fleeing profits.

As the rustic herder purposely overturned a cringing dove-seller's slatted seat in a recognizably swift motion, Pallu stiffened. "It's *Him*! Where are the guards?"

"If you want anything guarded, it should be your own men's tables," Eliezer admonished. "Tell them to gather the money!"

He was right. Pallu hurried along the porticos toward his stewards, who were sitting in spaces assured by bribes to the priests. Reaching the first table, Pallu rapped on it sharply, for the steward was watching the commotion, bemused. "Why are you just sitting there? Hide the silver before that fraud *Mashiyakh* scatters it everywhere!"

The man stared at him for a slack-mouthed instant, then picked row after row of neatly stacked silver from his polished table, placing it in the drawer beneath, trying to keep the coins in order. "Don't waste time being tidy. Hurry!" Pallu snapped.

Turning to the next several tables, he chased off the worshipers who were arguing with his men over fees, then cried, "Hide your silver!"

As he reached the third table to warn its keeper, Pallu heard coins falling, ringing thinly over the paving-stones behind him. He whirled about to check on the others and gasped, face to face with the cause of his turmoil. Elisheba's revered Rabbi Yeshua.

Even as his mouth formed threats against this rustic, Pallu froze, caught. The man's eyes gleamed, severe, but lucid and alarmingly, intensely ... *Aware*.

Uninvited, all of Pallu's secrets seethed upward, snakelike in his mind. The bribes, the lies to Levia and to Shelomiyth, the pretty young woman he'd seduced with false promises. Visions surfaced of the silver he'd embezzled from Elisheba's settlements to pay debts, paired with his murderous longings, cruelties, greed—all revealed themselves flagrantly, leaving him feeling utterly naked.

As if he truly had an eternal soul ... being comprehended by this ... commoner.

Still holding his gaze, the Galilean deliberately gripped the edge of the nearest table and dumped it over despite the steward's efforts to snatch it. Coins spilled, ringing chime-like over Pallu's feet and beyond, into the reach of others, many children. Pallu could only stare, betrayed by his own thoughts. How? From one glance. As if he had a soul.

"Out," the Rabbi Yeshua commanded, snapping the cord-whip downward, His voice and eyes so overwhelming that Pallu retreated in confusion.

Around Pallu, his stewards and worshipers shrieked, snatching the scattered silver. Clearly displeased, the Rabbi Yeshua brandished the whip again, ordering the stewards and unruly worshipers, "Out! Now! The Holy Words declare My Father's House is a place of prayer for *all* nations, but you've turned it into a den of thieves."

Pallu watched his cowering men scoop the remainder of their silver—his silver—into their tables' compartments and then struggle to escape the Gentile's Court.

Throngs of commoners clustered around the Galilean now, and He touched them as they begged for healings, while their children capered about, shrilling delightedly in Hebrew, "Hosanna!"

"Hosanna, Son of David!"

Pallu's benumbed thoughts finally cleared, translating their Hebrew, and its implications. *Oh save us, Son of David.* Pallu muttered, "No!" If these children were echoing what they'd heard from their parents, then the parents were mindless, openly shrieking for liberation from their Roman rulers. Worse, they were waving scraps of palm branches, living symbols of Israel's downtrodden kingdom and its thirst for rebellion against Rome.

Eliezer caught up to Pallu now, almost squealing he was so upset. "We've got to shut them up before the soldiers realize what they're shouting. They'll come down and massacre us all!"

"Let's leave instead," Pallu suggested tightly as his rage sharpened. His thoughts were again under his own control, all cutting toward revenge. He wanted that renegade Rabbi dead. Unless the Romans killed the man first.

***

"There now, what do you think?" Levia asked Elisheba, as Leah pinned Levia's dark hair high, coiling her braids within an extravagant new gold "fortress" headband.

Seated with Nathan on a small footstool opposite Levia's woven antechamber chair, Elisheba said, "With your new ornaments, you look as if you own half of Jerusalem."

"I deserve to be given half of Jerusalem, the way I've been treated," Levia sniffed, applying her cosmetics with deft touches to her lips and eyes. "Two days, he's been gone—and you understand perfectly what I mean."

"Yes." *I fear you are right,* Elisheba thought, watching her mother-in-law pucker her lips at the silver mirror. Nestled in Elisheba's arms, little Nathan cooed.

Levia kissed the air toward him, cooing in turn. "Oh, I should have named you Joseph. My perfect boy!"

Elisheba smiled, pleased, but with a tiny pang. How Joseph would have loved his baby brother.

A thud sounded at Levia's door and Pallu shoved his way inside, so furious that he seemed to be a living whirlwind, his robes flaring, his eyes glittering as he turned, his gaze searching the room. "Where's my writing box?"

"It's been so long since you've used it that I'm sure it's lost," Levia answered tartly, rubbing fragrant oil into her hands and then patting her face.

Pallu stared at her, specifically at her new headband and matching earrings. His eyebrows rushed together in a frown. "When did you buy those?"

"Yesterday," Levia said, still sharp. "I would have asked your opinion first, lord, but you weren't here."

"Don't use that tone with me or I'll have all your gold melted!" Pallu snapped. He glanced at Elisheba and his eyes narrowed as if he wanted to hurt her. "I saw your Rabbi Yeshua today, woman. He should have stayed in Galilee!"

Don't say a word, Elisheba warned herself, hastily lowering her gaze to Nathan's small perfect face, while Pallu ranted.

"He would have lived longer as a sheepherder. He's very good at that, you know. All commoners are."

Had there been another scene in the Lord's House? Had Lord Pallu lost more revenues? Her stomach churned its fear. But she defied Pallu, thinking, *Israel's King David began as a sheepherder!*

Shoving open a storage box, flinging scrolls aside, Pallu warned her, "False prophets tend to die badly, wallowing in their own blood. And often their faithful die with them. Remember that, woman, when you're tempted to follow another. Now, get out! And leave my son here."

Carefully mastering her emotions, Elisheba gave Nathan to Levia. But she didn't dare kiss the baby in farewell.

Would this be her final day here with her own son? She rushed down the stairs and through the courtyard, from room to room, trying to find Benjamin. To stay with him until the last instant, when she might be ordered away.

At last, breathless, her panic edging toward hysteria, Elisheba found Benjamin practicing his writing with Eran at a table in the reception room. Kneeling, she hugged her bewildered son, kissing his hair, fighting down her tears as she caught her breath.

Eran stood, alarmed. "Young Mistress, please, what's happened?"

"Oh, Eran," she exhaled in a whisper, "pray for your good Master!"

She had no need to say which master. The Rabbi Yeshua's name lingered between them, unspoken, understood.

***

Standing among a delegation of the nobility and flanked by numerous irritable priests and traders, Pallu faced the High Priest in Caiaphas' lavish reception room. "It's been two days and the Man refuses to allow any of us to conduct business in the Foreigner's Court, if He allows us in at all! He scorns our authority completely."

"And you—all of you—want to know what I will do to stop this man?" Caiaphas asked, a scowl furrowing his forehead. "I'll tell you then. We'll arrest him after the Feast of the Unleavened Bread."

Ten days yet! Pallu stifled his disgust. But he had to accept the wisdom in their decision. Arresting that fraud in the crowded Holy Courts surrounded by His fanatics would incite disaster.

One of the younger priests spoke, his eyes clear and earnest in his thin, bearded face. "If this Rabbi Yeshua doesn't proclaim Himself as king and *Mashiyakh* very soon, then the people will surely tire of His pretensions."

"We cannot risk waiting for the common People of the Land to become tired of their hero," Caiaphas answered testily. "What do they know? They're swayed by the promise of their next meal. And who are you, anyway? A student of Gamaliel?"

"I am Zerahiah, son of Ne'arjah," the younger priest admitted, retreating as if ashamed he'd spoken.

"You're supposed to be a priest, not a scholar. You sound almost sympathetic toward that man."

While Caiaphas scolded the errant priest, Pallu shuffled impatiently. Now, knowing that nothing would be accomplished for ten days yet, he was ready to leave. Before Levia spent all his silver.

***

Elisheba sat at a half-circle stone table set against a wall of the smallest reception room. Tapping her reed pen lightly in an ink pot, she murmured to Levia, "What else shall I write?"

Reclining on a nearby couch, Levia finished a yawn. "What? Oh, yes… 'So then, dear Marta, my greetings and fond kisses to your family. Let me receive word from you soon. I am eager to visit and talk with you face to face. I wish you blessings and…' Oh, just finish it nicely, Elisheba. I know you will."

Smiling, Elisheba traced her mother-in-law's idle words onto the parchment. She was just fanning the ink when an outburst of laughter and surly grumbling echoed from the corridor.

Glancing sidelong from beneath her lashes, Elisheba watched Lord Pallu and his guests enter the private reception room. Eliezer and Malchos had again shared their evening meal with Lord Pallu in the large reception room, and father and son were wine-warmed and smiling. Pallu, however, was frowning as if they'd dragged him into the small reception room against his will.

Hissing beneath her breath, Levia sat up, smoothed her gown, and drew her veil close against her throat.

"There, you irritating wretch, see?" Eliezer demanded good-naturedly of Malchos, while flicking a hand toward Elisheba. "Are you content?"

"As satisfied as I can be for now." Malchos halted beside the table and slid his ring-decked fingers caressingly over the parchment, making Elisheba lift her hands away from his perfumed touch. "She writes?" he asked Pallu, sounding as if he'd just learned Elisheba had a deforming scar.

"I suppose," Pallu grumbled. "Whatever women might think to write. I don't know."

"Oh, love notes and gossip!" Eliezer said cheerily, plumping himself onto a couch along the opposite wall. "There's nothing else for them, now is there?"

"Should they even be allowed such temptation?" Malchos asked, too sharp for Elisheba's comfort. "Women are so inclined to weakness."

"They're *all* weak, aren't they?" Pallu's tone suggested a previous argument, and worse, a comparison of Levia to some other woman, drawing a sharp breath of indignation from Levia.

Malchos leaned over the table, studying the parchment. His tight-lipped expression eased subtly as he saw Elisheba's writing for what it was—a kind note to one of Levia's friends.

"Thank you for writing my letter," Levia told Elisheba. "I'll sign it now." She traded places with Elisheba, her whole attitude an unspoken rebuke of

Malchos. He turned away, crossing the room to talk with Pallu and Eliezer.

"I wish they'd leave," Levia muttered to Elisheba. "I'm sick of them."

Levia no longer praised Malchos, Elisheba realized. Did she loathe him after all?

"They're all just alike," Levia continued softly, dabbing the reed in ink, "the same as Pallu."

"I wish things could be different," Elisheba whispered. "I'm sorry."

The men exchanged low jokes now, snickering like unruly boys. Elisheba leaned toward Levia. "I've no wish to hear any of this. May I go check on the children and be sure they're asleep?"

"Certainly," Levia murmured. "I don't blame you for leaving. The children are more delightful than our present company. I'll follow you soon."

Offering Levia a sympathetic hug, Elisheba stood and bowed her head politely before leaving. Levia smiled, but the men ignored Elisheba, as was proper. Their suddenly-raucous laughter echoed high, making her grimace in distaste as she stepped into the lamp-lit corridor.

The girls' sleeping chamber wasn't far away. Elisheba crept down the corridor, opened the door slightly, and peered into the dimly lit room. Malkah and the maidservants lay on their low beds, their eyes already closed. Baby Nathan was nearby, tucked into his basket, hushed and still. Zimiyrah, however, was whispering to herself as if she'd hidden toys beneath her pillow, naughty girl. Hearing her happy play, Elisheba couldn't bear to scold her. Softly, she crept away.

She was just leaving the corridor, heading off toward Benjamin's room, when swift-moving footsteps echoed behind her, making her turn. Malchos. "No!"

He flung an arm around Elisheba, lifted her off her feet, and swept her into a dark antechamber, stifling her protests, first with a hand, then with a wine-sodden kiss. The sour taste of him, the sensations of his hands groping beneath her veils and outer robe. She managed to turn her face from his, gasping, wanting to spit into the darkness.

Malchos set her down and whispered, "I've looked forward to this—having you as my wife. Isn't there a couch in here?"

"No!"

He pressed himself closer, kissing her throat. As if she'd given him any such right! Elisheba scuffled with him, their sandals rasping against the mosaic floor as she hissed, "Malchos! Stop! We're not married. I won't give in to you!"

"There's no reason you shouldn't." He shoved her back against a wall, pinning her hard with his forearm while tugging at her gown, his voice exultant in the darkness. "In two weeks, after Joseph's second burial, we'll be betrothed. None of this matters."

"To me it matters! I'm not shameless." She twisted about, trying to duck from his grasp, but he re-maneuvered his forearm tight against the base of her throat, choking her as he loosened her gown's thin gold belt. Blood thrummed hard in her head as she clawed at Malchos' forearm, kicking at him, struggling to free herself. The fool! He hadn't the least idea that he was almost crushing the breath from her. She choked out, "Malchos, stop!"

"Elisheba!" Levia's voice echoed outside the door. "Are you in there? You are! I know you are!"

Ignoring her, Malchos glared at Elisheba. "As you say, enough for tonight. But I warn you!" Shifting his arm from her throat, he dug his fingers hard into her shoulders, terrifying her with his strength. "Remember this: Never make me jealous! No writing notes, no sending messages that I've not read first. I'll find out everything you do. You'll be guarded as treasure in a fortress!"

Guarded? No, imprisoned. Sweat beaded over her skin as she rasped in a breath then coughed helplessly. He was so much worse than she'd imagined.

"Elisheba," Levia threatened, "come out before I come in."

Growling his disgust, Malchos pushed Elisheba into the doorway. Levia snatched her arm, scolding. "None of that here, Malchos! Kindred or not, you behave."

He leaned into the light and made a false smile at Levia. "Of course. Surely it was the wine."

"Oh, no doubt!" Levia tugged Elisheba into the corridor, complaining to her loudly. "Men! They do what they want and plead 'wine.' Well, not here and not now! Let him do without some fun. I saw him leave. I knew what he was after."

If only you knew, Elisheba answered in silence, shock threatening her senses. To think Malchos was celebrating the thought of the gathering of Joseph's bones. Looking ahead, she saw

Zimiyrah standing in the corridor, small and white-gowned, toys in her hands.

"Ama," Zimiyrah asked, her voice bell-clear, "why are you yelling?"

"Go to sleep!" Levia snapped. "And close your door."

"I'll stay with her ... please," Elisheba whispered, seizing escape, overtaken by tremors she couldn't control. Malchos was in the corridor now, his gaze chilling her.

When Levia nodded, Elisheba stumbled into the girls' chamber, closing the door. Already, Malchos and Levia were arguing outside, snatches of their fury becoming audible.

"... hush, you interfering woman! ... none of your concern!"

"... disgraceful! ... we still must answer to her father!"

"... it's all but agreed. I have every right!"

"No! You cannot presume so. This is an honorable house!"

Tiny Nathan continued to sleep. But Malkah sat up now, blinking, her sweet young face drowsy and bewildered. And Thamar and Leah scrambled from their pallets, lighting another lamp, listening wide-eyed as Malchos and Levia's angry voices faded away. Then the maidservants turned, gaping at Elisheba, obviously near-dying to ask questions she wouldn't answer.

Still trembling, a hand to her bruised throat, Elisheba sank onto Zimiyrah's vacant bed. The lamplight danced against the wall, glistening amid Elisheba's tears.

Zimiyrah dropped her toys, crawled onto the bed, and hugged Elisheba, then whispered consolingly, "Don't cry! I'm always in trouble. They won't be angry long."

Elisheba held her young sister-in-law and wept. Now she saw how her next marriage would end. Not in divorce, but with her own death.

Chapter 15

Was there no end to chaos this night? Eran huffed and propped himself on one elbow in his pallet.

First he'd been awakened by the Lady Levia, unmistakably furious and scolding some man who'd dared to answer her sharply. Then servants were hurrying through the courtyard, questioning each other. Now, Lord Pallu and his cousin Eliezer were outside, laughing, talking loudly. Not that he should complain, Eran reminded himself. This was Lord Pallu's household, but Eran would grieve to see Master Benjamin awakened when the little boy had fallen asleep so easily.

Getting to his feet, his limbs aching with the effort, Eran adjusted the solitary bronze lamp, which glowed on a stone table beside the wall. Master Benjamin remained unmoving in his low bed, his small round face quiet, eyes closed and tranquil.

The old man sighed, *Blessed are You, O Lord ...*

Even so, the rise and fall of voices outside was irritating. Unable to restrain his curiosity, Eran nudged an edge of the chamber window's protective cover and peered through the lattice. Lord Pallu, illuminated by torchlight, waved a scroll at his cousin, saying, "At least one of them is intelligent enough to demand money."

Eliezer snorted. "Well, how reliable can the man be? He didn't request much of your priest-friends, did he?"

Lord Pallu laughed. "Common men demand common prices. I believe he will fulfill his pledge. He's probably just trying to save himself."

"It's a shame Malchos didn't stay long enough to hear this. He'd be pleased."

Eran dropped the window covering, settled onto his pallet again, and deliberately plugged his ears. More dealings with corrupted priests. Whatever this bargain was, he didn't want to hear it. *Sleep,* he commanded himself. *Sleep until morning.*

***

Andronikos piled mint on the stone table and breathed the herb's fresh sharp scent as it permeated the morning air. Mint was good for many things, Andronikos knew, but not for curing the current worries knotting his intestines.

Earlier this week, he'd been secretly elated by the rumors sweeping through the marketplace in Jerusalem's upper city:

Master Iesous raised a man who had been dead four days. Who has ever done such a thing? He must be the Mashiyakh.

The priests and lords are all afraid of Him. He will proclaim Himself the Christos.

He will free Israel of the Roman oppressors!

Such approving talk convinced Andronikos that he'd be safe to follow the Rabbi Yeshua openly. But this morning, while in the markets choosing a

Passover lamb, the young merchant sensed popular elation becoming frustration against the *Mashiyakh*. Many were now declaring Master Iesous a fraud, for surely the true Messiah would immediately drive out the hated Roman conquerors and then establish His kingdom.

Their outspoken hostility compelled Andronikos to hesitate.

Should he speak in the Master's favor or not? Stephanos would advise against it. But then, Stephanos hasn't been himself lately. He must call upon Stephanos before prayer time. If—

Loukas charged into the shop from the courtyard. "Are we going up to the Holy House today?"

"Not today," Andronikos said, knowing what his brother was truly asking. When would they sacrifice their Passover lamb? "Mother is still cleaning the house. We'll probably have visitors tomorrow night for our Sabbaton feast. We'll prepare the lamb then. Today we work."

Before Loukas could grumble, two customers jostled each other on their way into the shop. A squabble erupted between a proud, tassel-decked Jerusalem scribe and an irritable, foreign-born tradesman, who waved his gold-ringed hands in the scribe's parsimonious face.

Obviously delighted, Loukas watched the quarrel, avidly listening to their foul language.

Andronikos wanted to wallop his brother's ears and send him off to help Maria scrub the kitchen. He also longed to wallop his customers' ears. Instead, as an example to his brother, he went to mediate with a smile and words of welcome.

***

Elisheba paused in her courtyard doorway, breathing in the cold night air, trying to settle her thoughts. Almost a year ago, Joseph became ill. Now, she had to accept marriage to Malchos. How? That brief struggle with him in the darkness last night had revealed more than she wanted to consider. He was brutal and obsessive. Worse, the gloating way he'd spoken of Joseph's second burial hinted at a long-held loathing of Joseph. She shivered.

And yet, what were her own problems when weighed against the life of the Rabbi Yeshua?

Lord Pallu had been jubilant during this evening's meal, their first informal Passover meal this year. Tender olive oil and herb-marinated lamb became like dust in Elisheba's mouth as Pallu announced the plans afoot for capturing "the fraud-prophet." A traitor had emerged from among the Rabbi Yeshua's closest followers.

"He will be caught this time. You'll see," Pallu had taunted Elisheba.

Would He? Elisheba closed her door and stepped into the courtyard, shivering beneath the cold, star-scattered sky. She could not retire until she conferred with Eran. They must find some way to warn the Rabbi Yeshua. Eran could depart on a "minor errand" for her at daylight.

Surely there would be enough time.

Drawing her mantle closer, she hurried through the courtyard to Benjamin's room. Light spilled softly from the edges of the ornate covered lattice, and she could hear Benjamin's clear voice questioning, answered by Eran, mild but firm. "Now, little Master, tomorrow is our feast day and you must sleep. You can play in the morning."

Elisheba rapped on the door. Answering, Eran smiled in greeting. Before he could say a word, Benjamin scrambled to his feet, square wooden game pieces clattering onto the floor. "Ama, will you play with me?"

"Not if Eran has told you it's time for sleep," Elisheba warned. Seeing Benjamin cast a guilty look toward his aged teacher, Elisheba said, "In the morning we will play, my son. But now, you obey Eran and pick up your game pieces."

Heaving a sigh, Benjamin picked up his wooden tablets, one by one, slowly, a new game emerging as he stacked them in a wobbly tower.

While he played, Elisheba beckoned Eran, keeping her voice low. "One of Rabbi Yeshua's followers offered himself as informant to the priests."

Eran listened, his quiet-dark eyes widening in horror, filling with tears as he sagged against the doorframe. "Then this is what I heard last night. Oh, blessed Lord Almighty, I should have understood. I should have *understood*."

***

He walked, leading His chosen ones through the chilling night.

The breath of His flesh arose in a mist, His heart of flesh pounding in growing despair. And with each step, He prayed—begged Father and Spirit—

against what He knew must happen. Let this coming terror be removed. Remain with Me!

His sandaled feet crunching over the rough path, Yeshua led His followers into the garden they used for prayer. As they walked, He gazed up at the stars. This last time as one of earth, Yeshua studied the heavens. And He remembered those very stars as He had first seen them, forming bright within Father's thoughts, comprehended by Spirit, given shape by Their spoken words.

Lights to fill darkness with wonder at the might and love of Father.

Lights to comfort those whom Father cherished.

Comfort me!

Reaching the garden, Yeshua turned to the chosen, perceiving their weariness, their confusion, their reluctance to be here. Even now, after all His warnings, they didn't understand—couldn't understand what was about to happen. He sighed. "My soul is crushed with horror, to the point of death. Stay here and watch."

They stared in bafflement—young Yochanan, impulsive Shim'on-Kefa, Mattityahu, T'oma and the others—still bound by their flesh.

Moved to compassion with knowledge of their weaknesses, Yeshua said, "Pray you aren't overcome by temptation."

He walked through the garden, into the hushed olive grove, and then dropped to the cold earth, aware of the Adversary lingering at the edge of darkness, waiting to rejoice over His spilled blood.

Satan! You, a being of the eternal, refuse to comprehend the truth. The flesh is nothing to me. Death is nothing me. Father and Spirit are All. Without Them—

Without Them... He gasped, tormented by the despair to come. Even as he mourned, one of Father's messengers stood before him, robed in eternal light, conveying strength for the agony to come. Yeshua drew in a sharp breath, feeling the bloodied sweat trickle down His face.

"Father! Take this cup from me! And yet, if I must drink it in full...Your will be done." *But if it can be removed...*

His soul writhed in anguish.

***

Prince of this world, he traced the shadow's precise edge, alert to the movements of his adherents, all of them watching as celebrants, onlookers savoring His earthly form brought low in torment. Such inglorious misery!

In sliverings of whispers and fear, he himself had persuaded the flesh of one of his own to strike against Him.

Y'hudah from K'riot, you know more than they! Who is this Yeshua to lead you to death? Save yourself!

The one called Y'hudah obeyed at last, in time-slowed steps, approaching Him, consigning His earthly being to death with a token-kiss of peace.

He is now within my realm!

***

Laughter and a high-pitched commanding whistle startled Elisheba from a restless sleep. It was still night. What was happening?

Rolling off her cushioned pallet, she slipped through her antechamber to her courtyard doorway, pried it open, and peeked outside. Lord Pallu was marching down the outer steps from his chamber, wide awake. Lordly indeed, he strode through the courtyard, sweeping on his richly tasseled, long-sleeved mantle as he beckoned his servants. "Is my litter ready? Come, come!"

He shoved one of his servants aside, making the man stumble and then rush to catch up with him.

The Lady Levia emerged on the steps above, watching him leave, her black hair falling loose like a heavy veil over her pale gown, eerie in the chilling moonlight. She turned as if to go inside then looked over the courtyard again, hesitating.

Risking criticism from tattling servants but desperate to hear the news, Elisheba ran through the courtyard, up the stairs. Levia waited, smoldering.

The instant Elisheba reached the last step, Levia tugged her inside the antechamber and slammed the door. "He's thrilled! He received word that they've captured your Rabbi Yeshua."

"It's true?" Elisheba dropped to her knees in despair, trying to catch her breath. No! A memory returned then, of the night she had begged for Joseph's life.

Y'shua... Take me to Him.

Joseph's last plea, and she had failed him. Now, almost exactly a year later, again, there was nothing she could do. Her will drained away.

"Elisheba, I'm sorry." Levia was pacing, fuming. "I know you've wanted the man to escape, though I still cannot understand why. And," she added fiercely, "if I were a wagering creature, I'd bet my gold earrings that my lord is going to see his new wife tonight!"

"I'm sorry," Elisheba mumbled, dazed. A breath away from sobbing, she said, "A year ago ... I was kneeling here. Pleading for my husband's final request."

Levia stared down at her, eyes wide, color fading. She burst into tears.

***

His emotions knife-edged, Pallu stood in Caiaphas' palace reception area, the open court, which was crowded with most of the members of Jerusalem's high council and their adherents. Elaborately branched lampstands glowed from each side of the courtyard, revealing everyone's consternation as they stared at the purpose of their assembly: the most rough-clad man among them, the Rabbi Yeshua. A livid welt stood out against the man's right cheek, for He'd been struck for insolence after an earlier confrontation with the former high priest Annas. Now, the reprobate *Mashiyakh* was being obstinate, refusing to speak at all.

Even when two intended witnesses finally matched their stories and testified that this Yeshua had vowed to destroy the Holy House of the Lord and rebuild it within three days—nothing less than blasphemy—the Galilean remained silent.

For a man who'd been so outspoken in public, this was a surprise. Pallu frowned. How could the fraud refuse to speak now? Wouldn't any such scoundrel, faced with death, be pouring out excuses and untruths in self-defense? And this nighttime trial, already on uncertain legal grounds, might be declared erroneous if the prisoner wouldn't defend Himself.

The High Priest, Caiaphas, waiting in his seat of honor, traded meaningful glances with his powerful father-in-law, for Annas had joined them to witness the trial's outcome. When the silence lingered, Caiaphas stood, strode into the midst of the assembly, and snapped at their prisoner. "Well? Aren't You going to answer? Explain the reasons for their testimony!"

The Rabbi gazed beyond him, mute.

Unused to being ignored, Caiaphas lowered his bearded chin, emphasizing each clipped word. "I command You under oath, by the living God, tell us if You are the *Mashiyakh*, Son of the Almighty Lord!"

At the mention of the Almighty Lord, the rustic looked the High Priest in the eyes. "I *Am*, as you say. And all of you will see the Son of Man, sitting at the right hand of the Almighty Lord, returning on the clouds of heaven."

For one breath of time, Caiaphas—with Pallu and every other man in the room—stared, clearly transfixed by the Rabbi's audacity. Pallu scowled. If the Almighty Lord ever bothered with the small matters of men, this fraud-prophet would drop dead now.

But the Rabbi survived.

Caiaphas blinked then recovered. Grasping his gold-edged garments, he shredded the neck of his outer robe, then of his inner robe, crying, "Blasphemy! Why should we need other witnesses?" Caiaphas turned, hands upraised in protest as he spoke to the council. "You've all heard this blasphemy. What's your verdict?"

Pallu growled his personal judgment, joining the council's outcry. "Guilty! He deserves death!"

The High Priest's guards bound and blindfolded the prisoner, wrenching his bonds tightly enough to make the reprobate gasp with pain. Then some of the council members spit in the rustic's face. Pallu waded through the throng and hit the back of the Rabbi's head, crying, "Prophesy for us, *Mashiyakh!* Who just hit you, eh?"

That was for my silver!

While others laughed, beating and taunting the Man themselves, Pallu struck the fraud-prophet with doubled fists, joyously fierce. *There's for the shame you caused me! And this*—he hammered the unresisting Rabbi again—*this is for deceiving my Joseph!*

***

His flesh hanging in bloodied shreds from the beatings, Yeshua stood on a pavement adjoining Pilate's residence. Pain and fatigue ground through Him as an ordinary Man, shaking His limbs. Pilate's soldiers surrounded Him now, tumbling dice and silver before His gaze, laughing, shouting their gaming taunts of "Basileus! Rejoice, oh King!"

Shoving Yeshua from mark to mark on the pavement according to the fall of their dice, the soldiers howled with delight at their own cleverness, for the dice determined His advancement along the stones and the dice decreed the articles gathered for the "king" during their game. "A robe for the King! Ha!"

They threw a red mantle over His torn shoulders, rolled the dice again, and barked out, "Have a crown, great king!"

The soldiers forced a crown of thorns onto Yeshua's head, and the burning spines sliced into His scalp, blood trickling downward from His wounds like dark-bright anointing oil. He cried out as one soldier clubbed at the makeshift crown, driving its thorns sharply along his skull, baring bone. Blood streamed down His face and neck, making His captors laugh, uproarious as drunkards.

Again the dice tumbled. The soldiers pushed Yeshua forward and slapped a rod into His hand as a mock scepter.

With another throw, one soldier shouted, "King!" and gathered up all the wagered silver as his comrades bellowed in disgust. Ending their game, the soldiers bowed before their living game-piece in mock servitude. "All hail, King of the Jews!"

Snatching the "scepter" from Yeshua's hand, they repeatedly smashed it into his face and head, beating him until his body reeled with the wounds and metal-bitter blood welled in His mouth. Wearied of their game now, Yeshua's tormentors spit into His eyes, then roughly clothed Him again.

As His captors led Yeshua outside into the morning light to die as an ordinary man, Satan accompanied the procession in a sweeping glow of triumph, as an eternal king newly anointed and parading to a coronation feast.

***

"Slow down, Kore," Stephanos warned, eyeing the crate they lugged between them. "If you break these stonewares, my father will …"

"Your father will forgive me. Mine will whip me instead," Kore teased, grinning, alarmingly unconcerned. Against his will, Stephanos grinned in return. Kore's vital nature was like a gift from the Lord, keeping Stephanos from thinking too hard. And from being uneasy when there was too much to be uneasy about. Wherever he looked, he saw danger. He heard whispers. Master Iesous was in the city and—

"Isn't this the house?" Kore demanded. "Let's hurry. By the way, don't we get some silver for being your father's delivery boys?"

"No, you're helping me as a friend, by the kindness of your soul."

"But I don't feel very kind now." Perking up instantly Kore joked, "What if I drop a dish?"

"Then forget your father's whipping. Old Kleopas will beat you instead. He's paid Father already, and you'd ruin his Passover feast with a set of broken dishes."

Shifting his hold on the crate, Stephanos knocked on the gate door. After much fumbling and clattering, a plump, gray-robed serving woman answered, looking bored. To the skies above, she said, "Ah yes, we've been waiting for these. More dishes to wash."

After they departed and the servant slammed the gate shut behind them, Kore asked, "Will your father go up to the Lord's House today?"

Silently blessing the Lord that Kore hadn't offended anyone in Kleopas' household, Stephanos said, "Yes, we're meeting Andronikos and Loukas there."

"I'll ask my father if we can meet you." They turned onto a narrow side street that cut across the business sector. A din of shouts and wailing echoed through the main street ahead. Brightening, Kore charged in front of Stephanos. "What's that noise?"

All the hairs prickled across Stephanos' scalp at the high, mournful keenings of numerous unseen women. What had happened? Who was dead? "Kore, stop!"

Unwilling or unable to hear, Kore charged ahead into the main street. Fearing for his impulsive friend, Stephanos followed. But as he reached the intersection of the narrow road and the wide paved street, Stephanos was forced to halt. Roman soldiers, brutally efficient, marched along the street, shoving aside the citizens to clear the path of a condemned man.

Condemned. "Lord!" Stephanos cringed, grasping a wall for support. Master Iesous, beaten and bloodied almost beyond recognition, staggered amid his captors as another man followed in distress, bearing a thick wooden beam. Condemned.

Unable to look beyond that first glance, certain he would vomit, Stephanos rushed back into the narrow side street, fears speeding his way home.

Chapter 16

Elisheba reached deep into her clothing chest, her fingers searching its far corner until she felt her purse. Pulling it out, she stared at its limp yellow contours. Less than a handful of silver. "Is this all?"

She hadn't paid attention to her spending money this past year. Foolish of her. She must request her monthly allowance; Pallu hadn't been paying her according to their contracts. But that wasn't important now. Eran must go to inquire about the Rabbi Yeshua, without Lord Pallu finding out.

Let the priests and council be forced to declare the Rabbi innocent. Please!

Her pace outwardly serene, Elisheba left her chamber and trailed along the courtyard to Benjamin's room. There, she tapped on the sunlit door. Eran answered, his face worried as she felt. "Young Mistress? How may I help you?"

"You'll need to buy supplies this morning." She handed him her purse, naming items used during Benjamin's lessons. "A new wax tablet, parchment, ink—"

"And a new cushion for my seat," Benjamin interrupted, snatching Elisheba's hand.

"And a new cushion," she agreed with a hug for her son. Quietly, she added, "Also, Eran, if you could make inquiries of the matter we discussed …"

"My new cushion?" Benjamin asked, listening intently. "I want a red one."

"You may have a red one," Elisheba promised.

Eran bowed. "Indeed you will, little Master." He nodded to Elisheba. "Thank you, young Mistress. Yes, I'll make inquiries. I pray to return promptly."

Silently blessing the Lord for Eran, who would seek answers where she couldn't, Elisheba beckoned her son. "Are your hands and face clean? Yes? Bring your toys then. We'll go play with your cousins."

***

Eran paused at the fabric merchant's booth, eyeing the change the man had given him for creating the agreed-upon crimson pillow. As he slid the remaining coins into their leather pouch, he asked the merchant, "What is the news today?"

"Where have you been, old man?" the full-bearded merchant asked kindly in Greek. "The markets have been full of noise. I saw the famed Master Iesous led out this morning to die. He's nailed up by now."

Nailed up. *Almighty Lord!* Eran held himself still, trying to remain coherent. "Where … where did they take Him?"

Leaning across his outside counter, the merchant gestured. "Down the main street from Pilate's residence, out the western gate. At the place of the Skull."

Do not let this be true!

As Eran turned away, the merchant called after him, "I'll have this cushion finished in three days. You'll come back after Sabbaton, yes?"

"Yes, yes." Eran nodded at the man and hurried toward the main road. Roman soldiers were stationed everywhere this morning, cool-eyed, bright-cloaked, their hands on their sword hilts, as if they were expecting riots. The crowds thickened as Eran pushed toward the huge stone-arched tower gate, passing through the chilling shadows of its sheltering room. There, seated at small tables, Roman officials glanced at Eran's empty hands, his servant-drab robes, his gray beard, and they looked away, uninterested. He had no goods to tax, no evident wealth. Eran hurried through the gate, his legs hurting. He wasn't used to moving so quickly, yet he couldn't rest until he knew the truth.

Beneath his breath, Eran whispered, "Ah, Lord, let the rumors be untrue!"

Scuffing down the busy road outside the city, he saw a crowd surrounding three tormented figures, nailed bloody and spread-armed against crossed, upright beams. Crucifixion was the Roman punishment of choice to publicly murder Jews and other unfortunates. Surely one of the most agonizing ways to die. Exposure. The merciless wounds. Thirst. Being unable to breathe…and the guards finally crushing your legs. He pushed the image from his mind.

Fighting horror, Eran approached the dying ones. Here was what he'd least wanted to witness.

The Master's eyes were purpled, puffed almost shut, His head sagging, blood drying in His dark, matted, thorn-wreathed hair. Crusted patches and streaks of blood laced His swollen face and lacerated arms. From His shoulders downward, the Master's flesh dangled in gory strips that sent shudders of horror through Eran's entire being. Was He already dead?

To Eran's shock, the Master pushed Himself upright in jaw-clenching agony against the huge spike in His heels and then sucked in a loud, liquid, drowning breath.

The entire world dimmed before Eran's eyes, and his senses spun, making him sway, forcing him to sit upon the hard, rock-patched earth lest he fall. Unable to look up again, yet unable to flee, he remained. Listening to the guards playing dice. To the women weeping nearby. And to the passersby flinging insults at his dying teacher.

"Save yourself, prophet! Come down and show us a miracle now!"

"Look! After all those miracles, He can't even save himself, the fraud."

Eran rocked back and forth, wailing inside. *Oh, Lord Almighty...save us!*

What use was life if the righteous were slaughtered and the jackals remained alive and triumphant? What was left for the humble if their good Master was killed with all their hopes? Nothing ... nothing.

"Eran?" Hands gripped Eran's shoulders. Young Kore, the rope-maker's son, knelt beside him, looking older and ashen. "I thought it was you. Listen! I saw Lord Pallu here earlier. Is it safe for you to remain?"

"Do I care?" Eran's voice cracked with tears and he gave up, weeping.

"I'm leaving," Kore said. "Please, come with me. You look half dead."

"Then let me finish the other half."

"Joseph's son needs you," Kore urged. He gripped Eran's elbows and tugged him to his feet. "Please, good Eran. There's nothing we can do here, except get caught!"

Hearing the young man's words end in an odd squeak, Eran looked at him. Was this wild boy beginning to break? Indeed, he seemed near an edge.

Eran summoned his strength. But he still couldn't lift his gaze to the Master Iesous again, nor the two men dying alongside Him, their groans of misery cutting at Eran's soul. He wobbled alongside Kore now, his whole being exhaling prayers of grief. So many righteous in his life had died. *Yet I remain. Why, oh Lord? Why?*

Tears streamed down Eran's cheeks, until his skin burned with the residual salts. Useless to wipe them away. *Let my life be finished, oh, Lord Almighty. Send me to Sheol now with Your righteous ones!*

Kore said not one word during their long, slow walk back to Lord Pallu's residence.

***

Waiting in the Court of the Gentiles before the Lord's House, amid a thousand men, young and old, Andronikos eyed the sun, agitated. It was near noon, almost the appointed time to enter the courts of the Lord and make sacrifices. Stephanos should have been here by now. Noon, the sixth hour, was the time, but if he waited for Stephanos, they'd be delayed here until the ninth hour, mid-afternoon, which would upset his busy mother. He had to return to the shop soon to let her to finish cooking their evening feast.

Beside him, Loukas goaded their tethered lamb, grimacing with impatience. Ordinarily, Andronikos would have encouraged his brother to be patient. But today, he felt no encouragement for himself or Loukas. He prayed for Stephanos to be safe. And he prayed for their Master Iesous.

Knots clenched Andronikos' stomach now, and his head ached with the effort of trying to not think. If all the whispers throughout the marketplace were true—and evidently they were—then Master Iesous was dying as they stood here. How could it be?

"Did you bring the knife?" Loukas asked, as the lamb gave a mild bleat.

"Yes. Don't ask me any more questions."

The tall, double-arched doors opened now, and white-robed Levites motioned the throngs of worshipers past the low railings of the outer courts and inside the first court, the Women's Court. Displaying proper veneration, Andronikos led Loukas past the priest's guards, who watched everyone closely.

Death was near—and not just for the lambs.

Andronikos guided his brother across the huge pale court and up the steps into the Court of the Israelites. There, Andronikos caught his breath, overwhelmed, as every year, by the sight of soldier-like rows of white-clothed priests waiting for the worshipers in formal lines, holding gold and silver basins.

But this year, Andronikos shuddered as the mighty doors closed, signaled by a resonating shofar, trapping him and Loukas inside the central court with hundreds of other men and youths. If a riot occurred now and the Romans decided to butcher them all with their sacrifices, the worshipers were trapped and defenseless.

As a chorus of Levites sang psalms and played their harps and reed pipes, Andronikos willed himself to move forward. Loukas picked up their unresisting lamb and walked beside him eagerly until they stood face to face with one of the white-clad priests. The priest waited, inexpressive, his beard trailing over his chest in two flowing black prongs.

From above them in the pinnacle of a southern tower, another shofar resounded, designating the sacrificial sixth hour. And before the high, carrying tones faded away, a cloudless, unnatural darkness poured through the skies over the temple, like ink blackening water.

"What's happening?" Loukas craned his neck toward the spreading shadows.

It wasn't an eclipse. The sun remained whole, but dark. Andronikos blinked, doubting his vision, as horrified gasps and murmurings swept through the Holy Courts. Even the chorus of Levites faltered then stopped singing, all of them staring upward at the oppressive sky.

"Surely this is a sign from the Lord," said one of the nearby priests. "What else can it be?"

The priest attending Andronikos and Loukas was no longer impassive. "If the Lord gives us such a sign that He is watching, then let us offer our sacrifices at their proper time. Now!"

"Lord … Creator of the Kosmos…" Too upset to finish his mangled prayer, Andronikos obeyed the priest, stepping forward, slipping his knife from his belt as Loukas held their lamb.

Loudly, as if to proclaim his obedience to the Almighty Lord, the priest prayed, holding out the golden basin to receive the lamb's blood as Andronikos swiftly cut its jugular vein. "Blessed are You, oh Lord, maker of the Universe!"

***

In the open courtyard, Benjamin kicked the small puffy leather ball across the pavement toward Zimiyrah, crying, "Ha! Catch it!"

Seated in a woven chair, embroidering a white robe with gold thread, Elisheba stared up at the suddenly dark sky. Where was the sun? It was as if a black robe had been flung across the heavens.

Roused by the strange darkness, Eran tottered out from Benjamin's room and sat heavily nearby, still shaken by the grief they dared not acknowledge.

Didn't signs fill the heavens when men dared to kill ones beloved to the Lord? And surely the Rabbi Yeshua was beloved.

"Is it night already?" Zimiyrah demanded, her lively, pretty face offended.

Benjamin stared upward, then called to Elisheba, "Ama, does this mean I have to go to sleep? I'm not tired!"

Malkah hurried to Elisheba now, not frightened, but questioning softly, "Is this a storm?"

"No, it's not." Elisheba dropped her embroidery to hug her frail sister-in-law. "There are no clouds. It must be a sign." She dared say no more.

Now Levia appeared, looking baffled, veils fluttering as she hurried down the steps from her chamber. As they all stared upward at the sky, unable to look away, Levia said, "I pray this doesn't wake our Lord Pallu. He's just now fallen asleep"

Elisheba averted her face. Indeed, Lord Pallu should be exhausted after beating and condemning an innocent man, then lingering to celebrate.

Yes, Lord Pallu should be tired after committing murder.

She hated him. And she didn't want to repent of the hatred. But staring up at the sullen sky, Elisheba cringed, assailed by sudden inexplicable guilt, feeling condemned, as she had just condemned Lord Pallu.

Crawling into her lap, Benjamin whispered, "Ama, I don't like this."

Still staring at the forbidding sky, Elisheba held her son close. "Neither do I."

***

Crushed beneath the onrushing tide of sins, He fought to breathe as the rift began. The Cup of Suffering blackened the skies about Him and then seeped inward to Yeshua's soul, provoking agony as Spirit tore away—with Father—abandoning Him. As They must.

Yet it was no comfort to understand that They could not remain amid the evils poured upon Him now. The separation became a mortal gash within Him, an enemy to His life. Suffering and mortal darkness took hold, expanding, pouring all mortal evils throughout His soul. Yeshua cried in protest, "My God, My God! Why have You forsaken Me?"

He had never been alone. Without Father! Without Spirit! He struggled to endure the torment. But existence without Them was unbearable. Shocking Him with its agony. With this new terror came overwhelming thirst, not just of the flesh, but of His burdened soul, weeping for the pure Living Water. "I thirst."

A man stuck a dripping, pole-supported sponge at Yeshua's face. He swallowed the liquid, gasping as acid-sharp vinegar burned His lacerated face and swollen eyes. But nothing compared to this inward agony. Nothing could quench this eternal thirst...the ceaseless fire!

Unfettered by Spirit's departure, the Adversary swept around Him now as dark light in the sky—the triumphant prince of the air commanding the submission of all to his dominion. Lion-like, he prowled, jeering, scenting all eternity's offenses gathered within Yeshua's mortal flesh. As Satan gloated, his adherents laughed with him...those fallen eternal princes dedicated to Baal and all the gods of men...deceivers of mortals.

Human onlookers mocked Him from the darkened road below, unknowingly encouraged by Adversary and his rebels. Pitying Father's children of dust, Yeshua pleaded, "Abba! Forgive them. They don't know what they're doing."

He writhed, accepting the Cup of Suffering in full. For Love. For Father's will... Spirit's desire ...

"It is finished. Abba. Into Your hands I give My spirit."

Exhaling, Yeshua willed His soul to depart its flesh.

Releasing Himself again to the Eternal.

***

Its Maker departing, the earth shuddered, groaning, trembling in horror. In the hillsides, rocks split like brittle wax, opening tombs shrouded in the darkness.

***

Chosen by lot this morning, the priest Zerahiah, son of Ne'arjah, held a golden measure-full of incense over the glowing altar in the Lord's Holy House. The tiny bells edging his robes chimed weakly with his movements, sounding smothered; he couldn't even see their gold-scalloped shapes in the darkness. The fire's light shone too feebly, overwhelmed by the blackness inside and outside the Lord's House. Even the golden lamps in the shimmering stands to his left seemed weakened. Zerahiah and his attendant-priests could barely see the walls nor the vast, thick, sky-embroidered curtain-like veil before them, which separated all the unworthy from the purity of the Holy of Holies.

His heart squeezing in fear within the black-shrouded walls, Zerahiah silently begged, *Adonai, take this darkness from us! Forgive our sins. Bless us again!*

Outside, a shofar's blast alerted him that it was the ninth hour, time for the incense offering.

Obedient, Zerahiah slid the heap of precious spices over the coals and anointed them with a golden flask, the sacred oil. As the rich, sweet fragrance lifted upward with the rising flames, he and his fellow priests revered the Lord Almighty in their prayers.

A rumble answered from deep beneath the earth, a groaning such as Zerahiah had never imagined. His attendants screamed and fled in terror, their bare feet slapping against the sacred stone floor. Too horrified to move, Zerahiah looked up at the vast thick veil protecting the Holy of Holies, and then gasped as a ferocious rasping of shredding fabric echoed violently throughout the Lord's House.

Jarred by tremors from the earth, Zerahiah struggled for footing. And he watched the heaven-patterned and impossibly thick veil rip downward in a dense reverberation, as if being torn by mighty, unseen hands. As the Lord, tearing His heavenly garments in grief at the death of a beloved One…

Seeing the massive veil fly apart, revealing the Holy of Holies to his sinful eyes, Zerahiah dropped to the wavering floor and screamed out his terror. He placed his forehead against the stone floor, his whole body trembling with the quake. "Now I must die!"

All the lamps and coals went out, as if snuffed by the hand of the Lord Almighty.

***

Even as It departed, they descended in victory, filling the hollows of the white and gold Holy House. This place He had inhabited until Yeshua of

Nazareth's inglorious death was now their own—mortal spoils of their celestial war.

***

"I thought I'd slept until evening," Pallu complained as he descended the steps into the courtyard. At the last step, he stared up at the mourning-dark sky. "What is all this?"

Sorry if the heavens disturb you, my lord! Elisheba looked away to hide her fury. In a chair beside her, as they'd been since noon, Levia cuddled little Nathan. Elisheba tried to calm herself by admiring Nathan's round-cheeked, dozing face. So like Joseph ...

"No clouds at all." Lord Pallu sounded disturbed now. "I've never—" A shudder rippled through the courtyard, intensifying within a breath.

"An earthquake!" Levia gasped, clutching Nathan tight.

Elisheba turned in panic, looking over at Benjamin. He was seated on carpets nearby with Malkah and Zimiyrah, all three children gaping at the trembling walls and the crumbling plaster. The pavement heaved beneath them, rippling like a living stone beast. The girls screamed. Benjamin's eyes went huge, his small face turned ghastly gray. "Ama!"

Elisheba scooted from the chair and fell. On her knees, she struggled across the uneven stones to her son, and then covered him and the shrieking girls. Above the awful rumbling, servants wailed in the kitchen and the ante-chambers, as if they were dying. Holding the sobbing children tight, Elisheba prayed in fragments of terror.

Let us live ... Lord! ... Almighty Lord ...

As the quake finally subsided, Elisheba lifted her head, still trembling. Eran huddled nearby on his knees, clearly too unsteady to move further, though he'd obviously tried to reach Benjamin. Now, however, his thin aged face was a study of grief as he glanced from the sullen sky to Elisheba. "Young Mistress, are you both well?"

Elisheba nodded and glanced over at her father-in-law. Lord Pallu sat on the pavement beside the steps, his legs sprawled, completely without dignity. He saw her looking at him and lifted his chin, glaring. Pallu straightened his robes and stood, a man out of patience with the world. "Shut up! Benjamin, stop crying. Little coward!"

***

"Little coward!"

Benjamin sniffled and straightened in Ama's arms, trying to obey Abba Pallu. Trying to be brave.

But another sob escaped him and Abba Pallu snarled, "You sound like a girl!"

Beside Benjamin, Malkah and Zimiyrah gulped as if they were choking.

To Ama, Lord Pallu said, "You're raising a weakling. This *will* stop!"

Benjamin felt his Ama tremble as if the quake were inside her. She began to cry without a sound. And she let him go.

Benjamin looked from Abba to Eran and saw his teacher also crying.

It was all wrong. Everything was suddenly bad again as it had been when his Abba died. Shivering, Benjamin felt watched again. Cold.

Little coward!

***

We're safe, Andronikos reminded himself as he stared at the cracks in the shop's plastered walls. No one had died.

Except, perhaps soon, the Master.

Pressing his hands to his head, Andronikos massaged his temples hard, trying to ease the ache. How could it be true? They'd condemned him so quickly.

It couldn't have been legal.

"All's well," his mother said, coming in from the courtyard. "The plaster can be repaired, no walls have shifted, none of the ceiling beams came down, and the sun is shining again. We're blessed."

Andronikos didn't feel blessed.

"Are you well?" Joanna asked, staring at him.

"Well enough." For a man who ought to be condemned for cowardice. "I'll tend the shop."

"Maria and I will have dinner prepared by sunset," his mother promised. "Our guests should be arriving soon."

Distant cousins from Corinth, Andronikos reminded himself, already wearied. He would have to compose himself and greet them properly. "I'll be ready."

He set to work, closing bins, putting away jars, and waiting on the few customers who hadn't been too unnerved by the day's events to finish their shopping. Fragrance for their homes, spices for their meals…. Andronikos' stomach knotted just thinking of food. He doubted he could eat their evening meal.

He was scrubbing the largest stone-work table when a shadow blotted light from the doorway. A servant, a Pharisee by the looks of him, hesitated in distress. "Please, am I too late? Can you help me?"

The man reminded him of Eran, elderly, gentle-eyed. Andronikos smiled, his headache easing at the sight of this kindly man. "Good sir, how can you be too late? The Almighty Lord has kept me here, waiting for you."

Sighing an inarticulate prayer, the servant said, "Thank you. My master has sent me to purchase myrrh and aloes for a burial, as much as this will buy."

He set a moneybag on the table. Lifting it, Andronikos heard the distinctively high clink of silver and felt its weight overflowing his hand. "I can prepare one hundred litras of ointment for this."

"Please, yes," the servant urged. "My master hoped for as much."

Andronikos dumped the silver into a pan on his scale, adjusting the metal beams until the silver balanced against them. Close enough. "Who is your master?"

When the servant didn't reply, Andronikos faced him again. The servant looked torn between the longing to protect his master's identity and wishing desperately to confide in Andronikos. Quietly, Andronikos said, "On my life, before our living Lord, you can trust me."

"I am sent by Nikodemos. Of the Sanhedrin. And his friend Joseph."

"Their names are safe here," Andronikos murmured. But the names gnawed within him, upsettingly familiar. Joseph, simply because the name was *Joseph*. And Nikodemos of the Sanhedrin because he was a known sympathizer of the Master Iesous. Andronikos didn't want to question the servant further. Pouring a small measure of new wine, he offered the stoneware cup and indicated a bench beside the door. "Sit and rest."

Again the servant sighed, easing himself onto the wooden bench and sipping from the cup, as if his day had been almost too much to endure.

Poor man.

Hefting two fifty-litra stoneware jars of myrrh ointment over to a row of spice bins, Andronikos measured out a scoop of powdered aloes and worked it into the myrrh with a paddle. He added scoop after scoop, mashing it together until the aloes mingled with the ointment perfectly, and the whole shop was filled with its spicy-sweet balsam fragrance.

While he filled the second jar, Maria entered the shop, sniffing the air like a little expert. As Andronikos expected, her dark eyebrows lifted and her inquisitive gaze went straight to the silver-laden balance. Just like mother. "You took another order?"

"Yes," Andronikos murmured, working down the heavy spice mixture in the second jar. "Please close the shutters for me. And tell Loukas I want his help. This order is large and we must hurry."

Perfectly obedient, Maria not only closed the shop's shutters, but she emptied the silver from the balance into a box and flicked a speck from one of the tables. All the while, she primly ignored the Pharisee servant, who very properly never once glanced at her, pretty as she was. She went out the door to the courtyard again, slight as a shadow. But there was nothing slight about her bellow. "Loukas! Andronikos wants you in the shop. *Now!*"

While Andronikos covered the weighty jars, Loukas trudged into the shop. "What?" he demanded, his frown bordering on rudeness.

"Wait, please," Andronikos commanded. Tonight, he would speak to Loukas of the great benefits of speaking with courtesy before customers. To the exhausted servant, he said, "My brother and I will secure these to your animal."

The servant stood, eyes bugged, mouth agape, revealing sudden panic. "I have no animal," the man confessed, clearly distressed at the thought of failing his master. "I beg you to forgive me. I was in such a hurry I ... I didn't think about carrying the jars."

Loukas rolled his gaze toward the ceiling beams. Andronikos nudged him. "Go get our donkey from the stable. *Run.* And then finish cleaning the shop and explain to Mother and our guests why I'm gone."

"Bless you!" the servant breathed, tears glistening in his eyes. "My master is even now waiting at the tomb. He wishes to anoint the body and wrap it decently before sunset. I just didn't stop to think ..."

Anoint the body. Wrap it decently.

Disquiet filled Andronikos, making his guts tighten. Might he be inferring to Master Iesous?

Andronikos squared his shoulders and gave himself a mental shake. Surely someone else had died today, not just the Master. A relative of Nikodemos.

Lifting one of the heavy jars, Andronikos pushed aside his fear. As a gift of kindness, he would help this poor man and then return tonight for the Sabbaton feast.

Chapter 17

A GARDEN TOMB. A tomb for a wealthy man. Not for a poor teacher. Andronikos reassured himself as he followed the servant into a beautifully paved open area, nestled beside a stone cliff tomb, surrounded by foliage, fig trees, flowers in bud. Master Nikodemos was burying one of his own family.

"Here," the servant said to Andronikos as they stopped before the low, open doorway of a pristine and obviously new whitewashed tomb. Andronikos drew in a breath. The evening light was deepening now, red-tinged with the approaching dusk. A flock of birds swept overhead, peaceful after the turmoil of the day. Lamplight flickered from within the tomb, warm and quiet.

Not wanting to enter the tomb and disturb the worthy Nikodemos and his family, Andronikos lifted one of the heavy jars and waited outside.

The servant went inside, exchanging sibilant whispers with others unseen in the tomb. A Pharisee appeared in the tomb's entrance, looking ill, his dark beard striated with gray, the pale edges of his tunic sleeves wet and stained pink.

Blood. Andronikos stared down at the newly paved court, swallowing hard.

"May the Lord Almighty bless you and give you peace," the Pharisee murmured sadly. "Thank you. I will take the jar."

Andronikos gave him the jar and returned to his patient, waiting donkey to retrieve the other jar. Willing himself to move, to not think too hard, he hauled the second jar to the tomb's entrance and waited again. At last, when no one came out to meet him, he stooped down cautiously, looking inside. Rimmed by shadows, lamplights flickered softly, revealing a body on a stone bed. A tortured form that had been a man.

Feeling horribly ensnared, Andronikos stepped inside, unable to keep from staring. Master Iesous ...

His face was calm in death, dignified despite the swellings and discolorations, the bruises and gashes, visible even within the low light. A slender cord bound the Master's wrists, keeping his lacerated arms together. His legs were also bound, but ripped as if clawed by wild animals. His flesh was torn all over—nearly flayed like raw meat—and a wound gaped beneath the heart, lethal. Perhaps death came before the wound. He hoped.

Someone took the jar from him. In shock, Andronikos blinked at the man, who was neatly bearded and well clothed, with somber dark eyes that oddly reminded Andronikos of his own father. He looked toward Master Iesous' body again, the marks of mortal cruelty finally sinking in hard. Was there no place spared by the Roman lash? No!

Blood-loving Roman fiends. They'd enjoyed doing this! Andronikos clenched his fists, longing to scream like a wild man. Longing to tear at the inhumans who had performed this butchery. *If only I could make you suffer as fully!*

"Were you a follower?" the Pharisee asked, packing the embalming paste of myrrh and aloes around the body, swift but careful, as if afraid of hurting the Master further.

Andronikos nodded, words refusing to emerge from his burning throat. If he spoke, he would begin to weep, even to curse everyone and everything, including himself.

"Bless you for coming," the well-groomed man said. He opened the second jar. After giving its lid to his servant, he began to apply the ointment to the Master's torn arms, quick and careful.

Again, Andronikos nodded stiffly. The sweetness of myrrh and crushed aloes perfumed the still air. Fragrance from his own shop, his own hands. But for Master Iesous, this should have been so much more than simple myrrh. It should have been spikenard.

"Indeed, Master Andronikos," the servant murmured, "you have been a blessing."

Unable to endure more of their blessings, their kindness, which he didn't deserve, Andronikos bowed his head. Ducking from the tomb, he stumbled toward his donkey as it nosed the fresh vegetation.

Catching the donkey's halter, Andronikos prepared to swing himself over the creature's back, until he looked across the garden and noticed two women sitting on a plant-sheltered stone bench. One woman was his own age, and lovely. The other woman was older and careworn, but both were modestly robed and covered, both weeping—surely followers of Master Iesous.

Watching them grieve, some of Andronikos' rage ebbed into compassion. He hesitated. The younger woman glanced up at him, but the older woman looked tearfully horrified that he, a stranger, had dared acknowledge them at all—as if they were immoral women. She stiffened, her very posture an unspoken command for Andronikos to leave them alone, as was proper.

He acquiesced, mounting the patient donkey and then riding up the path to the city. All along the way, he struggled to force away images of Master Iesous' tortured body in the tomb. How could any men inflict such wounds upon another? But didn't he long to do the same to the Master's tormenters? Could he become so cruel? Iesous had taught compassion and forgiveness.

I've learned nothing.

After stabling the donkey, he returned to the shop. Loukas was inside, leaning idly on a counter. "Close and bar the door, then you may go," Andronikos said, too oppressed to point out all the work Loukas could have done.

While Loukas eagerly locked the door with a loud thump, Andronikos went out to the central stone courtyard. He spotted his mother, talking to an entire family of distant cousins, whom Andronikos had never met. A husband and wife, one mother-in-law, and six freshly scrubbed children—all of them smiling, prepared to embrace and kiss him as if they'd known him for their entire lives.

Unable to smile or visit anyone, much less eat and celebrate, Andronikos put up a warning hand. "Please, forgive me. I'm unclean. I've just returned from a tomb."

"A tomb?" his mother echoed, her smile fading to concern. "Andronikos, are you ill?"

He shook his head, silencing her with an imploring glance. "No. But for the sake of others, I carried burial spices into a tomb. Continue the feast without me."

As they all stared, he took a basin and stoneware pitcher from a nearby table, went to his room, and barred himself inside, sick with despair.

***

Malchos seated himself uninvited beside Elisheba on a couch in the reception room. Thick unseen layers of his perfumes surrounded them. She shivered, almost pinching her nose, as Malchos breathed, "All I could think of today was you."

All he could think of was not having what he wanted. Elisheba looked down, her fear rising. Why did he want her so desperately? How else could she discourage him? Perhaps if she openly confessed her admiration of the Rabbi Yeshua then Malchos, a true Sadducee, would be repulsed by her foolishness. And then Lord Pallu would take Benjamin from her for years …. She had to maintain her composure. *Be rational. Think.*

Oblivious to her silence, Malchos leaned closer, whispering. "How grateful I was to hear that you'd survived the earthquake unscathed! You see, I already think of you as my wife. I've forgiven your rejection of me the other night. You won't suffer for it."

Suffer? Elisheba swallowed. Might he eventually plan punishments for her imagined flouting of his will? Sweat started, cold on her skin as she envisioned him beating her, perhaps finally killing her in preference to divorce. She had to escape him. She couldn't protect Benjamin if Malchos killed her and closed her corpse in a tomb.

Near enough to kiss her cheek, Malchos murmured, "Your rooms are already prepared in my house. Everything you could desire waits for you there."

Her desires? She was afraid to learn more of his. Right now, she desired only to survive him.

"You are so tempting! Tell me that you agree," Malchos urged, warm against her cheek, "and I will come to you tonight."

"For the sake of our good names, forgive me ... please." Quivering inwardly, Elisheba kept her voice low, aware of the Lady Levia and the children watching them. "Nothing's signed or sworn between us yet." As he opened his mouth to argue, she reminded him, "Please, I want no gossip among the servants. Please, please ... forgive me."

She hurried to sit with the children. She must show her father the bruises Malchos had inflicted upon her. She would beg Lord Pallu to consider someone else. No, she would lose Benjamin. Could she hide him away first?

"I don't like Malchos," Benjamin said as she sat down.

"Shh," she whispered, smoothing his curls. How would he react when Malchos took them into his household? If her rooms were already prepared in his house, then she would marry Malchos in a matter of days. Days! Elisheba shuddered.

Benjamin looked up at her now, disconsolate as he'd been after Joseph's death. Today's earthquake and the darkness had frightened him badly, as she had been frightened. And Lord Pallu's harshness only added to their miseries. Pallu had pointedly shunned Benjamin since the quake, wounding her little boy's spirit.

Aching, Elisheba watched her father-in-law doting over little Nathan, lifting him from Levia's arms, crooning praises as Nathan smiled, all sweet dimples and charm.

Of course she should have expected this. Shouldn't Lord Pallu prefer his own son above hers? Indeed, it was preferable that he no longer see Benjamin as his heir.

Why, then, hadn't he released her and Benjamin? Why wouldn't he allow her to take Benjamin and live with her parents? How could she win their freedom?

***

Sitting up, Benjamin sucked in a breath.

Shadows crept just behind the weak lamplight, promising soundless threats that raised the hairs on his head. And other thoughts whispered inside his own.

What can you do? Nothing. Why don't you run to your grandparents?

Even pulling the thick wool coverlets over his head didn't help. The whispers continued and the whisperers threatened, lurking, laughing unheard as if they waited with swords to slice him apart. *It'll be too late if you wait until the lamp dies out, Benjamin! You should run to Abba Pallu. Run!*

Terror gave him enough strength to drag the coverlets off the bed as he scurried to take refuge with Eran. "Eran, wake up!" But Eran was no help, burrowed beneath his own coverlets, eyes shut. He'd said almost nothing today. And he hadn't prayed tonight—as if there was nothing to pray for, though there *was!*

Benjamin shoved him, trembling. "Eran! Wake up. We need to pray."

"Little Master," Eran mumbled, patting him feebly, "go to sleep."

What was wrong with Eran? Didn't he care?

The whisperers waited, laughed cruelly, and watched. Benjamin pulled the covers over his head and huddled down near his aged teacher to pray alone. Tomorrow night, he would stay with Ama. No, he'd run from the whisperers. Now.

***

A current stirred through the grayness—but not of fear. The Holy Spirit swept among the hushed righteous, calling them joyously from rest to awareness.

Joseph turned, just as white light flared, slicing through the gloom in splendor more dazzling than the sun, banishing darkness. Drawing every soul's cry to Him, their King.

As one, they recognized Him. As one, they worshipped, overcome. And Joseph called out, "Lord!"

Even as he dropped to his knees in praise with the multitudes, Joseph felt life and light pouring through him like a song from the Spirit. Life from his white-robed King.

Exultant, the Lord stretched out His arms, revealing marks of earthly torment on His wrists as he called to them all, "Return to Me, for I have redeemed you! Sing for joy, O heavens, for the Lord Almighty has done this. Shout aloud, O earth beneath!"

Answering His triumphant summons, they shouted until Sheol itself shook for joy.

***

In adoration, John rejoiced, bowing himself again—too overcome for anything but worship. "Blessed are You, Adonai! Who is like You?"

"John."

The word touched through his soul, commanding, "Come."

John obeyed. Without words, by the Spirit's own insight, he comprehended his task and joined other souls chosen for their Savior's purpose.

To go to Jerusalem. To speak to the faithful who yet lived in flesh.

***

From the eternal, Joseph stepped—as bidden by the Holy Spirit—into darkness, into the earthly boundaries of his broken tomb. And there, he laughed, understanding in full what would be done.

For You, Adonai. Only for You!

Chapter 18

ALONE, ELISHEBA WANDERED through her silent rooms, nudging the flickering lamps, casting more spices onto the incense braziers, and fluffing pillows. When Joseph had lived, this was the time they'd kept sacred for themselves, clinging to each other, kissing, laughing, discussing everything precious of the body and spirit. There would be no such teasing-tender words with Malchos, however much she might try.

"Had I known our time would be so short, Joseph ..." What? What would she have discussed most of all? Love. And every mystery of his soul. She would surely have asked such troubling questions that Joseph would have shaken his head in bafflement.

Whom could she question now? No one. Except perhaps Eran. But he was in deep mourning, too distraught for mere words, as she could become if she remembered more.

She would speak with the old teacher tomorrow, and encourage him. Though the Rabbi's death had oppressed her soul to the point of numbness. But Eran would understand.

Eran always understood her. As he had understood Joseph. Indeed, Eran had quietly encouraged Joseph and his friends, and Elisheba, to seek the Lord Almighty through the Prophet John, and then to follow the Rabbi Yeshua.

Whatever eternal hopes she and Joseph had placed in the Almighty, they were inspired by the aged teacher. Elisheba saw that now. And because of Eran's faith, despite all the wounds and sorrows this past year, still her soul yearned toward Adonai.

She must rest in Him, or go mad. If she thought of Malchos, she would—

"Ama!" Small impatient fists thumped low at the ante-chamber door, scattering her fretful thoughts.

"Benjamin?" She hurried to let him in. He scuffed past, indignant, chin down, his gaze cast up at her, his coverlets trailing behind him. "What's wrong?"

He refused to say a word, but plopped himself firmly into the center of her pallet with the truculent air of one who wouldn't be moved.

But then, why move him? She welcomed her son as a respite from her loneliness. She wouldn't sleep anyway, so let him stay.

Even so, she would definitely talk to Eran in the morning.

***

Despite all their silent whisperings, their urgings, the child had gone to his mother. Not to his grandparents, who were the preferred ones—never being submissive to It.

His grandparents would instill within him their ways and worldly enticements. They must. The child had not yet made his choice. Meddlesome It *was still too close.*

Because of the mother. Because of the teacher.

In timeless patience at the edge of the boundaries It possessed around the mother, they waited. And smiled. For in his foolish slumber, the child turned away from his mother's prayerful, protective embrace. Away just enough to allow their spirit-wounding darts of fear.

***

Within the dream, amid clouds of dim gray, red, and gold, Benjamin saw his father—the only place he saw Abba now. This time, Abba was smiling, almost teasing, just as Benjamin remembered from their playtimes.

"He is dead," his grandfather Abba Pallu said, standing beside him in the mists, taking hold of Benjamin's arm. "Come away."

Sick with longing for the dream to be real, for his father to hold him and to laugh with him once more, as they had in life, Benjamin called out, "Abba?"

Don't be angry with me, he pleaded silently. *Don't say those things.*

His father turned, looking at him, his eyes dark-burning, making Benjamin shrink away, knowing what was coming.

What do you want? Why should I bother with you? Abba's eyes blazed darker, his voice hissing worse than anything Benjamin had ever heard. *You're sickening. A whimpering, shivering little dog that ought to be kicked. Ask your Abba Pallu to save you....*

Hands reaching out like claws. Abba was no longer Abba, but an enemy, his face shifting, twisting into smoking-fire ugliness, mocking him. *Oh, have I frightened you? What do you expect, Benjamin? You're going to die too!*

Trying to escape, Benjamin grabbed for Abba Pallu, then awoke, suddenly.

Still alive.

***

They writhed and turned about in alarm like dark feathers in a gale. Without warning, their delight in tormenting this small bit of flesh shattered like light in a broken crystal, wrecked by an unseen tide surging through their realm of the air.

Loathsome It swept them away from their quarry. The sheer impact of Spirit's power sluiced their beings through mortal walls like water dashed through sieves, stunning their screaming thoughts to near nothingness.

And light—His light—blinded their eternal senses, forcing them to flee. Into the darkness, away from the dawnlight.

Within the air, they regathered their legions and fought to right themselves within their shaken realm, until they were summoned by the outraged cries of their angel-lord master.

His *flesh has escaped us!*
We have lost...!

***

I'm being brave, Benjamin promised himself, swallowing his cries hard so he wouldn't wake Ama. *It didn't catch me.*

But he was sweating. Trembling. What if the dream returned? He needed a sword. He had to show Abba Pallu and everyone that he wasn't a coward.

Exhaling his fright, Benjamin rubbed at the tears he'd tried not to shed. A quiet tremor shivered through the room now. An earthquake? Benjamin stiffened, waiting. But nothing else happened. He relaxed and nudged himself closer to his sleeping Ama, inhaling the incense smells lingering in her room, comforting himself that everything was real and unchanged. Even better, the first bits of morning light glowed through the blue-covered lattice window, calming him.

His Ama turned and put an arm over Benjamin as if to protect him in her sleep.

But she couldn't protect him in his dreams. And as he stared wide-eyed toward the brightening lattice, another dream began—so big that it couldn't fit inside his head.

So huge that it stood tall and light-robed in Ama's room.

It saw him and approached, half-kneeling on the floor beside his cushioned pallet.

I'm not a coward. I'm not screaming. But Benjamin gulped at his fright, his heart thudding as his father leaned toward him, watching. Only watching.

Abba didn't change. Didn't turn evil. Didn't hiss or hate.

Instead he smiled with all the joy Benjamin remembered. And loved him with a look of brightness so strong and protective that Benjamin took courage yet again that this time, Abba wouldn't change.

Hopeful, he tested his dream in a whisper. "Abba?"

"Benjamin." His father touched his cheek, then mussed his hair, teasing-kind and *real*. "Don't be afraid."

"Abba!"

Ama woke. And screamed.

***

A man in her room! Not Malchos, but a stranger, touching her son!

Dragging Benjamin into her arms, Elisheba screamed again, using words this time. "Out! Get out! Leave us alone!"

"Abba!" Benjamin yelled, squirming, straining to reach the man.

"He's not!" Elisheba cried, looking the intruder full in the face, ready to claw, to kick, to fight for her son. "Get out!"

"Elisheba, don't be afraid," the man urged, still kneeling, smiling. Elisheba wavered, then stared, aghast.

Joseph's smile. Joseph's eyes. His wondrous, lively gaze, more vivid than ever. Impossible! "No ...."

"Elisheba, He came to me," Joseph said, with all the joy she remembered shining in that brilliant gaze. "Yeshua came to me."

A memory threaded its way to the surface of Elisheba's thoughts. *Yeshua... take me to Him!*

Everything grayed as thrumming filled her ears. She was going to faint.

"He's risen!" Joseph glowed with the words. "Death is defeated!"

Concentrating on regaining her senses, Elisheba lowered her head, sucked in her breath, then focused hard on his words. "Risen? Who?"

"Our *Mashiyakh*, Yeshua!" Joseph grinned at her, his entire being alight with exultation.

Such light didn't belong in her room ... or in this world. She was dreaming.

Benjamin struggled in her arms, hurting her as he broke away, lunging toward his father—who could *not* be alive. "Abba!"

Joseph curved an arm around Benjamin, resting his cheek in the little boy's dark curls, exactly as he'd always done. Benjamin sighed within his embrace, eyes closed, his expression blissful as a sleeper's.

"Don't be frightened," Joseph urged again, stretching his free hand toward Elisheba.

She shook her head at him, scared to believe. "No."

Tenderly persistent, the man leaned closer, still offering his hand. Recognizing the delicate lines in that hand, she gasped. How often she'd traced these very imprints in his palm—too precise and intimately remembered to be a dream. This was real.

"Joseph." Her thoughts scattered and regathered and her heart rejoiced, making her laugh even as tears stung her eyes. "This is impossible!"

She blinked and then stared at him, mesmerized. Oh, he was *beautiful*. He looked as regal as a king's son. No wonder she hadn't recognized him. And he loved her still, yet he looked at her differently, as if seeing and cherishing her spirit, not her physical form that he'd adored. The difference hurt. Nevertheless, he beguiled her even now.

Holding her breath, Elisheba tentatively touched Joseph's extended fingertips, trying to comprehend flesh that was no longer flesh of the earth, but perfected. A body no longer warmed by blood, but by light and life itself. And his garments were finer than any she'd ever seen. Whiter. His spirit, too—always so precious—now seemed intensified. As one prepared for something beyond this life.

The more she studied Joseph, the more she saw the truth. The difference between them was like comparing a dazzling gem to a dirt clod.

This is what the Almighty Lord intended for those who loved Him.

When she could finally speak again, she whispered, "You're truly alive."

He laughed, and all the light in the room seemed to emanate from his soul. "Very much alive! But more than this, I'm sent to tell you that *He* lives."

"The Rabbi Yeshua ..."

"Our same Lord! He freed us beyond death from Sheol."

"If you're alive, then He must be," she agreed, her heartbeat skittering, joyous at Joseph's elation. How spectacular he was! How perfect .... She gazed at him through a shimmering haze of fresh tears. More than anything, she longed to throw herself into his arms. Yet she didn't dare. Nothing of the earth remained in him.

Joseph's exultation softened, tempered by solemnity. Kissing Benjamin's hair, he smiled at his son in absolute love. Opening his eyes, Benjamin grinned and straightened. "Abba, this is my best, *best* dream!"

"My brave boy! My little Samson, never forget this 'dream'! Remember always that I love you," Joseph urged. "Remember too—always honor your Ama."

"You're leaving?" Elisheba reached for his hand. She must delay him. He couldn't leave her again. "Please, not yet! Can't we go with you?"

It was a futile question; she already knew the answer. Joseph shook his head. "You have more to do here. And I have one more task to fulfill." Joseph's eyes glowed again, dancing bright until she could *almost* see mischief there. "Whatever happens, don't be afraid. Amid everything that is yet to come, He remembers you and loves you. Tell everyone that He lives!"

With one last encouraging look, swift as a breath, he was gone like light merging into light from the lattice window.

Benjamin protested. "I wanted him to stay!"

"Who was he?" Lord Pallu's voice cut through Elisheba's room as he barged in from her antechamber. "Who was here? Don't lie! I *heard* you."

He'd heard? How could she explain? Elisheba turned to stare at Lord Pallu, who looked around her rooms for evidence of her liaison. He believed the worst concerning her behavior. Elisheba's mouth went dry. Her thoughts stuttered, refusing to form words.

"Abba was here," Benjamin said. "Abba walked out from a big light—a dream—and Ama screamed."

Pallu's face went rigid, eyes wide, jaw clenched. Growling, he bolted toward Elisheba and snatched her arm, wrenching her to her feet. "What's this game you're playing, eh? I hear you screaming, I dress, then come running to help you—as if you deserve it!—and I hear you talking to a man, begging him to take you both with him. You've been bringing men into my house!"

"No!" Elisheba gasped. How could he think so? "My lord, I give you my word; there's been no man for me since Joseph! I loved him and honor his good name."

"Don't lie to me! Your son's own words condemned you." Reaching down, Pallu grabbed Benjamin by the back of his small tunic, for Benjamin was already scooting away from his furious grandfather. "I heard you talking to a man; I saw someone."

"Who did you see?" Elisheba pleaded, seizing the hope that she could somehow reason with Pallu. But he dragged them both through the doorway, jostling Elisheba until she heard her sleeve's seam ripping.

"He was Abba!" Benjamin insisted, stumbling as Pallu forced them into the courtyard. His small voice raised, loud and defiant. "I wanted to see him and he was here!"

Lord Pallu wouldn't believe Benjamin or her, but what else could she say except the truth? "It was Joseph." Elisheba explained, her words tumbling over themselves. "He appeared to us, but not as he was, yet ... a living vision."

Pallu halted, staring at Benjamin, then at Elisheba. She hushed, trembling, waiting for him to slap her, to beat her in front of Levia, Malkah, Zimiyrah, and Eran and the servants who were gathering to stare, all blank-faced with shock.

But Pallu tightened his grip on Elisheba's arm, then hauled her and Benjamin fiercely from the courtyard through the formal, echoing stone corridor. "Enough! I want you and your weak-minded son out of my house."

By the time they reached the small stone gate room, Benjamin was sobbing. "I saw him! I saw Abba! I want to go to my Abba ...."

The watchman inside the small room scrambled to his feet in alarm. They'd caught him sleeping. Pallu glared at the man and snapped, "Open the gate!"

"Yes, lord." The man fumbled with the big lock as if he couldn't remember his job. The instant the door squeaked open, Lord Pallu shoved Elisheba and Benjamin outside. Benjamin yowled, tumbling in the street. As Elisheba caught her balance and whirled around to protest, Pallu slammed the door in her face without another word.

Hearing the dry, resounding clunk as the watchman dutifully locked them out, Elisheba gave up. They'd been cast out. She hurriedly kneeled and checked Benjamin, who clutched a scraped knee, tearful and grimacing in pain.

"My baby," Elisheba whispered. She rocked him briefly, kissed his salt-wet cheek, and finally lifted him to his feet. "We can't stay here. Come with me."

Sniffling, Benjamin whimpered. "Where are we going? To find Abba?"

"To my abba's house." Elisheba brightened at a sudden thought, amazed. "We're free. We're freed from Lord Pallu! Benjamin, we're going to have to walk for a long distance. I can't carry you all the way. I know your knee hurts, but I need you to be very brave and walk."

"I am brave," Benjamin argued, sounding congested as he limped beside her through the morning light. "Abba said so."

"He did, didn't he?" Though her feet were beginning to hurt—too tender against the stone pavings—she caught her breath in delight. Joseph was alive. Alive! Just remembering his glowing, beautiful face, she laughed. "He lives—the Rabbi Yeshua too!"

How was it possible? Yet what did it matter? If the Rabbi Yeshua was alive as Joseph, then how could she mourn? She wanted to dance, praising the Almighty Lord. It was difficult to walk straight, she felt so giddy.

"Benjamin, always remember how well your abba looked, and how happy he was to see you. Now … my mind's so scattered … where do my parents live again?"

A low whistle pierced the air behind her, and a man's deeply accented voice caught her attention, speaking Greek roughly as if it might not be his native language. "Look what we've found wandering through the streets, Porcius."

"And I thought our watch would end in boredom," another man responded in similar jarring accents. "Do you suppose her lover has thrown her out?"

Benjamin turned, looked over his shoulder, and then his eyes brightened, "Ama, they have swords!"

Soldiers. Romans? "Almighty Lord," Elisheba whispered, her elation vanishing instantly. And they were talking about *her*. "Turn around, Benjamin."

She hadn't considered her appearance—barefoot, her hair unbound and uncovered, her chamber gown loose and torn. And her throat still showed bruises from Malchos' abuse. *Lord, save us. I must look like a harlot thrown from some man's bed!*

To her horror, one of the soldiers strode up beside her, dangling a small purse of coins before her eyes as they walked. Though she refused to look at him, she couldn't help seeing his wide, powerful hands and his muscular arm. His voice was low, though businesslike. "How much do you ask, woman? Surely I could keep you for a week with this."

"I don't think she wants you, Gallus. She wants me." The other soldier made obnoxious kissing noises at Elisheba until she flushed. "I will give you twice as much, woman."

Others paid attention now as the early morning streets came to life. Servants leaned outside their gates, and rude porters laughed at her. Ahead in the street, another soldier turned to survey the commotion. Eyeing Elisheba, he called out, "Gallus! Porcius! Who is *that*?"

He fell into step with the other two and they began to discuss her as if she couldn't hear them. Her hair, her skin, her curves, and how she might have acquired those bruises around her pretty throat.

Elisheba picked up Benjamin, heavy as he was, and continued to walk, her gaze fixed on the pavings ahead. She whispered into her son's ear, "Don't look at them, my baby! Don't say anything. Remember what Abba said—honor me."

***

Morning. Stephanos rubbed a hand over his whiskered face and groaned. How could it be morning again when he hadn't slept? Each time he'd closed his eyes, he saw Master Iesous, flayed bloody and staggering out to die. And he remembered Kore visiting him yesterday, stone-pale, telling him of the Master's brutal death. His followers scattered, perhaps doomed. As Stephanos could have been. And might yet be.

Fear crept through Stephanos' soul like dark tendrils from a life-choking vine. He hated this weakness, this paralyzing terror. His parents were worried about him, and Stephanos suspected they should be. There was no reason for his panic, yet it remained.

Almighty Lord, take away this fear! Give me my life again.

His thoughts dazed with fatigue, he turned over on his pallet and saw a man's feet. The cleanest bare feet he'd ever seen. Here? How? Jolted, he stood and stared at the man who'd appeared unannounced in his closed room.

Wearing pure white robes, the man possessed a gaze so intense it seemed to cut into Stephanos' soul.

Trying to recognize him, Stephanos' blurred mind fumbled. The Baptist John. No. He was dead. Then who was this man? As he started to demand an explanation, Stephanos noticed the man's bloodless wound. A cut. All the way around ... his neck. A lethal wound. A beheading. As the Baptist died. "Who are you?"

He stared at the man's face again. The Baptist stared back boldly, undeniably *him*.

"Aw!" Stephanos flung himself away and tripped, bruising his elbows as he landed sprawled on the floor, squawking. "I'm dead? I'm dead!"

"Stand up!" the man snapped, impatient as the Baptist John had ever been in life. But his eyes glittered with all of the Baptist's zealous joy. "Why are you lying there? Our Lord's risen! Stop acting like a dead man and *get up*."

"I'm dead?"

"You're not dead, nor am I. See? I'm only changed." The Baptist reached down and swiped Stephanos' jaw, the blow light but vividly intense. "Now compose yourself. Get up and go tell the others the good news. Our Lord and Redeemer lives!"

"Our Lord?"

"The one you called Master Iesous. He's risen from the grave and sent me to tell you. Now, get up!" He leaned near, as if ready to drag Stephanos to his feet once more.

"Yes, yes, I'm standing." Stephanos struggled to his feet, wobbling.

Looking satisfied, John nodded at him and then simply vanished as if doors and walls were meaningless to his glorified form.

Alone again, Stephanos looked around. What had just happened? Could he be going insane? Might he actually be dead and within a spiritual realm? No, certainly he must yet be alive; his entire body shrieked its mortal existence. His heart thumped as if he'd run a race with Kore. His elbows hurt. The floor was cold and hard beneath his feet. Most important, his jaw tingled sharply where he'd been swatted by the Baptist. And if his jaw hurt ....

"The Baptist lives! Master Iesous lives!" And if Master Iesous lived ... surely He was the Christos ... alive beyond death. Nothing else mattered now. He had to tell Andronikos. And Kore. He'd start with them. He'd find the Master's disciples, the Almighty Lord's disciples!

Snatching his cloak, Stephanos dashed from his room and sped outside through his family's courtyard, then out the gate, whooping. Too ecstatic to finish dressing, he waved his cloak like a banner as he charged barefoot through the Upper Market streets. Merchants and workers stared while he rushed by, as if he were insane. He didn't care. What could they do to him? Nothing!

"Andronikos!" He reached the shop and hammered on the door until Andronikos finally opened the window, seeming seriously wary, a cloth dangling from his hands. "Andronikos!"

Andronikos shifted his cloth-wrapped grip on the shutter. "What? Has someone died?"

"No! Look!" Pointing to his jaw, Stephanos demanded, "Is there a mark here?"

Andronikos scowled. "Yes. There's a handprint. I see the outlines of the fingers. Who struck you?"

"You see an imprint!" Stephanos whooped and grinned. "The Prophet John struck me, that's who! He's alive!"

His eyes widening, Andronikos grabbed a wooden stave and prodded open the door. He waved Stephanos inside the shop and snapped, "Close the door and bolt it. But stay away from me. I'm unclean."

***

"He's gone mad," Andronikos whispered to his mother in the courtyard.

Joanna nodded, teary-eyed, watching Stephanos, who was half-dressed, wild-haired, his eyes shining avidly as he paced here and there, waving his cloak, describing to one of her cousins the scene of the Baptist appearing to him, striking him. "You wouldn't believe the mark on his throat— a cut all the way around. I couldn't believe it."

"Sit down, my friend," Andronikos interrupted, showing Stephanos to a bench, aware of their visiting Corinth cousins retreating nervously into their rooms. "Have you eaten?"

"I haven't even prayed yet," Stephanos told him brightly. "Or maybe I have. I don't remember, but it doesn't matter." He laughed again, rocking back on the bench, swatting his cloak on his knees like a jubilant boy. "You must think I'm insane!"

You are, Andronikos agreed silently.

His mother turned away, wiping her tears, becoming brisk as if she could restore order to Stephanos' rattled brain—and to reassure their worried cousins. "Maria! Get some bread from the kitchen. Loukas? Loukas! Bring me some wine. Andronikos, since you've already walked through the shop..."

Before she could command him, Andronikos said, "I'll get some myrrh extract to calm him down." Though he must again warn Stephanos that he had been inside a tomb and was ceremonially unclean. Not that it mattered. Stephanos was completely irrational.

He went into the shop and paused, exhaling heavily, shaking his head. *Blessed be You, Lord Almighty, but ... How much more trouble must we bear?*

Stephanos was a good man. It hurt to see him falling apart like this.

Covering his hand again, though likely the cloth availed nothing, Andronikos lifted an alabaster flask of myrrh extract from a chilly stone shelf and turned to his work table for a cup. Instead of the table, he faced an unexpected, impressively robed customer, who glanced around the shop as if he'd never seen it before. How had the man entered so quietly? Andronikos hadn't heard the door creak. In fact, the door was bolted shut—a worrisome detail.

Still holding the flask but trying to seem casual as he edged toward one of his stone cudgels, Andronikos asked, "Sir? May I help you?"

"Yes. *You*, merchant, do you have any gum?" the man asked in a perfect mimic of Kore's habitual greeting.

What? A chill slid over Andronikos and he froze. Only Kore, Joseph, and Stephanos had ever teased him this way. Moreover, this man's tone was distinctly familiar. The customer looked him straight in the eyes and grinned.

Joseph!

Air stuck like a rock in Andronikos' throat. Unable to breath, he dropped the flask, cracking and spilling it over the stone tabletop while he gripped the table's edge.

Radiating all the ease and confidence Andronikos had ever admired of his spirit, Joseph chided him, benevolence come to life. "Andronikos, don't be afraid. I have good news. Our Lord lives. We're redeemed!"

Redeemed? Andronikos wheezed in a breath, still clutching the table.

"You're my kindred now."

What?

"Do you hear me, brother?" Joseph leaned forward until they were almost nose to nose. Andronikos gawked, perceiving his dead friend's face. Every imperfection of Joseph's earthly life was removed. Such clear eyes ...

"Are you listening?"

Dry-mouthed, Andronikos nodded, trying to get past the shock enough to speak.

Joseph said, "You're to protect my son."

"Protect your son?" Perplexed, Andronikos managed to sputter, "That c...can't happen, unless ..." He froze again, choking down the disloyal thought. *Unless I marry Elisheba.*

There was no mistaking the glint in Joseph's eye.

He knows my feelings for her. A warming blush of shame crept into Andronikos' face, but Joseph didn't seem offended. Quite the opposite.

"You're to protect my son," Joseph repeated. "And tell everyone what I've told you, brother. Our Master Iesous lives. He's risen from the tomb!"

As if hearing an unexpected noise, Joseph glanced beyond Andronikos, toward the courtyard doorway. Andronikos followed his gaze, then heard his mother's footsteps. And her exasperated voice as she approached, calling, "Andronikos?"

When Andronikos looked back, Joseph was gone. But the windows and doors were still closed, and the myrrh extract spread in a thin puddle, dripping off the table's edge onto his feet. This happened.

Too shaken to walk, Andronikos sank to the floor just as his mother entered the shop. Seeing him go down, she gasped, "Andronikos!"

His mother rushed to hold him, checking his forehead for fever then testing his pulse. Andronikos patted her arm, mumbling. "I'll be fine. I've had a shock."

"You're flushed," his mother protested. "And you never drop things!"

"I'm going to sit with Stephanos. I just saw Joseph, son of Pallu."

"What?"

"That's exactly what I thought when I saw him." Catching his breath, Andronikos pulled himself to his feet and hugged his now-ashen mother. "By the way, you'll need to part with some of that silver you've been hiding. I have to marry Joseph's Elisheba."

It was his mother's turn to choke. Unlike him, however, she didn't go speechless.
"No! Andronikos, I forbid it!"

***

Light-swift, Joseph turned amid Jerusalem's streets, observing stones, bugs, shadows, animals, and humans all within the same instant, in perfect clarity. To exist in this form, in this new realm, was perfect joy. Movement, thought, and perception were all so effortless!

How had he managed to plod through life in a dull-sensed, burdensome body of earth? Blessed are You, Lord Almighty, Creator of the universe and all that exists!

What a wonder to sense his Creator with every breath, to recognize the Spirit at every turn. He'd never dreamed of such an expansion of all his senses. Such perfect orientation between himself and the Lord.

Another being of light appeared, his lordly bearing and vitality so extraordinary that Joseph was compelled to look at him. Countless beings gathered behind this lordly and glorious one, each mirroring their leader's majesty. Joseph recognized them now as fragmented memories from his earthly form expanded within this present realm, piecing themselves together to reveal patterns he'd failed to notice as a mortal man.

I have met you before. All of you.

Their magnificence invited comradeship, but his memories stirred anew, provoking wariness and loathing. You were the inspirations of so many troubles!

Come, *Adversary beckoned without speech, shifting his proud stance.* Reason with me. Listen to me. Things are not what they seem.

His appeal resonated, tangible and beguiling, but darkness emanated from the Adversary's core, as if he could not forever maintain a façade of light. Joseph scoffed. You are but a shadow of our Creator. And you lack what I revere: His love and His Spirit! *Though there was no need to communicate with words, Joseph commanded aloud,* "In the name of my risen Lord Yeshua, go!"

As one, the Adversary and his followers were flung back by Spirit. They scattered and fled through the air, trailing echoes of threats. If they'd been mortals beneath that impact, they would have suffered bloody wounds.

John drew near, impatient. We are summoned. *Even as John communicated this, Joseph felt their Lord's clear and vibrant call, and he smiled.*

***

Watching the new immortals depart, Adversary seethed. Do you believe you and your

Master have won all? Those you have loved yet walk the earth.

Chapter 19

Trembling with the unaccustomed exertion and acute distress, Elisheba set Benjamin down outside the gate to her father's residence. Behind her, the leering soldiers and discreetly curious onlookers, many of them servants of her parents' neighbors, watched her every move.

Word of this would spread quickly, she realized. By nightfall, virtually everyone in this area of Jerusalem would be discussing her shame. The thought was nauseating.

Whatever happens, don't be afraid, Joseph had said. *He remembers you.*

"Remember me now, please," she whispered to the Almighty Lord. Summoning her courage, she hammered her fists on the heavy cedar door.

Where was Joseph now? Did he know she was being perceived as a harlot? Couldn't he do something to protect her?

Sethi, her father's authoritative black-bearded gate attendant answered the door. Seeing her and Benjamin, obviously disgraced, he paused, no doubt trying to balance courtesy with morals and loyalties in his law-bound mind.

"Sethi," she begged, "let us in! Where's my lord father?"

As she spoke, Benjamin impatiently wedged his small shoulder between the door and the gaping attendant, and squeezed into the courtyard. "Abba Barzel, we're here!"

His self-certain action and his young bellow revived Sethi, who lifted his bearded chin coolly at everyone in the street, then stepped aside to admit Elisheba, as if she'd been expected to visit while looking so disreputable.

Stumbling into the courtyard, Elisheba leaned against the inner wall. While Sethi closed the gate, she sat on the pavement, fighting tears. Would her father receive her? Surely he wouldn't hesitate as Sethi had. Or disown her for this public shaming. *If he doesn't accept me, I'll have to go out to the streets. To those men.*

"We're here!" Benjamin yelled again, clearly confident of his welcome. "And I'm hungry!"

Sethi strode toward the kitchen, calling to the maidservants, "Cook some eggs for the young Master. Also, bring water and bandages. I'll summon our lord."

Too mortified to move, Elisheba wiped her face on her sleeve and stared down at her feet, now feeling and seeing the need for bandages. Her toes burned, abraded and bloody. And the dirty skin on her soles was painfully rolled up in numerous places like small gory parchments, exposing raw, bleeding flesh. Proof that she'd never walked the streets without sandals before. Why couldn't Lord Pallu have allowed her some sandals and decent clothes before shoving her outside?

"My baby!" her mother's voice gasped. Her robes loose and fluttering, Daliyah descended the stone stairs from the upper chamber down to the courtyard, where she knelt beside Elisheba. "What happened?"

Before Elisheba could muster an explanation, Daliyah screeched in outrage, her soft hands poised over Elisheba's torn feet as if afraid to touch her. "Oh! Your feet are torn bloody! And *look* at your throat! Who did this?"

"Lord Pallu threw us out. Ama, I didn't even have time to—"

Elisheba's explanation died on her lips as she saw her father hurrying from the upper chamber and down the stairs into the courtyard. Barzel's steps slowed, his eyes went huge. Drawing in a harsh breath, he clawed the neckline of his robe and tore it viciously, screaming to the heavens like a wild man.

Elisheba cowered against her mother, terrified. *He's going to disown me.*

***

Storming into Pallu's courtyard, Barzel grabbed Pallu's long-sleeved cloak, wrenching the man toward him, bellowing his accusations. "You threw my daughter into the street like a common whore! Do you think I'll let this go unanswered?"

"She welcomed a man in her rooms!" Pallu argued, just as loud.

"Did you see him?"

"No, but she was talking to him. I—"

"What did he say?" Barzel demanded, tightening his grip, shaking Pallu until the scoundrel's jowls quivered. "Tell me what he said!"

"I didn't hear him, but—"

"Of course you didn't hear him because there was no man in her rooms!" Barzel flung Pallu back, making him stumble and flap his arms, fighting for balance.

Recovering, Pallu brushed his robes vigorously, as if Barzel's touch soiled him. "Her son said—"

"Don't you *dare* quote my grandson! You threw him out too! You called him 'weak-minded,' and don't think he didn't hear you. He's recited every word you said." Smoldering, craving to choke Pallu, Barzel snarled, "If your little Malkah was in my household, in a similar situation, I would have sent her home discreetly for the sake of your good name. But you shamed my daughter—and me—publicly, over nothing!"

"I didn't intend to shame you," Pallu protested. "I was angry."

"Well, *I'm* angry too," Barzel answered through clenched teeth. "And I do intend this: I want *all* of my daughter's silver and properties restored to me by sunset, with the money Joseph pledged to pay as her settlement, her *ketubah*, when they married. Also, if you don't send your steward to me this afternoon with written accounts of how you've handled her dowry, I'll have writs issued publicly commanding you to do these things so everyone will know you for the cheat you are."

"Surely there's no need for you to do that," Pallu wheedled, so smooth that Barzel begrudged the man's calm. "Nonetheless, we need more than one day to gather all the documents."

"By sunset!" Barzel snapped. "It's more courtesy than you've shown me. *And*," he emphasized, forcing Pallu to look at him, "I warn you, sunset is only the beginning."

***

Pallu watched Barzel leave. If only the man would simply drop dead in his tracks. There were few documents to show him. None at all from this past year. He had dismissed his land steward and handled Elisheba's properties himself after Joseph's death. As far as the silver, it would take all the coins he could gather to repay Barzel by sunset. *If I have that much.* Sweat prickled in his armpits.

There would have been no threat of public disclosure if he could have married Elisheba off to Malchos; the man was so besotted with the little fool that he'd never checked her properties or silver. Pallu could have told him the girl was impoverished and Malchos wouldn't have cared. He should have sent her to Malchos this morning and let Barzel deal with his daughter's unsanctioned marriage instead of this unintended shaming, regardless of the very likely possibility that Malchos would cast out Elisheba by nightfall.

Frustrated over his lapse in judgment, Pallu rubbed a hand over his face, trying to think while coldly ignoring Levia, who stood on the uppermost step by their rooms, cuddling Nathan in her arms.

You're going to part with all those ornaments you've bought, he warned his wife silently. *And if that's all you lose, you should count yourself blessed!*

He would gather everything he could from his debtors now. He must also send for Joseph's bone box—his ossuary—from the stonecutters before they heard any whispers of his debts. They'd demand immediate payment, alongside his other creditors.

He would at least have his son's bones set decently to rest—a few days earlier than he'd planned, but it couldn't be helped.

It was a mercy Joseph hadn't lived to see his wife become a whore, and his son turn idiot. Seeing his Abba, indeed!

Huffing, Pallu went to wash himself. He would be clean until he entered his son's tomb, though he didn't relish the thought of touching Joseph's bones.

Eran. He'd have Eran perform the task. After all, the old man had tended Joseph's body last year. Now he must finish the job.

***

This is not my role; it's yours, Eran silently groused, carrying a lamp as he followed Lord Pallu down the slope to the hillside tomb. Other servants followed with the stone ossuary.

Eran longed to refuse to enter Joseph's tomb. To see his bones and to gather them into the ossuary would be the final acknowledgement that the young man was gone. Even now, after a year, Eran didn't want to face his loss. This morning, Eran had almost envied his piteous little Master Benjamin, crying that he'd seen his father in a dream—just before Lord Pallu dragged the child off to cast him and the Lady Elisheba into the street.

Surely she and her son had taken refuge with her father. But due to her disheveled, disreputable state, which was Lord Pallu's fault, and her vulnerability and beauty, there might be complications. Eran prayed as he walked. *Let the young lady and Master Benjamin be safe!* Had they reached her father's home? He must find out as soon as he'd finished here.

Eran watched Lord Pallu stride ahead of him toward the tomb, detesting him. The young Mistress and little Master didn't deserve such treatment. If Eran had anywhere else to go, he would leave Lord Pallu's household immediately.

As much as he loathed Lord Pallu, Eran also detested himself. He wasn't dealing with matters kindly and forgivingly as Master Iesous had taught. But life had finally cumulated into one intolerable sum of pain that was breaking his soul into fragments of ugliness. How easy it was now to slide into spiritual degradation, turning his thoughts against all mankind. *Lord, our God, Creator of the Kosmos, comfort your servant ....*

On the path ahead of him, Lord Pallu halted and cried out, "Who's defaced our tomb?"

Defaced? Eran's rage fled at the word. He paused behind Lord Pallu, gazing down the quake-twisted, whitewashed steps approaching the tomb's entry. Indeed, the great wreath-carved stone had been rolled ajar, leaving the tomb vulnerably open.

Who would wish to do such a thing? Robbers? Surely no one had touched Master Joseph's body. Raising his lamp, Eran crept down the damaged steps after Lord Pallu, the light wavering feebly within the dim-shadowed tomb. Ahead of him, Lord Pallu jolted to a stop as if wrenched hard by a cord. Turning to the other servants, he called out, "Leave the box on that first shelf and go outside."

Obviously glad to obey, the servants slid the stone ossuary rasping onto a stone shelf then scurried outside, up the steps.

In a breath-stolen whisper, Lord Pallu beckoned, "Bring the lamp here."

Eran obeyed unwillingly. Sidling up to the stone shelf-bed, he held the soft-flickering lamp high and glanced down at the burial clothes, bracing himself to see Master Joseph's stark skull within those wrappings.

Nothing. He leaned closer, nearly spilling oil from the lamp. Was he going blind in his old age? The spice-paste stiffened clothes lay on the stone shelf like a locust's shed husk, perfectly wrapped and tied as they'd been on the morning of Master Joseph's entombment. And yet they were hollow. How could that be? It didn't make sense. Hadn't he tied them himself? Yes, those were his own squared knots, undisturbed. Therefore, where were the bones?

"His bones became dust so quickly." Lord Pallu said, his voice echoing thin in the dim light.

Eran sighed, unutterable relief now stealing into his own aged bones, though he was also distressed. What had happened to Master Joseph's body? "Bones do not become dust so soon, lord."

Lord Pallu gave him a scornful look. "Set down the lamp and put his remains into the box."

"There are obviously no remains." Eran pressed the stiffened wrappings down, checking them to be sure. Nothing. To prove his point to Lord Pallu, Eran deliberately crushed and rolled the burial clothes like a rejected scroll. As he compressed the fabric and felt it give way, he also felt the heaviness lifting from his heart. Bones could not disappear from a tied shroud. Surely this was a miracle! Surely young Benjamin had actually seen his father alive, as he'd insisted with all his small might.

How Master Joseph would have enjoyed this. He would have laughed. He would! *It would be so like you, my fun-loving boy, to make my final task for you so light.* Inspired by the thought, Eran chortled as he hefted the lid from the stone box and shoved the stiff, empty wrappings inside.

"Are you drunk?" Lord Pallu demanded, obviously offended.

"No, my lord." Placing the stone lid on the wasted ossuary, Eran exulted. *He's not here! He's not here!* It was like a song, and Eran wanted to dance like a child. Unable to resist speaking his mind, he told the proud lord, "There is no other explanation: This is surely a miracle as in the days of the prophets!"

"You're deluded."

"I pray so, my lord. I do!" Eran wiped his eyes, still chucking. "Now I marvel at my little Master

Benjamin this morning, saying that he saw his Abba—"

"Well, you can go discuss this with him!" Lord Pallu snapped. "If you think I will allow you to return to my household after behaving so disgracefully here, you are mistaken."

"Thank you, my lord." He almost kissed the nobleman as he skittered past him from the tomb.

"And don't think you're claiming any more wages from me!" Pallu called after him.

"No, my lord." Eran capered up the stairs, his joints and limbs loosened, younger than he'd experienced in years, which was also a miracle. He would shovel dung in the marketplace. He would gather rubbish. He would teach unclean tanners' sons to write their names. What was that compared to this wondrous joy?

Reaching the top step, he beamed at the other servants and marched up the rocky slope to the city.

What was the meaning of this miracle? Eran lifted his eyes to heaven in an ecstatic appeal for answers. "Let me understand!"

And while he sought understanding, he must ensure that the Lady Elisheba and his Master Benjamin were safe. As he entered the city, he halted. Where could he go? He was destitute.

Who would hear him?

Who would not scorn the plea of a homeless old man?

***

"You cannot be serious," Joanna scolded her firstborn as she pried up paving slabs in the corner of her bedroom. "Barzel and his Daliyah are wonderful people, but they will laugh you out of their house, if they don't slam the door in your face first."

"I've been telling myself that too," Andronikos assured her. "But I find I'm not listening to me. Joseph said—"

Joanna snorted in disgust. He still sounded as if Joseph would walk in the door any instant. After she'd been arguing with him all morning. "You truly saw him?"

"Mother." Andronikos knelt beside her now, his dark eyes and voice lucid, reasoning exactly as his father would have done. "Consider that I *agreed* with you this morning. I said Stephanos had gone mad because he claimed he'd seen the Baptist John alive, did I not?"

"Yes," she said, irritable that they were even having this discussion, much less digging up her silver. Gritting her teeth, she lifted the lid of the wooden box hidden beneath the floor, while listening to her son's rationalizations.

"And although Stephanos has calmed down and become himself again, he's still insisting he saw the Baptist. You haven't been able to discourage him from that, and his parents won't either when they get here."

"He is calmer," Joanna admitted. Though she truly believed Stephanos' wits were failing with this illogical Baptist story. Oh, how his good parents would grieve!

Undeterred, Andronikos continued. "You found me sitting on the floor in the shop. You knew something had happened to upset me. Well, now I'm telling you again, I saw Joseph. We talked. And I fear if I deny it, he will come visit me again. Besides..."

His eyes lit up, mischievous now. "Why would I torture myself, arguing with you over nothing? This wasn't nothing! Joseph is alive. Stephanos says he saw the Baptist alive. And *they* each told us told the same thing: Master Iesous has risen from the dead."

"Oh!" Joanna pushed a hand at her son, stopping his words right there. "This is too much, Andronikos. Anything could have happened to account for such a story."

"Believe me, I do intend to find out what's happened. It's critical because there's more to my story." Leaning toward her now, Andronikos said, "Remember how I isolated myself from our guests because I'd gone into a tomb before our Passover celebration? Have I ever been so rude or missed such a good meal for nothing?"

"No, but ..."

Deathly serious, he said, "Listen, Mother. The tomb I entered was Master Iesous' tomb. I saw Him cold and dead like meat on a slab. I've never seen anyone so brutally beaten in all my life. He had a wound gaping open at the heart. Ordinary men don't recover from being speared through the heart, Mother. And what about the earthquake? What about the darkness? How can we reason away such unnatural darkness?"

He shook his head. "Believe me, I'll be asking others what they know; I refuse to be anyone's dupe. But if it's true that Master Iesous lives again, then we cannot deny Him as the *Christos*."

She stared at her son, too shocked to think. Except that she knew he wasn't lying. He wouldn't endure such turmoil without a good cause. It wasn't like him.

Cold and dead like meat on a slab. The Christos. How could these things be true? But the matter at hand now was her son's determination to speak to Barzel. And her own determination to prevent such a meeting. "Remember, Andronikos, you *were* inside a tomb. You're unclean. You cannot present yourself at Barzel's residence for four days yet." There. Argue with that.

"But if Master Iesous is risen, Mother—as I've been told and believe—then he is alive. Am I then unclean?"

"I ... I don't know." Such a turn in logic! A priest would be screaming. To cover her confusion, Joanna reached into the hidden box and hauled out her leather coin bags one by one, thunking them heavily on the floor. She hadn't intended to remove all the bags, fearing Andronikos was demented and would squander the silver. But he began to help her because they were so heavy. Nine ... ten ... eleven ...

She hadn't realized there were so many. However, Andronikos didn't look surprised. He lifted a bag, gauging its weight. "Mother, haven't you ever considered that a lender such as Iakobos could give us a nice interest rate on some of this silver? You know we can trust him. I've never heard a complaint from any of his business partners, and he measures every grain of spice I sell him. Perhaps we should also buy some land."

Her son was right. She should have been investing this. "There's more hidden beneath the bed," she mumbled, embarrassment mixed with relief that he seemed lucid. "I was simply continuing your father's habits. You know how he saved things."

Grinning, Andronikos said, "Father was wise, of course. I'm going to invite Iakobos to share a meal with us and to discuss this. But let's hide it for now and reopen the shop. I doubt I'm unclean, and we should—"

A tap on the door alarmed them both. Joanna rushed to answer. Maria stood there, her thin hands clasped beneath her chin, her dark eyebrows raised in curiosity as she tried to look past Joanna, into the room. "Mother, Yosef's old servant, the one named Eran, is waiting in the shop. He's asking for Andronikos."

"What's happened?" Andronikos leaned into the doorway. "Is someone ill?"

Maria shrugged delicately. "Eran seems well, though he's agitated."

"This seems to be the morning for agitation." Andronikos hurried to the shop.

Eran met him, seeming pleased yet a bit shamefaced as he knotted his thin fingers together. "Master Andronikos, I cannot say whether I should exult or weep. I have been cast out and must somehow earn my bread and a corner in which to sleep. When you joked with me recently about teaching young Loukas …" He hesitated, and then clenched his hands tight together. "Might there have been a cup of truth in that cauldron-full of banter?"

Andronikos grinned. "You mistook me, good sir; it was quite the opposite. I spoke a cupful of banter over a cauldron of truth. Loukas neglects his studies and I have no time to stand over him and compel him to work. Why were you cast out? What happened?"

"A great miracle has occurred. However, sir..." The kindly teacher swallowed, as if pained. "I fear that the young Lady Elisheba and my little Master Benjamin might be in dire trouble."

***

His footsteps echoing amid the frescoed walls, Pallu stalked through the hall of his residence. Again and again, Old Eran's words returned to him.

A miracle as in the days of the prophets!

Pallu almost spat at the old teacher's naive beliefs. For a word-learned man, Eran had proven himself a spiritual fool. Well, good riddance to the old sermonizer! One less mouth to feed. Three, actually, including Elisheba and Benjamin. Their banishments surely counted as a full day's work, though it was barely past the sixth hour at midday. Pallu scowled.

But what had he truly seen today?

First, this morning, he'd seen a gleam of light slipping *out* of Elisheba's bedchamber. That had disturbed him. Yet it was nothing but a trick of shadows.

Then, Elisheba and her son both claimed they'd seen Joseph. Liars! Elisheba had concocted the mindless tale to hide her own duplicity and then dragged Benjamin into her schemes to bolster her lies with the boy's innocence.

If she were still here, he'd slap her and banish her again. He would!

But now, Joseph's bones were gone, though the burial clothes were untouched. Admittedly, *that* unnerved Pallu. Yet there must be an explanation for Joseph's bones simply vanishing from the tomb. Somehow, that grim disappearance was part of a larger plot to smear his own good name. He must furrow out the conspiracy and thwart it quickly.

Other concerns pressed in too. Placating Barzel to avoid meeting his demands. Telling Malchos that he couldn't marry Elisheba. Yet, if he could change that, Pallu would. Perhaps he still could. Indeed, he must. That way, Elisheba's marriage portion could seemingly exist in parchment and ink.

Shrill feminine voices knifed into Pallu's thoughts. Levia's voice cut to him from the reception room as she upbraided someone, a woman who was evidently weeping and arguing in return. No doubt one of the maidservants had done something wrong. But why were they being so loud?

Pallu strode toward the reception room to make his displeasure known. He'd had enough commotion today. He would not endure his wife and servants creating more. Sweeping his full garments about himself, he entered the room and frowned.

Levia sat on one of the couches, exquisite as a disdainful queen in her soon-to-be-sold ornaments. And, kneeling at her feet, sobbing, was ... Elisheba? Pallu exhaled his relief. So the girl was pleading to return to his household. He could send her to Malchos after all.

Smiling, prepared to be generous, Pallu went to speak to the errant creature.

She turned, and he choked down a cry of rage.

His young mistress, Shelomiyth—not Elisheba—scrambled to her feet and unleashed a torrent of wrath, her usually sweet voice harsh with fury. "There you are, you liar! 'Merchant Yoazar!' Did you think I'd let you abandon me? We've learned who you really are. Traveling merchant, indeed! My father followed you after your last visit. We've discovered your friends in the Lord's House and left messages. At first, they refused to talk about you, but this morning, my father received this."

Drawing her slender form straight, she brandished a tiny scroll at him. Pallu snatched it, recognized the writing, and crushed it in his fist.

"Obviously you offended someone, and he sent us straight to you!" Shelomiyth sounded so pleased that Pallu's fingers twitched with his longing to slap her. Suddenly, her fragile prettiness and tempestuous nature were unappealing. Why had he ever trifled with her?

"Her father was also here," Levia said coldly, flaunting her disrespect of him by remaining seated. "He has returned to his home to retrieve written proof of your dealings with him, which I demanded."

"You will acknowledge me openly as your wife," Shelomiyth informed him, her small fists on her hips. "And this time, I want a settlement from you for the sorrow you've caused me!"

"See if you can get one," Pallu taunted. Why should he subject himself to such abuse? Indeed, he would not. "I'll leave, so you women can become better acquainted."

Both women shrieked with rage. Ignoring them, Pallu marched out of the reception room. In his defense, he'd been in a tomb and must isolate himself. He also had a score of letters to write.

If he could imbue one particular letter with poison, he'd send it to Barzel for betraying him to Shelomiyth's father.

***

Seated on a couch at their midday meal, Elisheba stared at her father, unable to believe what he was saying. "Abba, why?"

"Pallu deserved it," Not bothering to hide his glee, Barzel dipped his unleavened bread into a rich, salty olive paste. "Pallu boasted to me that he'd married the girl falsely. I've made him accept his responsibilities toward her." Smiling across the dining table at Daliyah, who was reclining with Benjamin on her own couch, Barzel said, "I'm also notifying Pallu's creditors and debtors that he's got no silver to his name. And I've sent men to seize his olive groves until he repays me."

"Oh, that will make him dance!" Daliyah's beautiful eyes sparkled with approval as she scooted a bowl of herb-scented baked eggs closer to Benjamin. He sighed, too contented with food to bother talking or—Elisheba hoped—listening.

Adjusting her bandaged feet, she murmured, "I'm not sorry you've made him responsible, Abba, but this will grieve the Lady Levia and the children."

Barzel snorted. "Well, let them give Pallu their grief and make his life a torment. I'm not done with him yet."

Elisheba squirmed to think of the misery in Lord Pallu's household. Levia and the girls would be affected for the rest of their lives.

Changing the subject slightly, Daliyah asked Elisheba, "Are you certain that you're free of Malchos?"

"I promised him nothing," Elisheba reassured her mother. Casting a wary glance at Benjamin, she added softly, "Malchos tried to force himself upon me last week, though I protested. I escaped him only because Lady Levia intervened for me."

"He's the one who bruised your throat?" her father asked, dangerously quiet.

"Yes, Abba. But he accomplished nothing else except to terrify me. Thank you for not insisting that I marry him."

"I never wanted you to marry that man." Barzel looked as if he wanted to go after Malchos exactly as he'd attacked Pallu. "I knew he had a false manner about him."

"We kept quiet only for Benjamin's sake," Daliyah said. "But we were very unhappy with Pallu for trying to marry you to such an unworthy man."

"However, in a few years even an unworthy man might seem preferable to no husband at all," Barzel warned his daughter. "After your little walk this morning, I fear there won't be an honorable man in all of Israel who'd marry you without serious misgivings."

Daliyah uttered a protest, but Elisheba shrugged. "As long as it's not Malchos, Abba, I don't mind."

Barzel shook his head. "I mind. And let's have no more stories of Joseph coming to life again, eh? My acquaintances would believe you're simple-minded; *no one* would consider marrying you after hearing such a thing. Therefore, it's best forgotten."

Forgotten? Impossible. Elisheba remembered Joseph's glorious face this morning, and smiled. She would cling to that image for the rest of her life.

Sethi appeared in the doorway now, smoothing his black beard, at his most dignified. "My lord, you have a visitor. Andronikos, son of Zebedaios, is waiting in the antechamber. Will you receive him?"

Andronikos? Elisheba glanced at her mother, baffled, as Daliyah flung her a questioning look in turn.

"You have no idea why he's here?" Barzel asked.

"None whatsoever," Daliyah answered.

Elisheba shook her head, praying Andronikos wouldn't mention her warning messages. The gossips would turn her innocent intentions into a full-fledged dalliance.

"He has said it's private business," Sethi announced. "Master Benjamin's good teacher, Eran, is with him."

"Eh-wan?" Benjamin asked thickly through a mouthful of eggs. He sat up straight, his face brightening as he chewed and gulped. "Please, I need to see Eran!"

"Very well." Barzel smiled at his grandson, clearly glad to indulge him. "Escort them in. And, Sethi, bring another cup and some more wine."

Oh! This visit *was* about Eran taking her messages to Andronikos. Elisheba winced. That would upset Abba. To hide her concern, she checked her bandages, tightening them. Soon, she heard footsteps and the rustling of heavy garments.

"Thank you for receiving us." Andronikos said, low-voiced. Something in his tone made Elisheba look up. He was staring at her bandages, obviously concerned. And she'd never seen him so finely clothed—in long red and blue robes with meticulously embroidered edges, rich but discreet gold tassels, his dark curls shining beneath his head-covering, gleaming and perfectly groomed. But his genuinely concerned expression stirred her wonderment even more than his handsome garments. Why was he here?

Her parents would notice her watching him. Hastily, she averted her gaze, much as she was tempted to stare. She eyed Eran instead, standing humbly behind Andronikos, his face glowing with such a smile that she almost forgot her fears and laughed. How good it was to see Eran happy.

"Eran!" Benjamin ran to his teacher, babbling. "I had a big-big dream! Abba came and talked to me, but Ama saw him and screamed." Benjamin gave Elisheba a sly, sparkling glance. "*I* didn't scream; *I* was brave."

"You were indeed, Little Master," Eran agreed.

Barzel sighed, the very portrayal of a loving yet resigned grandfather. To Andronikos, he said, "My grandson has a vivid imagination. Don't take him seriously. What did you wish to tell me?"

After an instant's hesitation, Andronikos replied, "I'm praying you will take me seriously, lord, despite my 'vivid imagination'."

Benjamin eyed Andronikos. "I haven't seen you in the market for a very long time. Do you have any gum?"

Eran murmured, "Wait for now, Little Master. You'll want to listen to Master Andronikos."

***

Barzel listened approvingly, revising his former opinion of this young Greek-Jew merchant. Andronikos was well-groomed and evidently prosperous and well-spoken. Benjamin liked him. And Elisheba, too, was listening, blushing, though she refused to look at the man. Very telling of her. Might this man be persuaded to marry her, for lack of a better, to salvage her reputation?

"... then I knew Stephanos had finally gone insane," Andronikos said.

Sensible. Barzel added this attribute to his silent list.

"I went into the shop to pour him some myrrh extract to calm him ...."

Compassionate, Barzel mused. Perhaps something could be done to improve his social standing.

"... he asked, 'You, merchant, do you have any gum?' and I saw the man was Joseph!"

Fool!

Before Barzel could say a word, Elisheba sat up on her couch, gasping, one hand to her throat. "Tell me what he looked like to you!"

Now the young merchant looked awed, a man who has seen the mysterious. "He looked perfect. Not a mark on him. We were almost nose to nose. I've never seen eyes as clear and bright. And his garments were like the purest white wool."

To Barzel's disgust, Elisheba covered her face and sobbed while laughing through tears.

"Did you give him gum?" Benjamin demanded.

***

Holding her weeping daughter, Daliyah listened, stunned. Andronikos, always so composed, was telling a story that would have been too unbelievable, except that Elisheba and Benjamin had described the same "Joseph" to her this morning. Impossible! Nevertheless …

Andronikos continued. "He said, 'You are my kindred now.' He also called me 'brother' and said, 'Protect my son.'" Inclining his head politely to Barzel, Andronikos said, "Forgive me, lord, but that *is* what Joseph said. I would never dare tell you this otherwise."

"Brother?" Daliyah choked, as Elisheba gasped. "Like a kindred redeemer?"

Barzel stood, sputtering. "I … If I ever let you marry … after such … such …!" Evidently unable to think of anything worse to say, he threw his hands in the air. "You two *deserve* each other!"

"If your daughter agrees, then I'm sure we can reach an arrangement, lord," Andronikos said, turning admirably businesslike. "Let's discuss terms."

Chapter 20

Sagging onto a low cushion in his parent's quiet main room, Stephanos sighed in near defeat.

His father, usually so reasonable, sat across from him, shaking his head. And his plump, always-doting mother, Sarrha, was dabbing at her swollen red eyes, trying to recover from weeping. "Please, understand … dear Stephanos … we're afraid for you."

"I know, I haven't been myself," Stephanos agreed, his thoughts dashing here and there, searching for a logical defense. "Please, forgive me. But you mustn't think that I've gone mad. I—"

"Well, what should we think?" Isaak interrupted. "You shut yourself away from us for days, you behave like a mourner at our Passover feast, and now you've run out into the market streets, half-naked and screaming like a wild man!"

Hearing his father describe the scene thus, Stephanos flinched. Yes, that sounded bad. Obviously his behavior this morning had looked much worse to others than it had seemed to him. *Blessed Lord Almighty, give me wisdom!*

How could he explain anything that appeared so insane?

"And when Joanna sent word to us that you were in a state...talking of seeing the Baptist as one sent from the dead ..." Sarrha lowered her head into her hands, crying again, rocking back and forth and drawing her cream-colored woolen head-covering across her face in despair, verging on a wail. "What girl would ever ... marry you?"

Nodding agreement, Isaak declared, "You've lost your mind."

They were obviously ready to lock him away until he "recovered." Stephanos gazed up at the cedar roof beams, thinking. A memory returned, of Master Iesous this past autumn, defending Himself before hostile critics in the windswept Court of the Gentiles.

In your law it is written that the testimony of two men is credible.

To defend his own maniacal behavior before a judge, Stephanos reasoned, the plausible course would be to have others testify for him as independent witnesses.

Legally, a judge must accept his testimony if Andronikos added his word to Stephanos'—as he had. But it wouldn't be prudent to remind his father of legalities right now. Grasping at his one true hope, he said, "Father, if you cannot believe me or Andronikos, then I ask you to at least test our words."

"How can we possibly do that?" Isaak demanded, pounding his fists hard on his knees, a gesture of disgust Stephanos rarely saw and truly dreaded. "It's nothing more than the two of you, saying that you saw something you can't prove. And we don't believe you saw anything or anyone!"

"Before you declare us insane, please seek out Master Iesous' disciples. Ask them if He lives, as Joseph and the Baptist John both declared. If Master Iesous is still dead in the tomb, then by all means lock me away because I've imagined everything."

As his father hesitated, Stephanos pointed out, "I haven't been anywhere else today. No one else would know my story, or Andronikos' story of Joseph. But if you find that others are saying similar things, independent of us, then how can you doubt me?"

Sarrha sniffled moistly, emerging from her head-covering, not looking at him. "I don't see what harm it can do. But, Stephanos, you must admit it's ... unlikely."

He could almost hear his mother's thoughts, substituting "insane" for "unlikely."

Shaking his head, Isaak finally muttered, "At dawn, we'll go. And you'll wear clothes this time! Also, while I am speaking to those men, those troublemakers, you'll keep your mouth shut, or I will bring you home and lock you away."

Stephanos felt himself diminished in his father's eyes. He sounded like Kore's father, talking to Kore.

***

Silent and tense, Elisheba sat with her mother on a couch as her father and Andronikos debated marriage terms. Barzel grumbled openly in front of Andronikos, using Greek. "When a *Libertine* tradesman can come into my home and conduct his own negotiations to claim my daughter, that day I must truly be desperate!"

Finished jotting his terms onto a wax tablet, Barzel shoved the tablet at Andronikos, tossing a slender wooden stylus after it, the stylus clattering discordant over the stone table. Elisheba winced.

Thankfully, Andronikos wasn't offended in the least. Reclining on the couch nearest Barzel's, he accepted the tablet and read it without so much as a grimace. Evidently finished, he nodded, picked up the stylus, and pressed in a stipulation of his own. "I can pledge to you in writing, for your daughter's sake, that she will be my only wife," he told Barzel.

"I was going to write that in," Barzel said testily.

"Forgive me, lord," Andronikos murmured. "Now, what about an additional settlement?"

Casting the young merchant a surly *don't-you-dare* look, Barzel said, "Didn't you read what I wrote? I'm giving my daughter a very generous settlement."

"Truly, the Almighty Lord will bless you for your kindness," Andronikos agreed, still pleasant. "However, I'm asking you about an addition to the *ketubah*—my immediate payment to her when this contract is signed. What additional sum will reassure you, lord, that I'm seeking this marriage contract sincerely, not for profit?"

Barzel sat back on his couch and stared as if Andronikos had upside-down ears. "Not for profit? What sort of merchant are you?"

"A spice merchant, and a blessed one."

They traded such long-level bargaining looks that Daliyah sucked in an irritated breath and whispered, "Just finish!"

The men seemed not to hear. Finally, as if testing Andronikos, Barzel said, "One hundred shekels. Can you afford that much?"

"I was thinking one hundred and fifty," Andronikos countered. Pressing notations into the wax, he said, "I'll bring the silver to you tomorrow. You may keep it or invest it for your daughter and her children as you please, though I'll request written records from your stewards."

"Yes, and I suppose you'll add a long string of conditions," Barzel said. But he sounded less irritable.

"If that will please you, lord," Andronikos agreed, so bland that Barzel snorted.

"My baby," Daliyah whispered loudly, assuring that everyone would hear her this time, "are you quite certain this is what you want?"

"Quite certain," Elisheba announced. Her father frowned, but not with his previous indignation. Did she imagine he was begrudging Andronikos a hint of respect? She prayed she was right. She wanted them to agree. It would finish this day well.

Everything was so dazing, from the glory of Joseph's dawnlight visit, to the shame of her public walk through Jerusalem's streets this morning, ending with an unexpected betrothal this evening. From mourning to elation. And all of it, including her shame, she now saw as blessings from the living Lord Almighty.

To Adonai she thought, *Blessed be Your name! Through Joseph, You sent Andronikos to cover my disgrace. I know this marriage is right, though gossips will talk. Who else will understand me as Joseph did?*

No wonder Joseph had given her that final dancing look.

When the initial negotiations were finished, Andronikos thanked her parents and wished them a blessed night. Elisheba exhaled nervously, limping as she followed Andronikos outside. Evening air cooled her face, and deepening rose hues tinted the courtyard's uppermost limestone walls, while violet shadows crept across the pavings.

Benjamin had gone out earlier with Eran. Elisheba saw them now, Eran all smiling patience as Benjamin's small hands and voice lifted excitedly, describing his "dream" of Joseph this morning. Hopping on the pavings and stretching his arms upward, Benjamin tried to express Joseph's height while Eran laughed.

"I pray he doesn't forget this day," Andronikos said. Smiling, he turned to Elisheba and looked straight into her eyes, something he'd never done before today because she had been another man's wife. How wonderful his eyes were, she realized. Rich brown, with golden glints and subtle laughter lines when he grinned. When he admired her... His glance, and the very fact that he was speaking to her now, proclaimed their new relationship.

"We'll all remember this day," Elisheba answered in Greek. Was it ridiculous of her to feel shy now, like any girl newly betrothed? Yet even in this first true conversation with Andronikos, she felt she could say anything and he would accept and welcome her words, though she fumbled between Aramaic and Greek. "When I saw Joseph this morning, I sensed that he was content to be gone. That was...painful."

"Yes. Though he was obviously concerned for you; don't forget that." Andronikos' voice softened, full of remembered wonderment. "I almost envied him."

"I begged to go with him," Elisheba admitted, struck again by the twinge of bitter-sweetness—delight and loss at Joseph's departure. "But it's clear that we've work yet to do. He told me to tell everyone that the Rabbi Yeshua, Master Iesous, lives."

"He told me the same. Tomorrow I'm going to speak to the Lord's disciples."

"Oh!" If only she could go herself! But her father would certainly refuse, and she was bound by his edicts until her marriage. As her betrothed husband, however, Andronikos could intercede with requests on her behalf. "Please, whatever you learn, will you visit tomorrow night and tell me?"

"You had no need to ask," Andronikos promised. "Whatever I learn, I'll tell you when I return to sign the final contracts."

Shy again, she murmured, "Thank you for coming here today and risking such insults to speak to my father."

"I was afraid Joseph would visit again to punish me if I didn't obey him," Andronikos admitted with a self-deprecating grin.

"I'd be afraid too. Almost." As their shared smiles faded, she asked, "Do you suppose he's still watching us?"

"Now there's a fearsome thought. But no, I'm sure he wouldn't bother to hide. I believe he's beyond us now, don't you agree?"

"Yes, it seems so." She studied Andronikos, delighted by his graciousness, and liking the sound of his voice, his warming smile, his strong-cut features. He was quite handsome, she confessed to herself. Her thoughts had always been so filled with Joseph that she'd never paid close attention to his friend. And that was as it should have been. From this time forward, however, she must think of Andronikos.

"You are a blessing to me," she told him, meaning the words with all her heart. Andronikos looked discomfited by her remark. But before she could decide why, Sethi emerged from the gatehouse, haughty as a nobleman, followed by a meek, gray-robed man, whom Elisheba recognized as one of Lord Pallu's loan stewards. Behind them, two of Lord Pallu's other servants followed, guarding a small wooden chest.

A very small chest. Edging closer to Andronikos, she murmured, "That's not enough silver to repay my dowry and my bride gift; I can tell just by looking. My father will certainly summon Lord Pallu to court."

Andronikos chuckled, his discomfited look suddenly gone. As she gave him a questioning glance, he said, "Calculating silver as easily as you do, you'll agree with my mother and my sister very well." Shifting the subject, he continued. "If you want Eran to stay here, then he can. Otherwise, I'll take him into my household and he can help me to civilize my brother, Loukas. Also..." He hesitated, glancing down at her bandaged feet. "I think you should go rest and soak your feet in salt water. Do you have some good ointment?"

Unable to stop herself, Elisheba said demurely, "I believe so. My mother buys all her spices and remedies from a very reputable widow named Joanna."

"I believe I can vouch for her." Smiling, Andronikos wrapped one warm, cloak-draped arm around Elisheba and turned her toward the doorway, urging, "Go. Soak your feet. I'll return to sign the final contracts tomorrow afternoon. But first, I'll speak to Eran."

Elisheba obeyed, feeling the inherent comfort in Andronikos' touch. Now, for the first time since Joseph's death, she felt safe. So protected that she almost looked around to see if Joseph was watching, perhaps guarding her.

He wasn't, of course. Yet her sense of security remained because of everything she'd heard and seen.

Because of You, Lord Almighty, King of the Universe ... creator of souls ....

***

"If they aren't here, then we won't wait. I've business to attend to this morning," Isaak warned Stephanos as they climbed squared, whitewashed steps to an upper room above a fabric merchant's shop.

Despite the early hour, the merchant had been courteous, informative, saying that his guests in the room above were, all-in-all, peaceful. A remarkable thing, given last week's events. The merchant also counted it as a good deed and a blessing for himself to give shelter to Master Iesous and His disciples. Isaak's flickering twitch of a grimace revealed doubt that the merchant's deed was a blessing, but he'd remained silent.

"I don't expect you to wait," Stephanos told his father, "Particularly not after we've traversed the entire upper city." He had to admit that Isaak was trying to be fair in giving him this final chance to justify himself. But that's exactly what this was—a final chance. His heart thudding heavily, Stephanos waited as Isaak climbed the last step and rapped on the door.

Sounds of voices, and—unexpectedly—quiet laughter greeted them as the door creaked open. A man leaned out, sleep-rumpled but alert and good-humored, smoothing his thick, dark beard and garments. Evidently judging Isaak by his bright "Libertine" attire, he spoke in Greek. "May the Almighty Lord bless you and give you peace."

Hearing his voice, Stephanos remembered the man. Matthaios.

"How may we help you?" Matthaios continued, unexpectedly serene for a man who had just lost his famed Master in such ruinous circumstances.

For the first time in his life, Stephanos saw his father become truly flustered, as if he hadn't considered what to say. "I ... we hardly know where to begin. I ..."

Quietly, Stephanos dared to interpose, praying his father would excuse his disobedience. "Please excuse me if I am offensive or intruding upon sorrow, but last week, I saw the good Master Iesous being led out to die. I admit, to my shame, I fled in fear."

"As did most of us," Matthaios answered with obvious reluctance, a humbled flush spreading over his keen face. "Only the youngest of us twelve, John, stayed until our Master died."

Aware of his father watching and listening, Stephanos pressed on, feeling ill, his very sanity set in a balance. "Yesterday morning, I saw ... a man who was dead ... alive again. And I was told, 'Our Lord's risen.' Please, can you tell me if it's true?"

Matthaios gasped as if he'd been punched. "How could you know this? Our Master appeared to us only last night, though the door and windows here were barred."

"You say your Master Iesous lives again?" Isaak demanded, casting a suspicious look at Stephanos.

"Yes, our Lord ate with us last night." Now, the same joy Stephanos had seen shining in the Baptist John's eyes gleamed in this disciple's eyes as well. "As I live and stand before you, He's risen! With the wounds in His hands and side to prove He died."

"It's true?" Isaak stared blankly at Matthaios, then at Stephanos as if questioning his own wits now, in addition to theirs.

"It's true!" Stephanos almost wept, sagging against the chilled rough wall, feeling himself redeemed, released from the terrors that had haunted him. "I'm sane. He lives!"

Clearly delighted by their reactions, Matthaios urged them inside. "You two are father and son? Please, come sit with us! How did you know this? Who told you?"

"One of the Almighty Lord's own messengers," Stephanos breathed, shaking now as a man recovering from a long illness.

Matthaios took Stephanos by the arm, supporting him. He frowned kindly. "I've seen you before, haven't I?"

"Yes. Last year. But you won't believe my story."

"We will," Matthaios assured him. Raising his voice, he called in Aramaic to his friends, who were hauling themselves up from their sleeping mats, "Here are others beloved to our Lord Yeshua, who've heard! They've come to share good news."

One of the men stood. Stocky, thick-curled and dark, his eyes sparkled with enthusiasm as he greeted them in full Galilean-accented Aramaic. "Welcome! I am Shim'on-Kefa."

"Simon-Peter," Matthaios translated.

"Thank you, we understand," Stephanos said in Aramaic.

Surely he'd been ushered into a new life. And his father would listen to these men, who were obviously unpretentious, ordinary men who wouldn't risk their lives for nonsense.

They were all standing, eagerly greeting Stephanos and the dazed Isaak as brothers. And they were all glowing with the same spirit.

Your Spirit, Stephanos thought, at rest with the understanding, though still shaken, wondering why he should be received among the Master's disciples. *Blessed are You, Almighty Lord, our God, Ruler of the Kosmos, who has restored Your presence to Israel.*

***

"You should have sent me word at once!" Malchos snapped as soon as Pallu set foot in the reception room. "I would have taken her away immediately."

"And *you* will speak to me politely, as your elder and host, in my own house," Pallu retorted. To show Malchos his place, Pallu sat on a couch, leaving the young man to stand before him like an attending servant, though well-dressed in crimson and gold. Smoothing his own plain robes, Pallu said, "Anyway, I was just writing a letter to tell you what happened. How did you know the girl was gone?"

"Hearsay," Malchos muttered, "from our own acquaintances who've been told by their servants that you threw her into the street with her son."

"Obviously, my servants have been talking," Pallu complained, taking a slender red flask of wine and a cup from a nearby tray. By the weight of the flask, he judged there was enough wine for two servings, but did he wish to drink with his rude young kinsman or let him stand? He would complain to his father and Pallu would never hear the end of the "insult." The boy was unbearably spoiled.

Irritably, Pallu said, "Sit down, Malchos. We can talk, and I'll spare myself the task of finishing that letter."

Malchos sat on the nearest couch, fidgeting and scowling as Pallu poured the wine. At last, Malchos leaned forward and demanded, "Tell me the truth. Did she invite a man into her room?"

Did she? Forcing himself to be truthful, Pallu said, "I don't know. I heard her talking to someone. And her son insisted that a man who appeared to be his Abba had been there with them. What was I to think? Naturally, I became angry and threw her out, as any righteous man would have done. I regret it, but the matter cannot be undone." Glancing at Malchos over the rim of his cup, Pallu emphasized, "You can't marry her now."

"I can," Malchos insisted, stubborn as ever. He downed the wine. "It doesn't matter to me what the common people say."

"It does now. Her father has betrothed her to another man."

"No!" His voice horrible, raw with insult and fury, Malchos rasped, "Who?"

"I don't know. Barzel isn't talking. Neither are his servants. What a blessing that must be," Pallu added darkly, "to have close-lipped servants." If his own servants had been as loyal, he wouldn't be dealing with this overwrought youth now.

"I'll break their contract by declaring it was written under false suppositions!" Malchos thumped the wine cup on the table and stood, sweeping his gold-threaded mantle aloft with his agitation. "I'll sue the man for stealing my wife."

"You'll gain nothing and smear your own good name," Pallu argued. "What might you say, Malchos? Will you falsely declare that he stole the girl without her father's consent? Doubtless, Barzel will testify against you, as would any of his friends or servants."

"They can't disprove a private contract," Malchos countered, sullen-faced. "I could win, with witnesses and a document of my own."

Pallu could imagine the sort of witnesses Malchos would bribe. However, Barzel would fight him legally, as Elisheba's father. "Barzel would declare that contract void, declaring it dishonors him. More to the point, Barzel would accuse us both of other crimes. May I remind you that you attacked her while you were a guest in my house?"

"That can be construed in various ways."

"Yes, and none of them to our own good!" Pallu thumped a fist on the table to gain his nephew's attention. "Can all your private dealings withstand public scrutiny, Malchos? Can they? Sit down. Have a drink and calm yourself. We'll think of some other way to settle matters. Trust me; you don't want her at such a terrible price."

"Yes, I do!" Smoldering, Malchos finished the wine but it didn't calm him. "I always envied Joseph," he muttered, "having her as his wife."

His hostility as he pronounced Joseph's name made Pallu sit up straight and stare. There was no mistaking the young man's covetous tone. "You sound as if you wanted my son to die."

Malchos went silent, blinking like a trapped thief. Looking away, he set down his cup and stood. "Forgive me for intruding, lord."

"You wanted my son dead?" Pallu stared up at his nephew, stunned. As Malchos departed in a glittering swirl of gold and crimson, Pallu leaped up, yelling after him, "You wished death on my son!"

What had he done? He'd sheltered a viper! Had Malchos poisoned Joseph? They'd been seated side by side last year at the Passover feast....

Though Malchos was out of earshot by now, Pallu yelled, "Did you kill my son?"

Silence answered. But anything seemed possible, torn as his life was. And the look on Malchos' face...

Nothing can be proven—and likely it's not true. Surely it's not true.

"But you wished death on my son!" Pallu flung Malchos' abandoned cup against the wall and watched the fragile red stoneware cup shatter, its shards raining crimson on the floor.

He left the reception room, cursing and feeling cursed. He went outside and crossed the large courtyard to Joseph's former rooms. Shoving open the door, he looked around at its emptiness. All of Elisheba's belongings were gone now, packed by Pallu's servants and returned this morning to her father's house by the servant Leah.

The one glowing, beautiful thing left in the room was the blue veiling the girl had fastened over the lattice window.

Drawn to its color, Pallu fingered the veil. A haze of dust motes and fragile webbings drifted from the cloth, scattering through the sunlit air. Undisturbed for months, offering silent testimony to Elisheba's virtue. No man had entered or departed through this window. Pallu stared at the dazzle of dust and light. What, then, had he actually seen? A light leaving this room through this lattice. No. He'd seen nothing. He couldn't have.

No bones in my son's tomb ....

No, he'd seen emptiness that proved nothing.

Now, accusing whispers seeped in at the edges of Pallu's thoughts. He'd slandered Elisheba. He'd failed.

Trying to force away the taunts cutting into his thoughts, to escape shivers of fear and wonder, Pallu fled Elisheba's abandoned rooms, slamming the door behind him.

He'd done nothing wrong. Nothing!

***

Unhindered, they circled and swept down upon their prey, adding to his tangled fears, binding him tight. Claiming his flesh-clad being.

A pitiable trophy within the eternal, nothing of concern, except to the rejected One: Him.

Each soul claimed for their master brought one sure victory as Loathsome It mourned.

Chapter 21

Nervous as a bride, though her wedding was months away, Elisheba checked her image in a silver mirror. She needed to look completely respectable and modest at all times, a goal shared by Leah, her personal servant newly acquired from Pallu's household.

"This will do," Leah announced, draping Elisheba's braided, linen-twined hair with a length of subdued violet wool.

His dark curls shining in a ray of morning light, Benjamin loitered beside her chair, impatiently rapping its palm-woven arm with his wooden toy sword, a gift from Andronikos. Were all boys so captivated by weapons and fighting? It seemed so. And in a bout between her chair and her little boy, her chair would lose.

"Please don't hit my chair, Benjamin."

"I won't." He swung the sword away in a wide arc. "Ama, where is Abba?"

Elisheba paused, her whole being exultant with the thought: *He's no longer in Sheol!* "He's with Adonai, Benjamin, waiting for us. Isn't that wonderful?"

"Why can't I see him again?"

"You will, later. Until then, you should remember him as you saw him last."

"But I do that already." Heaving a put-upon sigh, Benjamin lowered his sword and drooped against her chair. "When can we go?"

"Very soon. When Leah's finished with my hair."

"Aw!" His face scrunched tight with frustration. "Can't I go outside and play?"

"Yes, but stay with Eran. And let me know when Master Andronikos arrives."

As soon as Benjamin darted outside, Leah began to chatter of everything she'd seen and heard in Lord Pallu's residence before he sent her away last night—after furious resistance from the Lady Levia.

"The young Mistress, Shelomiyth, has come to Lord Pallu's residence every day, but he doesn't acknowledge her. The Lady Levia speaks with her, however. They talk about Lord Pallu as if they've decided to ally themselves to make his life a misery."

"I'm grieved that it's come to that. I know they're miserable." Testing a gold bracelet then rejecting it as too frivolous, Elisheba asked, "How are the children?"

Leah stepped back to check Elisheba's appearance. "I miss them, Lady. Our sweet Malkah will soon be of marrying age. No doubt we'll be forgotten at her wedding. As for Zimiyrah, she is still furious with her father for sending you and Master Benjamin away. She told me to tell you that she'd remember you always."

Elisheba paused for breath, feeling her throat tighten with the ache of loss. Malkah would be bargained off to some preferably rich husband. And Zimiyrah's bright spirit would be weighed down with punishments until she conformed to her father's will. *Lord Almighty, remember Zimiyrah. Don't let her become hostile to life.*

"Our little lord, Nathan, however, is becoming quite fat," Leah said, brightening, "with the most wonderful laugh. I pray there'll be something left for him to inherit after Lord Pallu has wasted so much."

"I pray so too." As Leah brought her sandals and stooped to tie them, Elisheba said, "Leah, please don't discuss all these things with the other servants."

"Oh. I won't." But Leah kept her glossy-dark head down, so intent upon Elisheba's sandals that Elisheba knew her warning had come too late. Leah had probably been chattering with everyone who would listen to her.

"Leah," Elisheba warned, "I'm serious. Don't make gossiping a habit. I'd hate to lose you over such a needless indiscretion."

Leah sat back, color flaring in her smooth, pretty face, her dark eyes penitent. "I'll remember from this day forward."

To soothe her maidservant, Elisheba asked, "Will you come with us?"

"With you, to follow Master Andronikos and his friends?"

"To hear you say it that way, our plans sound scandalous. Master Andronikos' mother will accompany me."

"Yes, Mistress, of course." Her voice bemused, Leah added with all the snobbery of a status-conscious servant, "I still cannot imagine that you'll marry a tradesman."

"Master Andronikos is perfect, a wonderful man and an excellent match for me, so never say that again." Elisheba faced her maidservant. "It's precisely that sort of talk that my lord father and Sethi will notice, and as my husband, Master Andronikos might be hurt. Therefore, for both our sakes, Leah, guard your tongue."

"Yes, I'll be careful."

Unconvinced, Elisheba stood and smoothed her garments, watching as Leah fussed with her own sandals and head-covering.

A sharp tap echoed on Elisheba's bedchamber door. Sweeping one end of her head covering over her shoulder, Leah hurried to answer. Sethi stood there, looking over Leah's head at the far wall. "Master Andronikos has arrived, young Mistress."

"Thank you, Sethi," Elisheba murmured, pleased to see Leah back away as if Sethi were unclean and might bite. Perhaps her warnings were effective after all.

She followed Sethi outside to the courtyard, which was crowded with family, servants, and her mother's red-curtained litter. Instantly, Elisheba saw Andronikos talking with her father, both so intent on their conversation that she had no doubt of their discussion, for they'd found they shared many interests. Business, silver, investments, and their families.

Daliyah, Joanna, and Maria lingered near the men, pretending to visit with each other, but obviously listening, with sidelong glances, to business talk.

Now, urged on by Loukas, Benjamin charged Andronikos with his toy sword.

Breath-swift, the young merchant caught the little boy's sash mid-attack and hoisted him off the ground, shaking him playfully. Benjamin's wooden sword clattered to the stones as Barzel laughed.

Benjamin laughed too, swimming helplessly through the air beside Andronikos, vainly swiping toward the ground for his sword. "Ha! Help, I can't reach it!"

Pleased by her son's joy, Elisheba teased, "Benjamin, what are you doing floating around like that? Get down."

"I c-can't!" he hiccoughed. But Andronikos set him down and turned to look at Elisheba.

His dark eyes gleaming, Andronikos said, "Blessed be the Lord, our God, Creator of the Kosmos, who brings forth such beauty for His joy!"

Andronikos was referring to *her*. Elisheba blushed, even as she wondered what it would be like to live with a husband so steeped in prayer. Joseph had just been learning to devote himself in prayer when he died, while her father prayed as a matter of ritual, not as a matter of being. Even now, Barzel was staring at Andronikos, obviously liking the young man all the more for openly praising Elisheba, even as he silently disparaged his future son-in-law's "fanatical" behavior.

Pulling a sour face, Barzel spoke dismissively in Greek. "I expect you to return before sunset, in time for our Sabbaton meal."

"We will, lord," Andronikos promised, with all the genuine courtesy that had won permission for Elisheba to go with his family on this particular afternoon.

Daliyah kissed Elisheba twice as if they'd be parted for months. "I'll be sure there's plenty of food waiting when you return. Now promise me you won't lose any of my cushions. If you do, I'll demand new ones."

"We'll be careful, Ama," Elisheba promised, including Joanna with a glance.

Joanna smiled, barely, still seeming uncertain about closing the shop and spending a pre-Sabbath afternoon outside the city. However, because of Andronikos' testimony, she was apparently curious enough to go listen to the Lord's disciples. Daliyah had also been curious about the gathering, but wouldn't for the world dream of going because Barzel deplored such a foolish waste of time. Listening to a pack of babblers praising their supposedly risen Rabbi—

"Where's *my* new cushion?" Benjamin demanded in a remembering voice, interrupting Elisheba's musing. "Ama, you said Eran would buy one for me, but I never got it."

"We must ask Eran. He might remember where he ordered it." On the day of the Lord's death. Had it been mere weeks since that awful day of violence and darkness? Impossible. The world was now completely changed, full of promise for their futures.

Planting herself firmly beside Elisheba, Joanna whispered, "It's not for me to ride in a litter. I'll walk with Maria and Loukas."

"But my lord father expects me to ride in order to remain hidden in public," Elisheba whispered back in Greek. "And you, my husband's mother, cannot walk if I ride. So, please, you must endure my company."

"Now, I wasn't arguing against your company," Joanna protested. "It's just..."

It's just not something she'd done before, riding like a pampered and wealthy female, Elisheba guessed. "Then I beg you to humor me. How else can we visit?"

"I'll keep watch over Loukas, Mother," Maria promised, looking as if she wanted to clout her younger brother already. "Please, visit with Elisheba and don't worry."

"I suppose." Joanna gave the polished, red-curtained litter a wary, sidelong glance.

Seeing her unspoken doubt, Elisheba smiled. Joanna liked her well enough as a customer in her shop. But now, perhaps, she was afraid Elisheba's Sadducee upbringing would corrupt her family. How could Elisheba reassure her that she wasn't too badly spoiled? *And I'm certainly no Sadducee. My soul lives!*

Determined to convince her future mother-in-law of the truth, Elisheba said, "Good! I have so much to tell you."

But Maria delayed Elisheba, whispering eagerly, "Convince her to let me stay and visit with you tonight, please!"

"You know I will. But you'll find me very boring."

"I wouldn't," Maria argued. "Please, ask her for me."

"You sound like a sister," Elisheba teased. Maria's eyes sparkled, promising a loyal alliance. Between Maria and Joanna both whispering at her, she already felt like part of their family.

More important, she turned to find Andronikos watching her, with Benjamin still hanging onto him as any little boy would with his father. Andronikos caught Elisheba's gaze and smiled appreciatively, staring at her as if no one else existed for him within that instant—making her blush with thoughts of such enticements as she hadn't remembered since Joseph's death. She allowed herself to return his smile.

Until she realized Joanna and her parents were watching, their eyebrows lifted in unison.

"Behave," Daliyah told Elisheba, but her voice carried, including them all.

Unintimidated, Andronikos grinned and snatched up Benjamin, hauling him off to their waiting donkey while the little boy whooped and yelled in pretend protest.

***

Walking slow-paced among the servants through a springtime breeze, Eran allowed his thoughts to drift contentedly as they departed the Holy City, descending the hillside path into the valley of Yehoshophat. Splashing through the Kidron stream, then passing shaded groves, they climbed the Mount of Olives—the long, four-summit ridge east of the gleaming Holy House.

The young Lady Elisheba and good Joanna were riding ahead of them in the red-curtained litter. Master Andronikos rode ahead on a placid donkey, also carrying and teasing the Little Master, Benjamin.

Eran smiled, hearing Benjamin's pure, bubbling laughter. *You are good for my boy,* Eran told the young merchant. *If he cannot have his own father, then he's blessed to have you.*

Indeed, Eran reflected, Master Andronikos' willing spiritual adoption of Master Benjamin was another joy wrapped within countless marvels. Surely these days, these miracles, would never be matched again—and of miracles, there had been many.

To satisfy his own curiosity during the past few weeks, Eran had spent much of his free time hiking about the stone tombs nestled in the hillsides surrounding Hierousalem. Most of the tombs were closed, sealed and whitewashed, the bodies evidently decomposing within. But here and there, he'd found evidence of quiet mysteries. Stones broken. Shrouds emptied.

And he'd spoken to other families who testified in amazed whispers of loved ones appearing to them from beyond death and time. Furthermore, each loved one had declared the perfect wonder.

The Lord Iesous had defeated the most feared adversary of life by conquering death.

He is risen!

Exhaling in delight, Eran gazed up at the skies. As he continued along the dusty road, his praise lifted in wordlessness. Surely, no syllables existed that were high enough or rich enough to offer his meaning, may the Lord's own Spirit intercede. Yet, he must try.

Blessed are You, Almighty Lord, King of the Kosmos, who has fulfilled all of the law through Iesous our Christos, covering us with His righteousness ....

***

"Andronikos said he'd thought you lost your mind," Kore said, tramping after Stephanos in a rush to catch up with Andronikos' family. "I say he should have left it at that. After all the wild stories you've both been telling me, I still think you've lost your minds. And you're trying to drag me into madness with you."

"Yes, we're certain we owe you some suffering for all the trouble you've hauled us into over the past few years." Stephanos walloped Kore so happily that Kore couldn't help grinning in return.

"Fine! Now, Madman Stephanos, tell me where you're taking me."

"To meet with our Master Iesous' disciples."

"To be bored out of my mind. I knew it!" But it was better than home, or his father's shop, coiling ropes and dreaming of faraway lands he'd never see. Even so, Kore felt he had to complain. "You know I don't like to be surrounded by herds of teachers, Stephanos; you're enough of one all by yourself. And

Master Iesous' followers are nothing without Him. So tell the truth. This is a joke, isn't it? You're all trying to get revenge on me somehow."

"If that's what you think, then..." Stephanos shrugged. "You can go home."

"And *work?*"

"Tonight is Sabbaton. You can rest then."

"Never mind. I'll stay."

Merging now with a large crowd on the rocky slopes, Kore looked around. Young scholars like Stephanos were talking here and there, all so serious that Kore longed to jostle them. Families with children were settling themselves for the afternoon with baskets of food. Very ordinary. The ones who truly interested Kore were the priests and Levites, usually so proud and reserved, now mingling with the commoners amid the crowd.

He nudged Stephanos. "What're those priests doing here? Don't they have work to do?"

"I'm sure they're finished," Stephanos said quietly.

Hopefully not. Bent upon hearing the truth, Kore ambled closer, listening in as several priests talked with two somberly-clad young Pharisees.

"How can we explain? The Almighty Lord's house feels like a tomb," one of the priests said, nervously brushing at the edges of his white robes.

"No, not like a tomb," another priest interrupted, his lean face so earnest that Kore knew he must be telling the truth. "It's as if the whole place *rebels*! Lamps won't remain lit. Doors refuse to stay closed at night...."

"The largest doors," the third priest added, obviously uneasy as if the admission cost him much to confess. "It takes twenty of us to close them each night, as it always has. But in the morning, the doors are open as if a mere breeze pushed them ajar."

"And there are voices," the earnest priest said, his eyes almost wild with a recalled fear, "whispering from the darkness. And laughter from nowhere."

"Zerahiah, you're imagining *that*: I've heard no laughter," the third argued.

"You haven't been there at night!"

Fascinating. Their stories were every bit as odd as Stephanos' and Andronikos'. Kore was about to question the fretful priests when Stephanos took him by the arm.

"Kore," Stephanos muttered into his ear, "Will I ever cure you of rudeness? Let's find Andronikos."

"You were listening too," Kore accused. He was right, of course. How could Stephanos not want to hear a pack of scared priests discussing confounding mysteries in the Holy House?

But Stephanos quickly became his usual near-perfect self. "You think everyone else behaves as you do, my friend."

"You do. You just don't admit it," Kore muttered. "Look, there's Eran." Though he tried to sound casual, Kore was relieved to see the old servant; Eran had seemed tottering near death last time they'd met. When Master Iesous was nailed up to die.

Kore hastily put the bloody memory from his thoughts as too much to face. Better to be glad that

Eran was still alive—the only other teacher he'd ever met, apart from the Master and the Prophet John, who wasn't stone-dull and pompous. *I'll speak with him later*, Kore promised himself.

Amazing that such a quiet old man had become so important to him, he mused. He must be turning sentimental.

His parents would laugh at him, but they'd be pleased, no doubt.

"There's Andronikos." Stephanos greeted their distant friend with a nod, smiling broadly as Andronikos lifted a small child to his shoulders. "Benjamin's with him. He's brought his whole family."

"Perhaps they'll feed us." Kore wished he'd brought food of his own.

Eran was the nearest and met them first, glowing with delight. "I owe you thanks, my young friend," he told Kore. "The Almighty Lord has blessed us beyond measure since our last meeting. Come. Let me walk you to Master Andronikos."

As they continued through the crowd, someone called out, "Stephen! Come here. Tell us your story again."

"Stephen?" Kore joked. "Why would you even talk to someone who can't be bothered to pronounce your whole name?"

From the corner of his mouth, Stephanos chided, "Lower your voice, please! It's Shim'on-Kefa, one of the Lord's disciples. And he's not Greek, so don't mock him, Kore, I beg you." More kindly, Stephanos added to Eran, "Come. I'll re-introduce you to them."

"That would be a joy, young Master," Eran said.

Boring. Only to humor his friends, Kore accompanied them.

They walked, he thought, straight toward the disciple, Shim'on. But within one blink, Kore realized they'd veered while walking straight. He saw no other explanation. An instant before, he hadn't noticed this Man standing in his and Eran's and Stephanos' way. *How did I fail to see...?*

Light robes and a brilliant gaze. And when this man looked him straight in the eyes, radiant with life, Kore's thoughts all muddled in his brain. Master Iesous? "You cannot be alive."

And yet... And yet...

"Almighty Lord!" Stephanos gasped, catching Kore's sleeve then kneeling. Around them, others were gasping, shrieking, also kneeling.

"Don't be afraid," Master Iesous called to the crowd, lifting both hands.

His hands. Kore stared, dumbfounded. His hands were healed and whole, but marked by those fatal spikes. *I saw those wounds inflicted.* How could he possibly be alive?

Still staring at what he didn't believe, Kore dropped like a rope released, trembling too badly to stand. Kneeling on the spring-chilled ground, he saw the Master's feet, unmarred except for the piercing marks of those same dire wounds. *I saw you nailed ... bloodied ....*

I saw him cold and dead in the tomb, Andronikos had testified.

"He cannot be alive," Kore repeated.

Eran supported Kore, teary-eyed, yet laughing. "He lives indeed!"

Finding his tongue, Kore whispered thinly, "Blessed be the Lord, King of the Kosmos ..."

***

Hearing the outcries, laughter, and weeping, Elisheba turned and saw Him. As her heart leaped, expressing her fear and joy, she sank to her knees beside Andronikos and the shocked Joanna, breathtaken. *Blessed be You, Adonai!*

***

Without lifting His eyes or turning, He saw the Adversary, who lingered even now, though helpless against the armies of the Eternal and Spirit.

Satan, blind as ever to the Truth.

Death was this Fallen One's final weapon, yet he stood defeated. And surprised. A sacrifice of love was beyond the Adversary's thoughts—this living dark light who never loved. In vain, he'd sought to destroy what Father and Spirit had planned before time. Now he comprehended the truth, terrible to his proud, ravening mind.

What is left for you, but eternal fire? Mourn and rave! Let your cries echo from these temporal skies down through the deepest chasms of Ghehennah! Yet even there, those forever parted from Father by their own choices are set beyond your reach. Master-Deceiver, you deceive yourself. You have nothing of your own—only what Father has allowed you. Still, you refuse to understand.

You have chosen.

***

If only he could attack. Yet he, rendered helpless for now, watched them, those Protected Ones redeemed from the forever-broken Sheol. Within eternal light, they permeated this mortal gathering of flesh, surrounding their Lord as an army.

Possessing glory denied me.

His whole being consumed, wrath-eaten, he contemplated the battle. How could he allow this war to be lost? Must he, once jeweled radiance amid the heavens and still a master of light, bow to eternal creatures once born as wearisome flesh?

No.

Until their time passed to the eternal, he would indict those who remained—according to his rights. Battle would follow battle. And he would pour out on his adherents an overmastering zeal for their cause.

My realm will stand.

He studied those who were yet mortal, contemplating their fears and weaknesses. Until It swept him back—an undeniable current, shunning him to the edges of darkness, protecting those undeserving ones.

Brooding, he watched. And waited.

***

Leaning against Andronikos as they sat among the crowd, Benjamin turned his face skyward, gladdened, feeling the sunlight warm on his face.

Ama, where is Abba?

He's with Adonai, Benjamin, waiting for us. Isn't that wonderful?

Why can't I see him again?

You will later. For now, you should remember him as you saw him last.

Closing his eyes, Benjamin lowered his sword and watched sunlight play red and gold-bright behind his eyelids. Now, safe in this crowd with Ama and Andronikos, it was easy to remember: he saw Abba again in the dawnlight.

Smiling.

Alive.

OTHER BOOKS BY KACY BARNETT-GRAMCKOW

The Blessing
May Somerville has suffered a year worthy of the Bible's Job, and the man who unknowingly prompted all her troubles has fallen in love with her.

The Genesis Trilogy
The Heavens Before
A novel of the Genesis Flood
He Who Lifts the Skies
A novel of Nimrod's kingdom
A Crown in the Stars
A novel of the Tower of Babel

DID YOU ENJOY THIS BOOK?

Please consider leaving a candid review on Amazon, Goodreads, or other sites where this book is sold. Thank you!

ABOUT THE AUTHOR

KACY BARNETT-GRAMCKOW is a freelance writer. She is the author of the Genesis Trilogy (*The Heavens Before, He Who Lifts the Skies* and *A Crown in the Stars*). Kacy has also written dozens of devotionals which have been published in a number of books and web sites, including the best-seller *A*

Moment a Day and the *Women's Devotional Bible* as Elizabeth Larson.

Kacy also writes fantasy fiction, inspired by the Scriptures and history, as R. J. Larson. She and her husband of over twenty years make their home in Colorado Springs, Colorado, with their spoiled Ratcha pup, Sean.

Printed in Great Britain
by Amazon